Conejos Library District
Maria De Herrera Branch

Winterwood

Dorothy Eden

WINTERWOOD

Coward-McCann, Inc.
New York

Dorothy Eden

WINTERWOOD

Coward-McCann, Inc.
New York

Chapter 1

FROM the moment of leaving the hotel the enchantment of the night had grown. The walk down the narrow streets over the humped canal bridges and through a cobbled alley that led to the opera house had been full of the strangeness and delight of Venice. By the end of the first act of the opera Lavinia was in a pleasurable trance. She wished the lights would not go up, for they would only bring her back to cold reality.

But even when the lights came on, the enchantment stayed. Leaning forward in the box, Lavinia scanned the well-dressed audience, noticing the plentiful glint of diamonds, the swaying of dark immaculate curls, the movement of a jeweled fan, the blur of faces set in the polite masks of pleasure.

It was a little time before she realized that not only was she observing but she was being observed. In the box next to her there was a family group, a tall dark-haired man, a woman with hair that was startlingly black against a pale delicate face and a young girl in a simple white dress, her curls resting on childishly thin shoulders.

It was the girl who had drawn her father's attention to Lavinia. Lavinia was sure she was not intended to hear the excited whisper, "Look, Papa! Isn't she beautiful!"

She supposed she was silly and vain to find a mere child's admiration so pleasant. She had been used enough in the past to accept any kind of admiration as her due, and to be unaffected by it. But her shattering experiences had marked her more than she knew. She had great difficulty in not leaning forward and rewarding the child with a friendly smile. She did indeed glance long enough to catch the man's eyes. They were remarkably intent. Although his face was in shadow, she was sharply aware of the arrested turn of his head. His interested gaze held hers longer than she had intended.

She lifted her chin and appeared to be scrutinizing the theater beyond his head. Then she moved her fan languidly, as if quite at ease with the fact that she was attending the opera unaccompanied, except by a maid.

She knew, however, that the frail-looking woman was speaking to her husband. She must have said she was chilly, for out of the corner of her eye Lavinia saw him rise and arrange an Indian shawl about her shoulders. Then he left the box. The lights had gone down before he returned.

From then on, foolishly, Lavinia found her attention divided between the stage and the occupants of the neighboring box. She drew her own conclusions about them. The languid, languishing woman was bored with opera, but had come to show off her clothes and her jewels. The child—her age looked to be about twelve years—was enjoying her first visit to a famous theater, and was rapt with excitement. She looked delicate like her mother, and had probably been taken abroad for her health. The man had no great love for operatic music, but had come to give his wife and daughter this treat. He seemed to be an indulgent father, for he kept glancing at the girl's absorbed profile. But when his gaze wasn't on her he looked moody, sunk in thought. He had a well-shaped head with a rounded powerful forehead. It was too dark to see his features clearly but it amused Lavinia to imagine them. He would have a strong mouth with a full lower lip betokening temper and sensuality, hands that were used to controlling a horse or a willful child—or a woman. He would wear his clothes with the easy distinction of the well-bred Englishman. He would be impatient of foreigners, arrogant, sure of himself, but contrarily kind and gentle. He would be an ardent lover . . .

Lavinia twitched her lips in impatience with herself for imposing on a stranger the characteristics which she admired in a man. The romantic evening was making her take leave of what good sense she had. She must concentrate on the stage, which was sufficiently absorbing.

In the next interval she determinedly leaned back out of sight of the occupants of the next box. She certainly had no intention of eavesdropping on their conversation. It just happened that it was too audible not to be heard.

The woman was speaking in a low voice with an undercurrent of weariness and dissatisfaction.

"I told you, Daniel, we can't allow her to travel until the doctor thinks her fit enough. The funeral was a great strain to her. And to me, too. I would never grow used to Venetian funerals. They seem so outlandish and barbarous, that procession of black-draped gondolas. And then the *cimitèro* with all that stone and marble and cypress trees."

"I must admit I found it interesting," the man answered. His voice was pleasantly deep, completely fitting Lavinia's image of him. "In spite of your aunt's copious tears."

"She's grown too Italian in her ways," his wife said disapprovingly. "I suppose it's not to be wondered at, after having an Italian husband and spending all these years in Venice. But I don't admire all that freedom of the emotions. I'm sure I would shut myself in my bedroom to weep in private."

"Which you do all too often."

"There are occasionally things to weep about."

"I suppose Mamma means me," came the little girl's high, clear belligerent voice.

"Why shouldn't I mean you, poor love?"

The man spoke with a touch of impatience. "We're at the opera. It's no place to talk of tears. Are you enjoying it, Flora?"

"Oh, *yes*, Papa. More than anything."

"Then let us call Aunt Tameson's illness a blessing, so that we have to stay in Venice longer than we intended."

"Yes, at least I'm not at home with that horrible Miss Brown," Flora said with satisfaction.

Her mother's voice came reprovingly.

"Miss Brown was not horrible, Flora. It was you who were. And I warn you that if you behave so badly again, Papa won't come to your help. He spoils you far too much already."

"Then it will be another week before Aunt Tameson can be moved?" Flora's father had tactfully changed the subject.

"That's what the doctor thinks. Though I've no faith in foreign doctors. I can't wait to get her home to Doctor Munro."

"Personally, I can't wait to get home to Winterwood."

The woman gave a long sigh.

"Don't be so insular, Daniel. Winterwood has been there long enough. It will still be there when we return."

It was a moment before the man spoke again. Then he said, "It was a mistake bringing Edward. The boy's got out of control."

"No! You're always unfair to him. You spoil Flora, and Simon, too, but my darling Teddy is always in the wrong."

"The Continent is no place for an eight-year-old."

"I agree, Papa. He's been *awful!*" Flora's voice was heartfelt.

"I hope Eliza is able to listen for him," the woman said worriedly. "She wasn't very well. I warned her not to drink the water, but she did, so she deserves her indisposition. If she isn't better tomorrow, everyone will have to stay indoors all day."

"Mamma, I must go to the Piazza to feed the pigeons. Papa—"

"Not now, little one. The curtain's about to go up. Anyway, Eliza will be recovered by the morning. And I daresay the sun will be shining, and the pigeons still there."

"If Eliza isn't recovered we can never travel back to England. I simply couldn't manage without her help. I want to get back as much as you, Daniel." There was a touch of hysteria in the woman's voice. "The whole thing preys on my mind, poor Aunt Tameson failing every day, and being such a stranger to me. And then Flora behaving so badly that Miss Brown gave notice. How could you, Flora? In a foreign country!"

"I was driven to it," Flora said complacently. "Anyway, Miss Brown only wanted to go about reading her guidebook and looking at statues. She used to leave me alone for hours. I told you."

"Flora!" her father said.

"S-sh! The curtain's going up."

When the curtain had come down for the last time and the applause had died away, Lavinia intended to slip out quickly with Gianetta, not pausing, as she secretly wished to do, to stare inquisitively at the family so near to her.

She found herself, however, unable to resist a parting glance, and to her astonishment saw the man swing the child into his arms, and carry her from the box.

People made way for them as they went down the stairs, the little girl's head leaning trustingly against her father's shoulder.

Lavinia had to follow. In the foyer she saw a wheelchair brought forward by an attendant and the child placed in it. Then she was briskly wheeled away by her father, his wife in her full rich skirts, following.

The child was a cripple! How very terrible.

Chapter 2

It was pure chance that Cousin Marion decided, the next morning, to call on an English friend who was staying at a hotel in the Accademia area. She said she would take Gianetta, and Lavinia could occupy herself in her own way. Again, as so often, Cousin Marion's decisions sounded like thoughtfulness when in reality they were nothing of the kind. She was afraid that her English friend might recognize Lavinia.

Venice—with its coverlet of sunlight over the onion domes of the Basilica of San Marco, the faded beige of the Doge's Palace, and the old old rust-colored tiles of the crowding houses; with its black gondolas drifting up the dark green water of the canals, and the flutter and whirr of alarmed pigeons when the great bell from the Campanile rang. In spite of being there in the humble position of companion to Cousin Marion, Lavinia had been enraptured by it. She had made herself bear with Cousin Marion's slights and petty humiliations. After all, she had been in no position to object to them, for what would she have done after Robin's trial if Cousin Marion had not taken her in? She had no money and no reputation.

Who wanted to employ a young woman who had been the chief witness in a murder trial, and involved in the highly questionable events of that terrible night when Robin, stripped of all his assets in one of his mad gambling sessions, had finally wagered his own sister —or rather her hand in marriage—to that revolting Justin Blake, who so badly wanted her. Justin had won and come drunkenly to Lavinia's room to claim her there and then. Fortunately Robin, sobered now by the outrageousness of his act, had followed. In the ensuing fracas Justin had fallen, cracking his head on the brass firedog, and died instantly.

The charge against Robin had been murder, later reduced to manslaughter. Even so, he had been sentenced to seven years' imprisonment, and was now in Pentonville prison. Poor unlucky Robin, shut in his squalid cell, while she was here, in lovely Venice, even though in such a humble capacity.

It didn't serve any purpose to analyze why Cousin Marion had decided to befriend Lavinia, because then one might decide that she, who had always been jealous of Lavinia's looks and popularity, might be indulging in a petty revenge. It was better to believe that she had been moved by true sympathy, and that her insistence on Lavinia's wearing inconspicuous clothes and keeping in the background was only because it would be disastrous for her to be recognized.

But even dressed as a colorless and meek companion, Lavinia had dearly looked forward to her evening at the opera. When Cousin Marion had suddenly felt unequal to going out—she suffered frequently from nervous headaches—Lavinia had been overjoyed to be told she could go if Gianetta, the Italian maid, accompanied her.

It was then that Lavinia had been seized by a mad inspiration. She couldn't bear to go to the lovely La Fenice theater in the only evening gown she now possessed, a drab blue silk of which Cousin Marion thoroughly approved.

Lavinia was only twenty-two and her recent harrowing experience had not ruined her beauty. She had been used all her life to being looked at and admired, especially since she had put her hair up and come out. She and Robin had been known as the handsome twins, not celebrated for their retiring qualities. It was Robin who had been the spendthrift and the gambler. She had been merely foolhardy.

Since the trial, however, she had wanted only to escape notice. Cousin Marion had been perfectly right in insisting that she wear colorless clothes and keep herself in the background.

But for the opera . . . Alone in Cousin Marion's bedroom, Lavinia had riffled through the wardrobe and seized on a rose-pink satin. It was a beautiful dress and would fit her, Lavinia knew. For all her cosseting of herself, Cousin Marion was not the type to put on weight. She was small-waisted and as flat as a board. Lavinia would fill out the bodice better than she would. And the color would be perfect for her.

Actually, it had been less a desire to take revenge on Cousin Marion than a madness caused by the spell of the ancient city that had seized her. She must dress to suit its beauty.

If the dress, why not jewels, too?

After a moment she had decided to leave her own modest pearls unchanged, but she found the key to Cousin Marion's jewel box and took out those delectable diamond earrings, long graceful pendants that swung from tiny crescents, and had the greatest pleasure in putting them on. They had been a perfect foil for her upswept fair hair, her glowing cheeks and the gleaming rose of her gown. She believed she had never looked better.

It was foolish to let a dress, and a borrowed one at that, be so important. But it had been like coming alive again. Lavinia had called gaily for Gianetta and burst into laughter when she saw the girl's amazed face.

"But, *signorina*—pardon, milady—" Then her brown finger pointed in horror. "It is the *Signora's* gown!"

Lavinia had twirled the billowing skirts.

"Doesn't it look wonderful, Gianetta? Don't I look wonderful?"

The girl had clasped her hands in admiration.

"Ah, *molto bella, molto bella!*"

She knew that the man in the neighboring box at the opera had noticed the gown. It had been because of the way it had set off her looks that he had looked so long at her. She wasn't in the least sorry for her audacity, even though a long stare from a stranger in a theater could mean nothing except a temporary lift to her morale.

She was thankful, however, that Cousin Marion had not missed the gown, which had been safely returned to the wardrobe that morning. She was also delighted to have some time to herself. She meant to stroll around the Piazza, looking in the shop windows, small treasure troves whose contents were far beyond her reach, and perhaps being wildly extravagant and drinking morning chocolate at Florian's.

She didn't admit that she hoped she would see the family of last night again. The child had said something about feeding the pigeons. But who knew at what time she would do this, or if the unknown Eliza had recovered from her stomach trouble?

There were the usual small knots of sightseers in the Piazza. The predominant language was English, or perhaps that was because the English seemed to have the most carrying voices. Certainly, the gentlemen in their tweed jackets and caps, and the ladies in muslin or organdy, holding parasols to protect their delicate skins from the fierce Italian sun, looked exactly like people one would see at summer country parties at home. It was a pity, Lavinia thought, that the English sprinkled the globe so completely.

However, in spite of the familiar look of the people, the Piazza San Marco was delightfully foreign. When Lavinia had tired of her window-shopping, she allowed herself to be seated at one of the tables outside Florian's by a waiter with a seductive smile and a friendly, *"Buon giorno, signorina!"* And then, showing off his English, "It is a beautiful day."

Lavinia agreed that it was, and unashamedly enjoyed the waiter's admiration. He must see, by her neat prim dress, that she wasn't one of the wealthy English, yet he still paid her the tribute of devoted attention. And it *was* a beautiful day. Where, in England, could one see such blue skies, or be diverted by such scenes? Or indeed sit alone at a café table without undue attention being paid her? She was simply comfortably regarded as one of the mad foreigners, but a very pretty one. She was astonished to find herself feeling almost happy.

She had finished her chocolate before she saw the girl in the wheelchair. She was sitting in the middle of the Piazza surrounded by fluttering pigeons. Apart from the pigeons she seemed to be completely alone.

Lavinia looked among the strollers for her father, that tall dark-haired man, or her mother, or even someone in maid's uniform who seemed to be attached to her. There was no one. Even from this distance Lavinia could see the child's tenseness. Her hands were gripping the sides of her chair. Her small shoulders looked rigid. She seemed to be on the verge of tears.

On an impulse, Lavinia sprang up and went across to her. "Forgive me, dear, but are you in trouble?"

The girl wore a pink cotton sunbonnet that obscured her face. When she lifted her head sharply to see who had spoken to her, Lavinia saw, not the tear-streaked face she had expected, but a vixenish one.

"Who are you? Why are you speaking to me?"

"I wondered at your being here alone. Can you manage that conveyance by yourself?"

"No, I can't," the girl snapped. "What is it to do with you?"

"Well"—the child was so angry that she was almost amusing, a cross little doll with a flushed face and blazing tawny eyes—"aren't you pleased to hear someone speaking your own language, for one thing?"

"I should have known at once that you were English." The bright eyes swept over Lavinia's plain gown with contempt. "Who is in your charge?"

"A quite elderly lady," Lavinia answered agreeably. "Or she would seem elderly to you. But she has gone to have morning coffee with friends, so I have all this time to myself." Slyly she added, "Have you let your maid have time off, too?"

"Oh, that tiresome Eliza's ill. And my brother, who promised to stay with me, ran off. Papa will be furious when he hears."

"Is the sun too hot for you? Shall I move your chair away?"

"No, don't touch it. I'm perfectly comfortable."

"If you will forgive me for saying so, you look very flushed. I think it is the heat."

The girl pressed her hands to her cheeks.

"It's none of your business."

"But is it good for you to be so hot? I wish you would let me move you into the shade. Perhaps an ice—"

The tawny eyes were furious, like a trapped fox's.

"Are you being *sorry* for me? Because I don't like people to be sorry for me. I'm perfectly all right until Edward comes back."

"Then why don't you look at me?" Lavinia asked. "You only gaze over my head as if I'm not here. You did better in the opera last night."

The startled gaze did, then, meet Lavinia's.

"I've never seen you before! I don't know what you're talking about."

"Oh, I realize I looked better then than I do now. I was in the next box."

"That lady was *you!*"

Lavinia smoothed her gray poplin skirts.

"I suppose I don't look much like her now."

Interest had taken the place of hostility in the child's eyes.

"No, you don't. Why are you so dull-looking now? Are you a servant?"

"In a way, yes. Well, yes, I am completely. Though I hate to admit it. Just as you won't admit that you hate being helpless in that chair."

The girl suddenly said, abruptly, "I had been crying. I never let people see me cry."

Lavinia had to feel a reluctant sympathy.

"Neither do I. My name is Lavinia Hurst. I know yours is Flora because I overheard it last night. I couldn't help hearing. And your brother is Edward."

"My mother calls him Teddy—like a baby. Whose was the dress?"

"The dress?"

"That beautiful one you were wearing. Did you steal it?"

This was no child. She was a prematurely old woman, her thin face, its delicate bones much too close to the surface, precocious and observant.

"No, I didn't steal it. I borrowed it."

Flora looked disappointed. "Oh."

"In a way, I suppose it was stealing because I hadn't asked permission."

"From your mistress?"

"Yes."

"Is she hateful?"

It was surprising what a relief it was to talk to someone, even a child. "She is, at times."

"What will she say if she finds out about the dress?"

"She won't find out. I smuggled it back safely this morning. The earrings I wore were hers, too. Oh, goodness!"

"What is it, Miss Hurst?"

"I've forgotten to put the earrings back. They're still in my bedroom. Oh dear, if Cousin Marion finds out—"

"What will happen?" Flora asked with the greatest interest.

"I don't know. I'm quite sure she'd like to cast me in a dungeon."

"Or make you walk the Bridge of Sighs."

"Or send me to the ga—" Lavinia cut the word off abruptly, the game suddenly no longer a game.

"The gallows? Is she as horrid as that?" Flora obviously reveled in disaster. "Then let's think of a punishment for her. I know— Oh, *Papa!*"

A shadow had fallen across them. Lavinia looked up swiftly to see the man standing there, and knew that this was exactly what she had hoped would happen when she had crossed over to Flora. She hadn't been so deeply concerned about the child's distress. It had merely been fortuitous.

He had a square dark face, a stubborn and slightly brooding face with that jutting forehead and the dark clever eyes.

His attention, at first, was all for Flora.

"What are you doing here? Where is Eliza?"

"Oh, she's sick still; isn't it tiresome? Mamma said I would have to stay indoors, but I told Edward to bring me. Don't scold, Papa. He was perfectly able to. He's very strong. But he got tired of feeding the pigeons and ran off. He did it deliberately to tease me. He's really a thoroughly wicked boy. But it serves him right—I'm to have an ice, and he's not."

"An ice?" The man's eyes were on Lavinia. "Perhaps you will remember your manners, Flora, and introduce me to your friend."

Flora gave a peal of laughter.

"She's not a friend, Papa. She's only a servant. She's Miss Hurst, and her mistress—" Flora's voice became uncertain as she watched her father's expression. "I don't mean she's a servant all the time. Last night she was at the opera. What do you think, Papa? She was the lady in the next box to us. Doesn't that surprise you?"

"On the contrary," the man's voice was cool, "it doesn't surprise me at all. I recognize her perfectly." He gave a small bow. "How do you do, Miss Hurst. I am Daniel Meryon. Allow me to thank you for rescuing my capricious daughter. And what was this about an ice? May I have the pleasure of ordering them for you? And joining you?"

"Oh, Papa, you're not angry after all."

"Let us say, not with Miss Hurst. I'll deal with you and Edward later. Did you enjoy the opera, Miss Hurst?"

"Oh, very much," Lavinia answered composedly, "though I confess that of Mozart's works I prefer Cosi fan Tutte. All the same, I've never heard a better Queen of the Night. Only once, at Covent Garden—" She stopped, aghast. Could she ever learn to be anything but herself? Instead of keeping to her role of self-effacing companion, as soon as she was with an attractive man she was prattling like a debutante.

His voice was perfectly polite.

"You are a music lover, Miss Hurst?"

She nodded. "I am, but unfortunately lately I haven't had much opportunity to go to concerts. Last night my cousin wasn't feeling up to going out, so I went with our maid. Do you enjoy opera, Mr. Meryon?"

"Not in the least. But my wife does, and Flora, I hope, will."

"Oh, I adore it, Papa. When can I have a gown like the one Miss Hurst stole—I mean, borrowed—"

Lavinia resisted a desire to slap Flora sharply.

"Your daughter means the one I was wearing last night. It was my cousin's. She has a more complete wardrobe than I have. Fortunately, we are the same size."

There was no doubt about his interest now. Although Lavinia had known it was there all the time beneath his polite fencing. Her heart was beating rapidly. She had never known such brilliant sunshine, such wonderful architecture, such well-mannered tourists, even such charming pigeons as these that had their habitat in the Piazza San Marco. She had never felt so radiantly alive—nor so aware of potential danger and heartbreak. She had faced that judge, in the criminal court, with his old lizard-wrinkled skin and hooded eyes, with far more equanimity than she was now facing Daniel Meryon.

Which was quite unreasonable, for Daniel wasn't going to sentence her dearly loved brother to death or imprisonment. And after today she would never see him again.

"I should explain that I am acting as companion to my cousin," she said, deliberately heightening his interest. For it must be quite an intriguing situation to even a highly sophisticated man to find that the beauty of the previous evening was one of that obscure race of women, a paid companion, meant to be useful but invisible. Her eyes were dancing. "Flora is speaking the complete truth when she says I am a servant. But that doesn't mean I'm not able to enjoy all these new sights and sounds. I was taking a morning stroll in this quite fascinating square when I came across your daughter in distress. Now if you will excuse me, I must go back to the hotel in case my cousin has returned."

"But you were going to have an ice with us!" Flora exclaimed indignantly. "Are you running away from Papa? You had time to stay before he came."

"Flora is a martinet," said Daniel Meryon easily. "I'm afraid you'll have to obey her. And were you, by any chance, running away from me?"

He had such an inquisitive face. It would be very difficult to conceal anything from him. On the other hand, it would be a quite irresistible game to try. Across the years she could hear her governess' voice, "I'm sorry, my lady, but I can't control Miss Lavinia. If she sets her heart on anything, she intends to get it, willy-nilly," and Mamma's resigned answer, "We can only hope life will teach her."

For the next half hour, surely, it wouldn't do any harm to forget what life had already taught her . . .

She sat down gracefully.

"Certainly, if it pleases Flora, I can stay for a short time. I would enjoy an ice. Already it's so hot, so different from our own climate. Are you making a long stay in Venice, Mr. Meryon?"

"Where did you learn to be so expert, Miss Hurst? You answer one question with another."

She had never believed in dropping her eyelids in pretended modesty. She gave him her full wide gaze.

"I hadn't thought you so dangerous that I had to run away."

It was Flora who enjoyed what she assumed to be a joke.

"Oh, Papa isn't dangerous. Are you, Papa? What did you think he would do, Miss Hurst? Beat you as he does Edward sometimes?" Then, with her too acute intelligence, she seemed to sense something that excluded her and she exclaimed pettishly, "My head is beginning to ache. Do hurry the waiter with our ices, Papa."

"Certainly, my pet. Here he is now." Daniel gave the order to the waiter, and then picked up the conversation smoothly.

"You were asking how long we intended to stay in Venice, Miss Hurst. That isn't certain yet. My wife has an aunt living here. She is suffering from heart trouble, and has expressed a wish to die in England. So naturally we intend to take her there, as soon as the doctor says she is fit enough to travel. That should be within a week or two, we hope. Unfortunately, she had just suffered a shock before we arrived, and that didn't help her condition."

A shock. The funeral Lavinia had heard them discussing last night? She couldn't ask, since that conversation hadn't been meant for her ears.

"Just think what an entourage we will be," said Flora, with her adult precocity. "Me in a wheelchair, and Great-aunt Tameson scarcely able to walk. I don't care for her, but at least she's someone who can't run away from me."

Lavinia saw the quick pain in Daniel's face before he said impassively, "You are probably wondering about Flora, Miss Hurst. She hasn't always been in a wheelchair. She had an accident in the hunting field a year ago, and damaged her spine. The doctors say she will certainly walk again one day, but it's impossible to say when. So in the meantime, she must be very patient."

Flora frowned with great impatience.

"Oh, Papa, you're talking just like everybody else. How can I be patient? I'm so bored, I could die."

"At least you're a lucky girl to be in Venice," Lavinia pointed out. Already she found she wanted to take the pain from this man's, this perfect stranger's, face.

Flora pouted.

"You needn't think this is a holiday. Even here I've had to see specialists. And in Paris, and Lausanne."

"Naturally," said her father. "Aunt Tameson wasn't the only reason for this trip."

"She was for Mamma," Flora said sulkily. "She thinks far more of that horrid old lady than me. And she loves Edward best of all."

"Now, Flora—"

"It's true! She hates having a crippled daughter. She's ashamed of me. And she says it's all my own fault for riding Chloe."

"On the contrary, darling. She blames me for letting you. And she's quite right. I should have forbidden it."

Flora was clenching her hands, on the verge of a tantrum.

"I ride well. Much better than Edward. I was quite able to manage Chloe. She stumbled in a rabbit hole. It wasn't my riding that made her fall. I've told you a hundred times, Papa!"

"It was an accident, pet. We all know that. Now forget it and eat your ice."

Lavinia felt it was time to go. Besides, she had suddenly remembered Cousin Marion's diamond earrings. They must be returned to her jewel box before Cousin Marion came back.

Flora immediately said, "Are you going to be scolded for staying out too long? I wouldn't like to be you, poor thing."

"I can manage," Lavinia said coolly.

Daniel stood up and bowed.

"I think Flora has no doubt of that, Miss Hurst. Neither have I."

He overestimated her self-control. Tomorrow Cousin Marion intended to move on to Florence. This was goodbye. And already she knew how little she wanted to say goodbye.

Again it was Flora who made the diversion.

"Oh, Miss Hurst, don't forget about the earrings! We don't want you locked up in prison.

"But don't worry, Miss Hurst." The irrepressible voice floated after Lavinia. "If that happened, Papa and I would rescue you and carry you off to Winterwood. Winterwood is our favorite place in the whole world."

Chapter 3

Cousin Marion was sitting on the couch in her bedroom. She was still dressed in her large Leghorn straw hat and thin silk shawl. She was holding the diamond earrings in her hands. Her face was pinched and ugly with anger.

"So you're a thief, too!"

"You've been looking through my drawers," Lavinia exclaimed.

"And is that so reprehensible, after what you have done?" She dangled the earrings. "I just happened to find these." She paused, then said almost conversationally, "What else have you taken?"

"I haven't taken anything, Cousin Marion. I merely borrowed your earrings last night. I meant to put them back this morning. I know it was wrong, but please try to understand. I'd got so tired of looking drab." She saw the implacable face of her cousin, and realized that there would be no understanding. She gave a small shrug, and added fatalistically, "I wore one of your dresses, too. Since I'm apparently to be hanged, it might as well be for a sheep as a lamb."

Cousin Marion was momentarily shocked out of her anger.

"How can you be so flippant! I can't say my friends didn't warn me, when I proposed to befriend you. They all said I'd regret it."

"Then your friends were right. They'll be delighted." Lavinia threw off her straw hat and pushed her hair back from her hot forehead. Suddenly she was very tired.

"I didn't steal your earrings, or your dress, Cousin Marion. I simply borrowed them to wear, and I enjoyed wearing them. But I didn't harm them. And I'm not a thief."

Cousin Marion, with the illogical mind of a stupid woman, immediately pursued another suspicion.

"And who did you fascinate? That must be why you borrowed my things, to fascinate somebody. I suppose it was too much to expect that you wouldn't be looking for another man."

Lavinia went rigid.

"Cousin Marion! Please be careful what you say."

"I shall ask Gianetta. You needn't think you have that girl in **your** pocket. She shall tell me who you walked home with—if indeed you came home before morning. Now I believe everything they said about you, that you were mad for admiration, that you would pursue any man."

Lavinia's chin was in the air, her voice was ice.

"Cousin Marion, I have done nothing. I was merely desir—admired by a man whose sentiments I did not return. What happened was an accident, as you know very well. It's true that Robin and I may have led frivolous lives. But we're neither immoral nor liars." She drew herself very straight. "I'm sorry for you with your meanness and your jealousy and your curiosity. You think you can find out about life only by questioning me. I'm tired of your sly insinuations."

"Lavinia!"

"You're a hypocrite, Cousin Marion. You pretended to be doing me a service when all the time it pleased you to have me here to humiliate. Secretly you'd like to have been in my place."

Lavinia looked down at the crumpled figure, seeing the sallow face and the spiteful, frightened eyes. How could she ever think she needed to be grateful to a poor thing like this? She was only grateful for having been given the opportunity and the courage to leave her.

"Keep your diamonds and your expensive dresses. Don't think anyone is going to look at you in them. I'm giving you my notice from today, from this afternoon."

Cousin Marion's small pale eyes had watered into furious tears.

"It's *my* business to dismiss you."

"Then do it, pray."

"And without a reference. I don't know where you'll get another position, I'm sure."

"I shall manage."

"I can arrange for you to travel back to England in the company of some suitable person." Cousin Marion was recovering some of her authority. "I won't have people saying I treated you badly."

"I would prefer to go alone."

"Now, Lavinia, for goodness sake! Come down off that high horse. I did think you'd have at least conquered the sin of pride. All right, then, I didn't mean to dismiss you; I only meant to humiliate you, as you say. How do you think I'm going to like it, wandering about Europe with an Italian maid? But at least you'll do me the goodness to allow me to arrange your return to England."

How heartless the sun was for rising the next morning as if nothing had changed. By common consent Cousin Marion and Lavinia avoided each other's company. Lavinia methodically packed her modest belongings, wondering what dreary friend of Cousin Marion's she would accompany home. Then, anxious to get out of the hotel, as if the golden sunshine and the gaiety of life of the Piazza would dismiss her troubles, she tied the ribbons of her straw hat under her chin and set forth.

The day was completely her own. At least she could use it by gazing with last poignant affection on this lovely city.

She sincerely hoped she wouldn't encounter Flora or her father. That would only involve awkward explanations, and another farewell. If she hadn't forgotten Daniel Meryon's face, he was one person about whom she was determined to have good sense. Further acquaintance with him could bring nothing but disaster.

"Miss Hurst! Miss Hurst!"

She hadn't walked a dozen yards from the hotel before the imperious voice reached her ears.

She looked back to see Flora being pushed by an elderly woman in a servant's cap and apron.

"Miss Hurst, what do you think? Papa has said Edward must be kept in his room this morning as a punishment for leaving me yesterday. Did you get into trouble, too, for stealing the earrings?"

Lavinia had to laugh. For no reason at all, this abominable child had made her spirits rise.

"I told you a dozen times I didn't steal them."

"Well, Papa and I were not so sure. We decided it would be only what your detestable cousin deserved."

"Miss Flora!" The elderly maid was scandalized. She didn't look as if she approved of Lavinia, either, staring at her suspiciously.

"It's all right, Eliza. I was only joking. Miss Hurst, is your cousin letting you free this morning? If she is, would you take me to feed the pigeons? Edward isn't allowed out, and poor Eliza isn't entirely recovered from her sick stomach."

"Miss Flora, there's a forward minx! I beg her pardon, miss. She's got above herself lately. As if this lady has time to spare pushing you about."

Lavinia had been about to agree with Eliza, and walk on. But just for a moment there was something unbearably forlorn in Flora's face. It was an unguarded and unintended expression, for in a moment Flora was saying with her usual acerbity, "Let Miss Hurst answer for herself, Eliza. You have got time, haven't you, Miss Hurst?"

"I daresay I could spare you an hour," she heard herself saying carelessly, thinking of the ghost beneath that small aggressive face. They were alike, she and Flora. They both concealed ghosts.

"Well, I must say I would be thankful," Eliza said. "I'm still feeling peaky, to tell the truth. And we must be well for when we begin traveling with your great-aunt, mustn't we, Miss Flora?"

"If she doesn't die first," Flora said heartlessly. "There was one funeral, Miss Hurst. The remains were put on a gondola, and it was draped with black velvet, and the gondoliers were dressed in black from head to foot. And they glided away over the blue sea and just seemed to be swallowed up. Mamma and Papa and Great-aunt Tameson followed in another gondola, and they said the grave was under cypress trees. And it was terribly hot, and there were crickets making an awful racket all the time. But I believe the blue sea swallowed her up," she said dreamily. "That's the nicest thing to believe."

"Who?" asked Lavinia, with the strangest stirring of eeriness. "Who was it that died?"

"Oh, just one of Great-aunt Tameson's old servants. I don't know what the fuss was about. Except I promise I'll be just as upset for you when you die, Eliza."

"Bless you, I'm sure, Miss Flora. Then, if it's really all right with you, miss, I'll go in out of this murdering sun. How Miss Flora enjoys it, I don't know, her being so delicate and all. Likely the master will come out to fetch her in. He usually does."

You're crazy, Lavinia said to herself. You'll see his face again, and it will be harder than ever to forget.

"You're very quiet, Miss Hurst. Are you angry with me?"

"Shouldn't I be? I don't enjoy being buccaneered into doing things."

Flora twisted around in the chair. "Don't you like me?"

"I think you're a very willful little girl."

"Mamma doesn't like me, either. I'm not pretty, like her, and I can't walk. She only loves Edward."

"I know. You told me that yesterday. Perhaps it's because you aren't easy to love."

"But I am, I am," Flora said passionately.

Lavinia found her both unlikable and comic. She had the pathos of the very young and intense. She was going to be hurt too often if she lived with such intensity. The sneaking thought came that that was something Lavinia could help her avoid. I could speak from experience, she thought wryly.

"I think your papa loves you very much."

"Yes, now he does because he feels he was partly to blame for my accident. He wasn't to blame, of course. I was showing off. I always have had to, because Papa loved Simon and Mamma loved Edward. I was just in the middle, and only a girl."

Lavinia willed herself not to have her sympathies touched. What was the use? She would never see Flora again.

"Who is Simon?"

"My elder brother. He's thirteen, and he's at school. He's Papa's favorite."

"I think you talk too much about favorites," Lavinia said. "Well, what are we going to do this morning? Feed the pigeons, then have an ice, then walk all the way down the Merceria to the Rialto bridge and come back by gondola? That way, we'll pass those wonderful old palaces."

"Great-aunt Tameson lives in one of them," Flora said. "She's a contessa." The information was flung out before she added, her face sparkling, "That sounds like a wonderful morning, Miss Hurst. Much much better than Eliza would have given me. I wish you could be with me always."

"That's nonsense. You didn't set eyes on me until yesterday and then you despised me for being a servant."

"No, no, I didn't despise you. I only thought it a pity. So did Papa."

Lavinia's voice was careful. "Did he say so?"

"He said you looked much more suitable to be sitting listening to the opera than looking after a detestable cousin."

Cousin Marion was right again. She must subdue her looks and her high spirits.

"Then perhaps I'm not suitable to be pushing one young woman about Venice in a wheelchair."

"Oh, you are, Miss Hurst, you silly. Look, I have some money to buy grain for the pigeons."

Flora was too observant. She noticed Lavinia's silences, and the way her eyes dwelt lovingly on the dazzling scene. Later, as they walked slowly down the narrow winding street that led to the Rialto, she kept pausing to look at unexpected views, the little humped bridges over sluggish backwaters, the flowers—morning glory and geraniums and nasturtiums—cascading from window boxes, lacy iron balconies, dark windows from which who knew what face peered, patches of sunlight as yellow as mimosa.

"Why are you sad, Miss Hurst?" she asked.

"Do I seem sad?"

"You look as if you're seeing all this for the last time—as if you might be going to die."

In a strange way the beauty here was mixed with death. There was a chilly smell of decay in the old walls and the dark green water of the canals. Flora was too perceptive.

"Well, one can't stay here forever," she said cheerfully. England, without Robin, without a reputation, without money, would be a kind of death—how did Flora know?

Flora, indeed, had divined something else. She was gazing at Lavinia with her intense tawny eyes.

"Your cousin found out about the earrings!"

"Yes, I'm afraid she did. I wasn't going to tell you."

"Did she scold you dreadfully?"

"She wasn't pleased. As a matter of fact, we have decided to part. I am going back to England, perhaps tomorrow."

"Miss Hurst, you *can't!*"

Lavinia laughed a little at Flora's dismay.

"Why not?"

"Because I'm enjoying our friendship. You can't leave until we do, and that won't be for at least another week. Miss Hurst, do stay."

"I don't think that's possible, you silly child."

"Aren't you enjoying being with me?"

"A certain amount, yes."

"You don't want to go, do you? It's not as though you have Winterwood to go back to. What do you have to go back to?"

"Frankly, not very much. But that isn't your business. Now let us find a *trattoria* where we can have an ice before we go any further."

"The doctors say I'm to be humored," Flora burst out.

"And as far as I can see, you make sure that you are. What am I doing at this moment but humoring you? I didn't plan to spend my last day in Venice pushing you about. But here I am."

"Papa will be upset."

Lavinia's heart jumped. "What can it possibly mean to him?"

"He likes me to be kept happy and amused."

Lavinia stopped dead. "Really, Flora, you are the most presumptuous child. Why should I, a stranger, be ordered to keep you happy and amused? You're behaving like a duchess, and a very spoiled one, at that."

Flora gave only the ghost of her usual uninhibited giggle. She had become very pale. Lavinia was a little alarmed.

"I think all you need is some refreshment. We'll have our ice at that little place ahead, see? We can sit at the edge of the canal and watch the gondolas going by. The next time you come to Venice you'll no doubt be old enough to be serenaded in a gondola."

Flora shrugged her narrow shoulders. She had sunk into a gloomy silence, and when it came, merely toyed with her ice. She remained entirely silent during the somewhat nerve-racking business of lifting her chair into a gondola, and only spoke once all the way down the Grand Canal. That was to point out a small elegant *palazzo* in terra cotta stone, with a very handsome wrought-iron gate at the top of its water steps.

"That's where Great-aunt Tameson lives," she said. "They carried the coffin down those steps. It's a good thing they didn't slip and let it fall in the water."

"You're very morbid about that funeral," Lavinia said.

"I found it interesting," Flora said with dignity. "But Great-aunt Tameson doesn't want a funeral like that. She wants to be buried with her little boy Tom. His grave is in our churchyard at home. Great-aunt Tameson used to live at Croft House, not far from Winterwood. That's when she was married to her first husband. He died on the field of Waterloo. Then little Tom died of diphtheria, so her heart was broken and she came to Italy and married an Italian count. He died, too, and left her all his money. Isn't life sad?"

"The poor Contessa seems to have had her share of misfortune. What a curious name, Tameson."

"It's only the female for Thomas. I expect her parents wanted her to be a boy."

Lavinia laughed.

"You're determined to be gloomy, darling."

Flora's head shot up. Her tragic eyes besought Lavinia.

"I hadn't made a friend for simply ages, until I met you."

Lavinia made her voice flippant, touched against her will by Flora's melancholy.

"As you say—life is sad."

Flora shrugged away the arm Lavinia had laid on her small bony shoulder. "And don't call me 'darling' if you're going to desert me. That is simply the height of treachery."

When they got back to the hotel she refused to say goodbye. Although Lavinia looked about, and lingered longer than necessary, there was no sign of Daniel Meryon. Only Eliza was there to receive the child, and take her away.

Flora sat with her chin sunk, her shoulders hunched, and ignored both Lavinia's farewells and Eliza's scolding about her bad manners.

Finally Eliza made a resigned gesture to Lavinia, and wheeled Flora away.

So that was the end of that strange, diverting and really quite enjoyable encounter. Now one must get down to facing reality.

Cousin Marion was grimly pleased. She had already found some people who would undertake to see Lavinia safely home in return for some small services from her on the way. They were a Mr. and Mrs. Monk, who had formerly traveled without a maid, but Mrs. Monk had been ill in Italy, and felt she could not set out on such a long arduous journey without some female assistance.

"Naturally I've not told them the truth about you," Cousin Marion said virtuously. "I've merely said family reasons are taking you home."

"Family!" Lavinia said bitterly. Could Cousin Marion be so stupid as not to realize that her only family, darling Robin, was in prison for seven years?

"You will have to invent an elderly aunt," Cousin Marion said briskly. "The Monks are leaving first thing in the morning. Mrs. Monk will be sending for you sometime this afternoon, when she feels able to interview you."

Another one of those who enjoyed imaginary illness, Lavinia thought drearily. She supposed she must do her best. And to give Cousin Marion her due, she seemed a little sorry that she was going.

"Why did you have to be so foolish?" she asked. "Perhaps you didn't mean to be dishonest, but you will ruin your life if you go on doing these impetuous things. I suppose it's your nature. Frankly, I believe you attract trouble."

Lavinia nodded, too dispirited to reply or defend herself. And anyway, what Cousin Marion said was true. Trouble did pursue her.

Soon after lunch the summons came. The small page, who could speak only a few English words, managed to indicate that the *Signorina* was wanted in the suite on the ground floor.

"Now look modest," Cousin Marion called after her. "Mrs. Monk particularly wanted to know if you were a quiet modest person. I told a lie. I felt that under the special circumstances the Almighty would forgive me."

She supposed she could keep her eyes downcast, but she couldn't keep the distressed color out of her cheeks. Lavinia followed the agile page boy down the stairs and along a corridor until he stopped and tapped at one of the handsome carved doors. The Monks were obviously affluent people. This looked like the entrance to a palatial suite.

A woman's voice called faintly but imperiously, "Come in," and the boy stood aside to allow Lavinia to enter.

The first person she saw was Flora in her wheelchair, her little old woman face wearing a triumphant expression. A boy with a mop of black curls was trailing a kite about the room, intent on his game and ignoring everyone else. Behind Flora stood Eliza, the elderly maid, her mouth tucked in disapprovingly. Almost reluctantly Lavinia looked for the other occupants of the room. The woman with the imperious voice lay on a couch, her head with its mass of night-black hair resting on a fragile white hand, a tea gown with frothing lace ruffles draped becomingly about her. Flora's father stood at one of the windows with its opaque circled Venetian glass. He was framed by the deep embrasure, looking, in that setting, with his faint melancholy, like a portrait of a Venetian nobleman.

"Miss Hurst—" Flora began, and was instantly silenced by her mother in that weary but supremely arrogant voice.

"You look surprised, Miss Hurst. Didn't the boy explain that my husband and I wanted to see you?"

"No, he didn't. That is—" Lavinia was vividly aware of Daniel Meryon's eyes on her. He thought she was occupied only in looking at his wife, and was giving her an amused yet curiously tender and disarming look.

"He couldn't speak English, Mamma," Flora pointed out. "No wonder Miss Hurst is confused."

"Silence, miss. The first thing Miss Hurst will have to do—that is, if I decide to engage her—is to teach you manners."

The little boy with the kite raced around the room again, then stopped in front of Lavinia and regarded her critically.

"You're to be Flora's companion, but you won't like it. She's a tyrant. Isn't she, Eliza?"

"Now, Master Edward—"

"Teddy, come here, and be quiet!" said his mother, in her dying-away voice. "You know my poor head can't stand noise, darling."

"I think it's time Miss Hurst was told what we want of her before we scare her away completely," Daniel put in. He had seemed so detached from the scene that his sudden voice startled even Edward into momentary stillness. "My daughter, Miss Hurst, as you have probably guessed, has set her heart on having you with her when we go back to Winterwood. I gather that you are contemplating leaving Venice almost immediately, so that's why we sent for you at once. Naturally my wife would like to ask you some questions about your background and so on."

"I shall want to know a great deal," said Charlotte Meryon with only slightly concealed suspicion and hostility.

"Then ask her, Mamma, and she'll tell you," Flora said. She was very pert and confident now. Those desolate airs this morning had been merely an act. "I couldn't eat any luncheon, Miss Hurst, and I cried for two hours. Then I had a fainting turn, so Mamma agreed to send for you. Didn't you, Mamma? I explained how awful your cousin had been to you," she added. "And it isn't true that I'm a tyrant. Edward is speaking lies."

"Flora! As you can see, Miss Hurst, this child is completely out of hand. The doctors said she was not to be thwarted, so this is what happens." Charlotte was pretending, not successfully, to be tolerant toward her crippled daughter. Lavinia could feel the dislike. For the first time she felt a little sympathy toward Flora's extravagances about not being loved. They seemed to have a basis of truth.

All the same, interest in the Meryon family couldn't quell her indignation about the high-handed manner in which they seemed to be arranging her own future. It wasn't only indignation she felt. Apprehension, too. Good sense told her to turn and walk out of this room immediately. She knew by the pull of her eyes to that watchful face by the window that if she allowed herself to be cajoled or bribed into working for these people she would spend too much time listening for his voice or his footstep. She knew the impetuousness of her nature all too well. Indulging in a strong attraction for a married man was no way to start a new life. She must travel back to England with the elderly Monks and forget this brief madness.

In any case, why should Charlotte Meryon assume, as she was doing, that everyone was so willing to obey her commands?

"I will be frank with you, Miss Hurst, and tell you that only dire circumstances would bring me to engage a complete stranger like yourself even if you can produce all the necessary references. But we have had one calamity after another. Haven't we, Daniel?" Her large eyes, curiously pale, like lakes of shining colorless water, sought her husband's. "I have an invalid aunt to be got to England. There is my daughter, a helpless cripple, and I myself am far from strong." Her hand fluttered over the table beside the couch on which there was an array of bottles. "I am subject, on the least exertion, to prostrating headaches. So we are a melancholy lot of invalids and in urgent need of help. It seems that Flora—"

Lavinia could listen to no more.

"I think you are under a misapprehension, Mrs. Meryon. I don't accept employment with this impulsiveness any more than you offer it. Besides, I am not at all the kind of person you require. I agree with you that your daughter is a little overexcitable, and even though she is an invalid I hardly think it necessary to humor her to this extent. She has merely had a passing whim. She will forget it."

"Miss Hurst!" Flora exclaimed, her eyes wide with outrage. "How can you be such a traitor?"

"We said goodbye this morning, Flora. Don't you remember?"

"But I'm saving you from your horrid cousin."

"You're thinking entirely of yourself," Lavinia said. "You haven't deceived me in the least." She faced Charlotte Meryon again, noticing that the pale perfect face wore a look of displeasure, and also some surprise. She obviously had not been told that Lavinia had none of the humility or meekness to be expected from someone in her situation.

"My arrangements have been made for traveling back to England, so I am quite unable to accommodate you," she said. "I'm afraid this whole thing is my fault. I shouldn't have spoken to Flora in the Piazza. I had no idea she would imagine herself so attached to me. But she will get over it. Now if you will excuse me, I have a great deal to do. I make an early start in the morning."

She turned and went quickly before anyone could speak. She would not weaken for the woman on the couch, whom she already unreasonably disliked, but Daniel Meryon had only to say, "Do this for me," or the crazy spoiled forlorn little creature, Flora, to catch her hand, and she would not have been so sure of herself.

She heard Flora's wail, "Miss *Hurst!*" and Charlotte's "Daniel, what a preposterous young woman!" and young Edward's sudden derisive hoot, "Flora's a crybaby!"

It wasn't she who was preposterous, but they.

Nevertheless, it had been she who had deliberately sought Flora's acquaintance on the chance of her father appearing. And he had appeared, and for a little while it had been irresistible to plunge into a forbidden excitement.

Where was her recklessness now?

She knew only that she would find it intolerable to be ordered about by a woman like Charlotte Meryon. She knew that type, self-indulgent, vain, clinging, and unfairly using her frailty as a weapon. If it were frailty. One couldn't deny her loveliness. That black hair and white face and those great colorless eyes had an almost eerie beauty. Daniel must want to indulge her whims as much as he did Flora's. Lavinia already knew it would be unbearable for her to watch that. She couldn't assent to this impulsive scheme.

But, had it been cruel to deny Flora? She was shockingly spoiled, to be sure, but she was also struggling with a certain amount of gallantry with her illness which, unlike her mother's, was genuine. She had a sharp, alert mind that it would be a challenge to guide. *You* guiding an innocent child's mind! *You!*

"Didn't you like them?" Cousin Marion asked sharply. "Please don't be difficult now and refuse this opportunity. You might remember you're in no position to pick and choose."

"I haven't seen the Monks yet," Lavinia answered. "It was a mistake."

"A mistake? How could it be? Then who did you see?"

"Some strangers. I wasn't the kind of person they were looking for. I told you, it was a mistake."

Later she did see the Monks, a thin old paper-faced couple, absurdly alike. She agreed to be ready to leave with them at seven o'clock sharp in the morning. She was wryly pleased with herself that for once in her life she was doing the sensible and conventional thing, and for the rest of the day was utterly miserable. Only Cousin Marion's everlastingly complaining voice saying that she might at least make herself agreeable on her last evening induced her to put on the dowdy blue silk and accompany her cousin down to dinner that evening.

She prayed that the Meryons would not be dining at the same time. Another onslaught from Flora would be too much.

Cousin Marion, as usual, thought the waiters were too slow, the food foreign and indigestible, the room too hot. In the middle of her stream of complaints she suddenly demanded, "Who are you looking at?"

They had come in—Charlotte and Daniel, and Edward, dressed in a smart dark blue velvet suit. There was no sign of Flora.

Neither Charlotte nor Edward noticed her, but Daniel did. Across the room he paused to give her a slight bow, and then went on. She noticed that when they were seated he had his back to her.

And that was the last she would see of Daniel Meryon, a pair of broad shoulders, and that square powerful head turned away from her and attentively toward his lovely wife.

But where was Flora? Ill? Crying in her room? Having a tantrum?

"Lavinia, I was speaking to you. Who are those people? Have you acquaintances here you didn't tell me about?"

"They're only people I spoke to in passing. They have an invalid daughter. I felt sorry for her."

Cousin Marion's gimlet eyes bored into her. But she read nothing in Lavinia's face, for she said disappointedly, "I can't admire this freedom you have with complete strangers. Your own nature is your worst enemy. Do, pray, try not to give Mr. and Mrs. Monk any nasty shocks, or I shall be held responsible."

"I'll never see them again," Lavinia murmured.

"Who? The Monks? That's not the point. You should try to be remembered pleasantly."

Did that matter? She supposed it did. For it was surprisingly painful to think how she had hurt and disillusioned Flora. She hoped the child wasn't really ill.

At last the day was over. Cousin Marion was in bed, her light out; Gianetta had retired; and Lavinia was expected to have done the same.

But the moon was shining on the lagoon. The air was balmy. By leaning far out of her window she could just see the domes of the Basilica gleaming silver. To complete the magic, someone far out on the lagoon was singing an aria from *La Traviata*. It was unbearably beautiful, unbearably sentimental and sad. And Lavinia had an overpowering compulsion to stand on the side of the canal just once more, letting the moonlight and the calm wash all the bitter realities out of her mind.

She put a shawl over her head, covering the fair hair that betrayed her Englishness, and took the precaution of going down the backstairs. Wandering alone in Venice at night would be what Cousin Marion would term her final folly.

"Gondola, lady?" the smiling gondolier, his eyes gleaming in the flaring quayside light, asked.

She shook her head reluctantly. Besides, she doubted if she had the fare. Cousin Marion was not exactly generous with money.

Someone took her arm. A deep, familiar voice said, "Yes, gondolier, please. Take us as far as the Rialto. Step in, Miss Hurst."

She was caught off balance. That was her only possible reason for obeying. She had started so violently that if she hadn't stepped into the gondola she believed she would have tumbled into the canal.

"Whatever do you think you're doing?" she asked Daniel Meryon.

"Fulfilling your wishes, I believe. You were longing for a gondola ride by moonlight, weren't you? And why not? It's very romantic. One should never leave Venice without having done it."

"Mr. Meryon, of all the presumption! Are you trying to kidnap me?"

He laughed, pleasantly. "You do have a tendency toward drama.

If that were my intention, I would have instructed the gondolier to take us down the small back canals. Have you seen them? They're very narrow and dark and quite sinister. There one can feel Venice's cruel past very distinctly. Have you noticed it? The romance of all this, the moonlight, the decorative palaces, is only a veneer."

Lavinia impatiently dismissed his conversational discourse.

"What about your wife? Flora?"

"My wife has retired with a headache. Flora, I hope, is asleep. The doctor gave her a sedative."

"Why did she need it?" Lavinia asked in a hostile voice.

The gondolier had swung his boat round and out into the open stream. It rocked a little, and Daniel supported her as she inadvertently swayed against him.

"Let me answer that with another question. Why do you need to be persuaded to come back to Winterwood with us?"

"Persuaded! Whatever do you mean?"

"Because you do want to come, don't you? I really can't think why you feel it necessary to stand on your dignity like this."

"Mr. Meryon— I simply don't understand what you are talking about."

"You were very kind to Flora." He didn't seem to have noticed her indignation. "I don't think you did that casually. You may think her spoiled and unlikable, but you recognize her tragedy and her courage. She is a very lonely little girl. You noticed that. That's why I think this isn't just a matter of indulging her whims, but of you being the best possible influence for her." After the briefest pause he added, "My wife agrees, though reluctantly. She thinks you rather too pretty, and wonders how you come to be in this position."

"As for that—"

"No, don't explain. I don't particularly want to know. Flora and I accept you for what you are to us. Isn't that enough for your sense of dignity?"

To her complete fury her voice trembled. "Your wife will scarcely accept that."

"As Charlotte rather aptly put it, 'beggars can't be choosers.' We really are in desperate straits for help. Oh, she will ask endless questions, of course. But aren't you flattered that she should distrust you for being pretty?"

"Mr. Meryon—please believe me—I'm not suitable for this position. You know nothing about me. I'm not even honest."

"You mean that business of borrowing your cousin's jewelry. If I may be frank, she can scarcely do it justice herself."

"You're very rash to dismiss a thing like that so lightly."

The gondolier, rowing rhythmically, suddenly began to sing. He had a fine lyrical tenor voice. The lapping of the water against the boat was a gentle accompaniment. The lights from the shore were so much dimmer than the moonlight. They were bathed in luminous light; the water was velvet black, the ripples like the fin-silver of fishes. Daniel had made no answer to Lavinia's last protest, as if suddenly he had become caught in the magic of the night. She knew that she had. She seemed to have sailed away from the past and the future, and was experiencing an extraordinary sense of release and freedom. She sensed that he was, too, although she could scarcely presume to divine his thoughts. It was a bit of moonlight madness to have the intuition that he, too, had been glad to momentarily shake off ties and troubles.

If the gondolier didn't stop singing she would find herself agreeing to any proposal, no matter how fantastic.

"You have an extraordinarily innocent face," Daniel said, and the spell was gone forever.

"What makes you say that?" she demanded suspiciously.

"Only because your cousin seems to have made you feel you have committed some black crime. I assure you Flora and I will be more tolerant when you are at Winterwood."

She tried to revive her indignation. She was altogether too conscious of his arm against hers. Gondolas were not made for prim behavior. However had she allowed herself to get into this situation?

Because you wanted to, the voice in her head said. Be honest for once. He has spoken nothing but the truth. You do want to go to Winterwood; you do want to be persuaded; you did cultivate Flora's acquaintance; you did deliberately go outdoors alone this evening. And you were utterly miserable at the thought of those dead-and-alive Monks with their parchment faces. Be honest!

But you know where this will lead you. You'll fall in love with him and begin to hate Charlotte's lovely face. Going to Winterwood will be deliberately impaling yourself on a stake, walking on nails . . .

But couldn't there be some way out of the hurting?

If you made Flora happy, for instance, not because you like and admire her, but for his sake, because he cares. If you were able to help her to walk again, wouldn't that recompense you for your own hurt? And wouldn't Robin be happy to know you had such a good position?

Anyway, Daniel Meryon knows what he is doing. His eyes are wide open. He's only flattering you because he wants his own way for

Flora's sake. He's happily married. His wife is very beautiful. He's
adult and conventional and sophisticated. Those tender glances
come easily to him. You must learn not to read anything into them.
You must learn to control your destiny.

But, oh, to live again . . .

The song had ended. The dark curve of the Rialto bridge loomed
ahead. The gondolier expertly swung the gondola around. They were
headed back for San Marco. The world was returning.

"Very well," Lavinia said in a low, determined voice. "I'll come. If
your wife will agree."

"I will agree, Miss Hurst."

Then, with his unpredictable disturbing behavior, he lifted one
of her hands and put his lips to it.

"The gondolier expects us to be a little romantic," he said calmly.
"Don't let us disappoint him. Besides, that is only part of my gratitude."

"Then pray don't show the rest of it," she said tartly.

He laughed with enjoyment. It was a pity it was too dark to see his
face. She would like to have seen it when it was full of pleasure, no
matter what the reason for the pleasure. She had a feeling it was not
often like that. At least the dark safely permitted her a smile of sheer
relief, and a growing delight. Practical considerations surged through
her head. She would have some more precious days in Venice. She
would insist on taking sole charge of Flora, and begin earnestly to
like the child. The Monks would have to be told, of course. But their
dull, petulant old faces had got past feeling much of either pleasure
or disappointment. They would have to delay their journey for a
day, and find some other companion much more suitable than herself. Which would be all to the good as, in the height of frustration
and despair, she might have yielded to the temptation to push them
off the appallingly slow train that bumped and rocked its way across
Italy!

She suppressed a small gurgle of amusement, and her companion
looked enquiringly at her.

"Would you have tipped me overboard, Mr. Meryon, if I hadn't
finally agreed to your request? Is that why you inveigled me into a
gondola?"

"Perhaps."

"You don't know who I am. You're trusting your daughter to a
complete stranger."

"I know that you enjoy the opera; I know that you speak like a lady; I know that you have come to your present situation through bad fortune."

"Bad fortune! Yes. How do you know that?"

"I expect your parents died and there was less money than you had anticipated. Probably your father was a spendthrift and left you forced to keep yourself. I only make a guess, but obviously you have been well-educated. And—forgive me for saying so—you must have found your cousin less than stimulating company."

It was all so harmless, and so exactly what she had already planned to tell his wife.

"You are very perceptive, Mr. Meryon."

"So is my wife."

Was he hinting that she must be careful—supposing that innocuous story were not the true one?

But it turned out that he was thinking of something else entirely.

"It might be just as well not to mention my method of persuasion. Charlotte regards riding in gondolas at night a highly frivolous pursuit."

And was accustomed to not trusting her husband? Since she couldn't ask that question, Lavinia fell silent.

They were slowly getting nearer to the San Marco water stop, the lights of the hotel, and yet another beginning to her life. The little red light bobbing on the prow was pretty, but much too dim to show the way.

Chapter 4

In high dudgeon Cousin Marion, with Gianetta, departed for Florence. She had washed her hands of Lavinia forever, she said. That elderly nondescript couple, the Monks, who should never have left the safety of their fireside, decided that Lavinia was much too flighty for their taste, and also departed, thanking their lucky stars that they were spared such an unreliable traveling companion.

So the die was cast.

A little later Charlotte Meryon sent for Lavinia to come to her bedroom.

This time Charlotte was alone. It was impossible to know whether she was pleased or displeased. Her huge eyes rested speculatively on Lavinia. She was holding a fan, which she moved languidly now and then. It was a hot morning and the heat evidently made her limp and tired. There was no vestige of color in her face, though this seemed to add to her strange attraction. She was still in a negligee and her heavy black hair was tied back loosely as if she hadn't had the energy to put it up.

"My husband tells me that you have been persuaded to change your mind, Miss Hurst. May I ask why?"

Lavinia decided on frankness.

"I have fallen in love with Venice and would dearly like a few more days here. That, and the prospect of traveling with two elderly very dull people, made me regret my rather hasty decision yesterday."

"You think we will make more amusing traveling companions?"

"I wasn't thinking in terms of amusement, Mrs. Meryon."

Charlotte moved her fan rapidly.

"Perhaps you were overcome with pity for our daughter?"

"Yes, I feel great pity for her. Though, if you will forgive me saying so, I don't think it's good for her to make a weapon of her helplessness. I should like to treat her as a person who is normal in every way."

"Have you expressed this opinion to her father?"

"No, not yet."

"I expect you will. You seem to be a very opinionated young woman."

Lavinia bit her lip and said nothing.

Charlotte's great eyes looked over her fan.

"I will warn you at once that my husband doesn't enjoy gratuitous advice any more than I do. However, let us keep to essentials. I must know something about your background. Who were your family? What education have you had? Why are you in the position of having to support yourself?"

The story Lavinia had rehearsed came easily. She had so quickly become an accomplished liar.

"I was brought up in Somerset, Mrs. Meryon. My father had a small estate. I had a governess and was taught all the usual things, music, sketching, French and a little German, the English poets, dancing, of course, and riding. Then, just before I was to come out, my parents were killed in an accident. The dogcart they were driving in overturned. Papa liked fast horses, and—" It was still too painful to talk about, the frantic shock and disbelief, Papa dead, and Mamma dying, beautiful black Caesar with a broken foreleg, shot.

"He sounds like my husband," Charlotte commented. "This passion Englishmen have for horses. Well, go on. Wasn't there some other member of your family who could take over bringing you out? Were you an only child?"

"Yes." Forgive me, Robin, she thought, but it's safer this way. "The reason I couldn't come out was that it was discovered, after my father's death, that he had a great many debts. There was nothing left for me. So my Cousin Marion offered to have me as her companion. I'm afraid we finally found each other quite incompatible. It was mostly my fault, I admit. I hadn't been brought up for that sort of life."

"Have you any reason to think you will be more successful in our employ?" Charlotte asked.

"I shall do my best, Mrs. Meryon."

"Your position won't include wearing fine clothes to the opera."

"That was foolish of me," Lavinia admitted.

"Yes, it was." Charlotte seemed to be summing up Lavinia's appearance, perhaps reflecting on her youth, for the daylight showed faint lines about her own eyes, and for all its perfection her face had a lack of freshness, a worn and delicate look, as if the heat or the traveling, or anxiety, had drained her. Already she seemed exhausted by this interview. She pressed her fingers to her temples.

"I am a martyr to headaches. Only someone who suffers similarly can understand how I feel."

"I'm sorry, Mrs. Meryon," Lavinia murmured, the thought coming that Daniel must show insufficient sympathy.

"I am forced to spend half my life on a sofa. I can't describe the effort this trip has been. But it was absolutely essential to make it for my poor aunt's sake. She wrote to me expressing her wish to die in her native country, so what could I do but regard it as a sacred trust. Have you had an experience of nursing, Miss Hurst?"

"A little," Lavinia answered.

"Well, that's a blessing, at least. As my husband has told you, we have been left entirely in the lurch by Eliza's getting ill and that wretched Miss Brown's leaving us in Switzerland. Although I must be fair to her and say that my daughter tormented her. I must have your promise, Miss Hurst, that if you undertake this journey with us you will not desert us halfway. After we reach Winterwood is another matter. Shall we regard this as a trial arrangement?"

"Certainly, Mrs. Meryon. Nothing could suit me better."

Charlotte sighed with relief. She had saved face. She had been forced to engage Lavinia, but had done so on her own terms.

"Then I hope you are ready to begin at once. My husband and I will be at my aunt's *palazzo* all day, so I shall want you to stay with the children. Please pay particular care to Edward. He is a high-spirited child and loves to do what he calls his disappearing trick." Charlotte smiled fondly and went on, "Tomorrow I will want you to pack my aunt's belongings. Eliza is coming today to help me sort them out. It's all so exhausting in this heat. And I worry continually about my poor aunt. She isn't fit to travel, but insists on doing so."

"It would be terrible if she died on the way," Lavinia said.

"Don't even begin to think of such a thing," Charlotte spoke with a peculiar intensity. "It simply mustn't be allowed to happen."

Lavinia very soon had sympathy with the departed Miss Brown. She knew that Flora, self-willed, pampered and highly disturbed as a result of her crippled condition, would be difficult, but Edward proved to be nothing less than a fiend. He refused to obey, was ill-mannered and noisy, and tormented Flora until she was in furious tears.

"I told you, Miss Hurst. Mamma ruins him. She thinks he can do no wrong. He's her pet. How do you like being a pet?" she demanded viciously of Edward.

"How do you like being a crybaby?" Edward retorted. He really was a beautiful child, with his rosy cheeks and glossy black curls. He was the exact opposite of Flora with her waxen peaked face and straight brown hair. She must have been a plain child even before her accident. No doubt her mother had always been disappointed in her. Her best feature was her eyes, which could blaze into a tigerish color when she was agitated. But even they became a disappointing hazel when she was dejected or tired. The Italian sun had brought out a faint dusting of freckles on her cheekbones, which were causing her distress. She wanted to put rice powder over them, and sulked when Lavinia laughed at her vanity.

"If you're going to behave like Miss Brown I'll be sorry I ever persuaded Papa to employ you," she said spitefully.

"Old Brownie," Edward put in. "Flora was awful to her. Miss Hurst, can I go out and play?"

"Not until Flora has had her rest after luncheon. Then we will all go for a walk."

Edward behaved as if he hadn't heard her. This, Lavinia was to find, was a characteristic of his when people didn't say what he wanted to hear. He appeared to be quite contentedly occupied playing with his toy soldiers, and Lavinia, giving her attention to Flora, couldn't have said when he disappeared.

It was the stranger bringing him back who startled her.

He walked into the room after the most perfunctory tap at the door, dragging a pouting Edward by the hand.

"I found this young man wandering in the Piazza. I thought I had better bring him back"—he had given Lavinia a casual look, then looked again, with some intentness—"since I hardly think you had given him permission to be out, Miss—"

He waited in the boldest way for her to say her name. He had expected her to be Eliza, and was inquisitive as to her identity. She hadn't the slightest idea who he was. He had a handsome highly colored face, though it verged on coarseness, with thick lips, and bright bold eyes. His clothes suggested the dandy. He had a look as if he were about to break into laughter. His lips were slightly parted and seemed to quiver.

What was so funny?

"No, he wasn't supposed to be out," Lavinia said coolly. "Thank you for bringing him back. I'm afraid I don't know who you are."

"Oh, he's Mr. Peate," Flora put in. "He's a relation of Great-aunt Tameson's."

"Jonathon Peate," the man amplified. "A nephew of the Contessa. And, you neglected to say, Miss Flora, a friend of yours." In an exaggerated gesture which made Flora wince, he lifted her hand and kissed it. "Ma'am! Your servant. Aren't you going to introduce me to your new companion?"

His gaze was raking her again, and, unaccountably, Lavinia was nervous. She believed he was just one of those too familiar and breezy men whom she had occasionally encountered among Robin's friends. Yet there was a sharpness in his look that could have suggested more than mere admiration.

"She's Miss Hurst," Flora said offhandedly. "Did Edward invite you to visit us, Mr. Peate?"

"How do you do, Miss Hurst?" The man bowed, then said in a loud jovial voice which no doubt he thought appealed to children, "I have just rescued your small brother, Miss Flora. I must say you don't seem very grateful."

"Mamma and Papa are out."

"Then can't I have a short visit with you? Miss Hurst, will you be so unwelcoming as our small invalid?"

"I am not an invalid!" Flora said between her teeth.

"Oh, sorry, sorry. I quite realize that. You have very sensitive toes, princess."

"Toes?" Flora said coldly.

"I seem to tread on them rather often. I hope Miss Hurst will be more charitable toward my clumsiness." He was laughing softly now as if his amusement couldn't be held back any longer. "After all, I believe I have done you a good turn, Miss Hurst, in bringing back young Edward. It would have been bad luck to have been hauled over the coals on your first day."

"How do you know that it is my first day?"

"Deduction, my dear young lady. You were not here yesterday. I wish you well with these charming little imps of Satan."

Lavinia made no answer. She had already decided that she disliked Mr. Jonathon Peate intensely, although she had to admit he had a certain virile attractiveness. He hardly seemed the kind of friend Charlotte and Daniel would have, yet he was behaving with great familiarity. Indeed, he was quizzing her again with that slightly disturbing intentness. She supposed he was the kind of man who would not think someone in her position worthy of the best manners.

Flora's outspokenness matched their visitor's.

"How long are you staying, Mr. Peate? You were not invited."

"Pardon me, princess." Mr. Peate bowed with a great flourish.

"Then I must leave. I merely thought your papa or your mamma might be in."

"They're not. And don't call me 'princess.'"

"Flora!" Lavinia felt she had to make a halfhearted protest, even though she secretly approved of the child's rudeness. But Mr. Peate merely seemed amused by it. He gave his merry laugh and said that he would have to call again.

"I shall look forward to improving our acquaintance, Miss Hurst."

He was still laughing softly as he left.

"Isn't he abominable?" said Flora intensely. "He always calls me 'princess' and behaves like that just because he sees it makes me angry. I can't think why Mamma and Papa have him here."

"Why do they?" Lavinia asked.

"He's a cousin of Mamma's, though she had never met him. They have both come to see Great-aunt Tameson, so of course they have to be friends. I am sure Papa doesn't like him."

"And your mother?"

"Oh, she says family things are important. I don't agree at all. When I am grown-up I shall certainly refuse to speak to Edward."

This made Edward, who, as well as his gift for detaching himself from conversations in which he wasn't interested, had a sharp ear for ones that concerned him, spring up and come over to Flora's chair.

"Won't you even say good morning?" he asked with great interest. His lively little face was highly attractive when it lost its look of obstinacy and self-will.

"Never. You are too odious."

"Well, so are you. You'd better be careful what you say to me because you can't run away. I'm going to pull your hair until it comes out in my hand."

"No, no! Stop him, Miss Hurst! He's a devil! Miss Hurst!"

It was a pity that Charlotte chose that moment to return. This was the signal for Edward to burst into loud sobs and fly to his mother's skirts, and for Flora to sink into a white sulkiness.

"There, there, my baby!" Charlotte raised indignant eyes. "What have you been doing to him, Flora? You're the eldest, and should know better. Miss Hurst, this was one reason why I was glad to have Miss Brown leave. She seemed unable to keep order."

"I believed I was engaged to look after Flora only," Lavinia pointed out.

"Yes, yes. Edward will have a tutor when we get home. But while we are in these straits I do expect you to lend a hand. I have just had a most trying hour with my aunt, and my head is aching. Teddy, pray think of Mamma's poor head, and stop making that noise. Miss Hurst, I would like you to come this evening to visit my aunt, and take her packing in hand. If you could see the things she wants to take!" Charlotte pressed her hands to her brow. "One would think she was planning to spend a lifetime in England when really, at the most—" Charlotte saw Flora's too watchful gaze, and shrugged her shoulders, indicating wordlessly her aunt's imminent death.

"How is she today?" Lavinia asked.

"Astonishingly well. And that is making her very difficult. She wants to see everything. This must be shaken out; that must be wrapped in cotton wool; her jewelry must be carried by hand; the gown she wore to a royal reception, heaven knows how many years ago, must be packed in a trunk of its own. There are pictures, ornaments, furniture. But those simply must be got rid of. I think you, a stranger, might have more influence with her, Miss Hurst. My husband simply won't have the patience to travel back to England with a whole caravan of luggage."

Now that they were off the tricky subject of the children, Lavinia felt more sympathy.

"Certainly I will do what I can, Mrs. Meryon. By the way, a Mr. Peate called."

A curious expression passed across Charlotte's face. It was there for the merest second. It was quite unreadable.

"Oh, Jonathon! Did he say when he would call again?"

"No, not the exact time."

"He's like all men, expects one to be at his beck and call." There was a note of irritation and fluster in Charlotte's voice. "He could be of much more help to me with Aunt Tameson if only he were of some use in a domestic crisis. But I find men quite helpless in a sickroom or in organizing a house. Well, we women must bear the burden. Come with Mamma, Teddy. She might just possibly have a sweetmeat for you."

Flora watched them go.

"You see, Miss Hurst. Edward is Mamma's pet. He will grow up to be a milksop, Papa says. How lucky you were to be an only child. You would have all your parents' love. Did it make you very good?"

"Do I look good?"

"Not in the least, thank goodness. Miss Hurst!"—Flora's voice seldom lost its agonized intensity—"Don't let Mr. Peate look at you like he did."

"I can scarcely alter his expression. What was it you didn't like about it?"

"I can't explain. Anyway, I don't like him. He laughs when there's nothing funny. We never met him before we came to Venice. Don't you think that odd?"

"Sickbeds have a way of gathering strangers together. Perhaps Mr. Peate is fond of your great-aunt."

"He's fond of her money, more likely."

"Flora, what a very cynical thing to say. Did you hear someone else say it?"

"I heard Papa and Mamma talking. Papa said she was to send that fellow packing, but she said how could she when Great-aunt Tameson wanted him. And, anyway, one didn't behave like that toward relations. And it would look as if we wanted all the money if Mr. Peate was got rid of."

"Got rid of!"

"I should like to push him in a canal on a dark night," Flora said broodingly. "I don't like him. He looks at Mamma, too. It's a pity Great-aunt Tameson is so rich."

"Is she?"

"Oh, yes, dreadfully. But I'm sure she doesn't care a bit about money now. She only wants to be under the stone angel with little Tom. I pray I am never rich in case someone like Mr. Peate stands by my bedside."

Chapter 5

MR. PEATE was not standing at his aunt's bedside when Lavinia was there. The old lady lay alone in the vast room. A servant had shown Charlotte and Lavinia in, and had then left. All the windows set in their medieval Gothic arches were shut and the room was stiflingly hot. Candles burning in a branched chandelier of Venetian glass added to the warmth. Their light was reflected in several mirrors so that the room seemed overilluminated, and yet curiously dark. The darkness came from the dark red damask walls and the heavy curtains. The face of the old woman in the bed was almost the color of the candle flames, a pale yellow, in which gleamed a pair of berry-black eyes. There was a strong smell of violets, which, blended with the heat and the candle smoke, was a little sickening.

"How are you this evening, Aunt Tameson?" Charlotte asked. "It's very hot in here. Don't you think you should have a window open?"

"And be poisoned by the smell of the canals!" For all her look of frailty the old lady had a surprisingly strong voice.

"After all these years you must have grown immune to that. Did you eat your supper?"

"Such as it was. Who is that?" She pointed a forefinger at Lavinia.

"This is Miss Hurst, whom I was telling you about. She will be helping me with your packing. She agrees with me that we can't travel laden like camels."

"What's it to do with her?" the old lady asked tartly.

Charlotte sighed. "I'm only pointing out that you'll have to discard some of your belongings. Almost all your clothes must be given away. You really can't keep ball dresses from the eighteen-thirties."

"How would you like to throw away the dear treasures of a lifetime? Don't be too overriding, Charlotte, or I will be sorry I sent for you."

"I'm not being overriding, aunt. Merely practical. We have filled three trunks already. Tomorrow, with Miss Hurst's assistance, we will finish."

"Is this young woman trustworthy? Where does she come from? Why haven't I seen her before?"

"I explained all that to you. She has agreed to look after Flora."

"I have a great many valuables," the old lady grumbled. "I shall wear what I can, but the rest—"

"The rest are locked in your jewel case, which I personally am looking after. Please don't be difficult, Aunt Tameson. You know that Daniel and I want to move you as soon as possible. This can only be done with some assistance. So you must make up your mind to trust Miss Hurst."

As I have had to, she might have added, from the resentful glance she gave Lavinia.

The old lady held out a hand to Lavinia. It was the sad hand of an old woman, blue-veined and knotted with age. It was also heavily be-ringed. Lavinia noticed that, although the hand was emaciated, the rings seemed strangely tight, pressing into the flesh.

"You won't be too cruel, will you, Miss Hurst?"

"Aunt Tameson, are you suggesting I am cruel!" Charlotte exclaimed. "That's unfair. I couldn't be doing more to help you. But someone has to be a little practical."

"Practical people are so dull. I was never one of those, thank goodness. I don't believe Miss Hurst looks very practical either. She's too pretty. Why isn't she married?"

"Now that's her business, aunt." There was an edge to Charlotte's voice, as if this were a question she herself would have liked to ask.

"I expect Daniel engaged her. A man always has an eye for a pretty woman and by the look of him, your Daniel's no better than others." The old lady sounded malicious. It seemed as if she didn't care too much for Charlotte, perhaps because she resented being dependent on her.

Charlotte sighed. "I have explained, Aunt Tameson. We needed extra help. We hadn't expected Eliza to get ill, and if you must know, we hadn't thought you would be so feeble. Actually, it was Flora who took a fancy to Miss Hurst, and the doctor has said her wishes aren't to be crossed, though I must say I don't entirely agree with that. So now you have the whole story, and it's time we left you. You must try to sleep. And no walking about in the night counting your possessions. I've ordered Fernanda to sleep in here and see that you don't wander."

The old lady looked crafty and petulant.

"Why shouldn't I look at my possessions while I still have them? Soon enough they'll be gone."

"And you'll be at Winterwood, not needing any of them. Forgive me if I sound hard, but you know this is the doctor's orders. You must rest and get strong for the long journey."

"You mean otherwise I'll be listening to those screeching cicadas for all eternity. I'd rather have an English thrush singing on my grave."

"And so you shall. We'll take you safely home. But you must promise to be good."

"Oh, I'll be good, since I must. Only let us get started. We haven't all the time in the world. Am I unfaithful, forsaking Lorenzo to lie with my little Tom? But Tom came before Lorenzo. He was my baby. And there was his father. Once I loved him very much. But I was so young. Only seventeen. And he had to get himself killed at Waterloo before little Tom had a chance to know his papa. I must say though," her eyes twinkled with some dry amusement, "Willie would have been astonished to know that I would be dying a countess. I wonder which husband I shall choose on the other side, Willie or Lorenzo. I admit that I enjoyed Lorenzo's title and money. Poor Willie was only a captain of Hussars. But I don't suppose there are any titles in heaven. I daresay we are all leveled into the same dull position."

"How can you be so irreverent, Aunt Tameson?"

"Now don't be cross, Charlotte. I enjoyed my title and I shall dislike giving it up. That is the truth."

Charlotte seemed upset as they left the gloomy room.

"I can't tell you, Miss Hurst, how these visits to my aunt upset me. The old will be so morbid, and I hate death."

"I think perhaps your aunt is frightened, too, Mrs. Meryon."

"Oh, no, she is very strong-minded. Anyway, I don't believe she means to die at all."

It seemed as if the words slipped out without Charlotte's intending them to. She immediately went on, "Naturally Daniel and I hope she will enjoy a long happy time at Winterwood. That's why it's important to make this journey as easy as possible for her."

Lavinia had noticed a peculiar musty smell in the house, as if it had been shut up for years. Now, in the flickering candlelight of the large marble-floored *sala*, she saw dust on the heavily carved furniture and the statues and ornaments. The floor looked as if it hadn't been properly swept for months.

There had been the same musty smell, overlaid by the clinging violet perfume, in Aunt Tameson's room.

"Are there no servants except that one we saw?" she asked.

It was a casual question, and shouldn't have prompted such a sharp, suspicious look from Charlotte.

"Why do you ask?"

"Nothing has been properly dusted. What are the other rooms like?"

Charlotte threw up her hands.

"Don't talk about them. Chaos! I wouldn't have told you this if you hadn't mentioned it, but my poor aunt has really grown quite eccentric. After being used to a horde of servants when her husband, the Count, was alive, she apparently decided she couldn't stand their noise and chatter and dismissed them all except a girl to clean and shop, and the old one who died. She has been living here in virtual isolation, seeing nobody, and thinking herself poor. That's a hallucination of the old, I believe. You saw the way she can't bear to throw anything away. But please don't talk of this, Miss Hurst. One doesn't gossip about one's relatives' infirmities."

"Naturally I won't talk about it," Lavinia said stiffly.

"I particularly meant to Flora. That child is a jackdaw for gossip. She mustn't be allowed to think her great-aunt peculiar. Nor must Edward. Children develop secret nightmares about things like that. I want them both to be fond of the poor old lady. They may give her a little pleasure in her last years."

Charlotte, Lavinia divined, would have liked to have said last months, or even last weeks. Naturally she couldn't be expected to have any fondness for an aunt she hadn't seen since she was a child. But she scarcely needed to be a hypocrite. Or did she? Wasn't it better that way, pretending an affection and concern she didn't feel. At least it gave a more civilized veneer to the affair, and the poor Lady Tameson could deceive herself that she was being cherished.

Lavinia had found the long strange day quite exhausting. She thought she would sleep soundly, but contrarily it was too hot and she was too strung up and queerly apprehensive. She hadn't seen Daniel at all. She had had her supper with the children, and gone to her room after they were settled in bed. Then she had begun thinking of the lonely old woman a prisoner in the dusty *palazzo*, and this had taken her depressed thoughts to Robin, who was even more of a prisoner. Finally she had got up to throw open the long narrow window and see if the moon was shining on the lagoon as it had done last night.

She thought its beauty would soothe her. It was very late, past midnight, and there was only a small knot of gondoliers lounging on the quay, talking vociferously, as usual. But no—there were still some strollers. Two people, a man and a woman, walked slowly down the humped bridge over the canal and toward the hotel. As they approached the door, the woman put her hand on the man's arm, indicating to him that she didn't want him to come farther. She wore a dark cloak and was heavily veiled. The man took off his hat and bowed exaggeratedly in a mocking way. Then he laughed. His laugh was quite audible and completely recognizable. It was that of Jonathon Peate.

Lavinia was almost certain that the veiled woman was Charlotte.

There was something peculiarly clandestine about them. Charlotte, if it were Charlotte, was hurrying from him as if she were extremely anxious to get away. Yet she paused to look back and he waved. As if he had her under some spell . . .

The next day Charlotte left Lavinia in the downstairs drawing room of Aunt Tameson's house to fold and pack a pile of clothing and other objects.

"I hope you have been trained to pack neatly, Miss Hurst."

Lavinia said with truth that she had. Three months in Cousin Marion's employment had taught her that. But she doubted if she could constrict this mass of belongings—feather boas, bonnets, gowns, fans, buttoned boots, boxes of gloves, parasols, a large Bible with gilt clasps, bundles of letters tied with lavender ribbon—into boxes.

Over everything hung the violet perfume, making the large room, darkened by closed shutters, stifling and full of ghosts.

The silence was unbearably oppressive. The whole house was silent. It hardly seemed that there was an old woman still living upstairs. No wonder Lady Tameson wanted to be taken away to escape the ghosts of the past. There was not even the cheery chatter and bustle of servants, for Fernanda, the plump, slatternly maid, couldn't speak English.

Charlotte had asked Lavinia if she spoke Italian.

"No more than a few words."

"Then if you want Fernanda for anything you'll have to use sign language. But you shouldn't need her. And don't disturb my aunt. She's resting."

It was obvious that Charlotte, having had to employ Lavinia against her will, was now going to make the utmost use of her. Flora had threatened to make a scene when she had heard that Lavinia was not to be at her sole disposal that day, but calmed down when told that her father would be taking her and Edward out.

With the scent of the Contessa's past gaiety cloying her nostrils, Lavinia thought wistfully of the children, perhaps taking a gondola ride with their father, or eating ices in the Piazza San Marco while the great bells rang from the Campanile, and the pigeons wheeled with rattling wings. She worked hard, slowly reducing the pile of objects to be folded and packed. A long necklace of black and gold Venetian beads, a pair of lavender kid gloves, an elaborate program tied with silk cord from Teatro La Fenice—*Il Trovatore*—a set of the works of William Shakespeare in red leather with faded gilt lettering, a Venetian leather box containing the Count's decorations. Thirty years of a woman's life.

Once a door closed somewhere. Once Fernanda called something upstairs, but the answer, if there was one, was inaudible.

Lavinia, suddenly suffocated, opened a shutter, and the hot sun struck her in the face. Water sucked beneath her, leaving slimy green marks on the ancient wall. The black prows of passing gondolas dipped and rose; a gondolier was shouting vociferously, his voice dying over the water.

She imagined long-ago guests arriving here for parties, the ladies delicately lifting their skirts to climb the slippery steps, the great lamps over the doorway glowing, and the sound of violins coming from this mirrored and polished room.

Now the mirrors were empty, or almost, since they had nothing to reflect but shrouded furniture and trunks that could have been coffins. Was all the house as gloomy as this room? Lavinia suddenly had the impulse to explore.

She went softly up the marble staircase and, tip-toeing past Lady Tameson's door, which was closed, began opening doors along the corridor. The rooms were all bedrooms, all furnished with massive four-posters and heavy wardrobes, all empty, all musty, with a mingled scent of canal water and age. She was examining a *prie-dieu*, obviously meant for more devout guests, when she heard quick, firm steps on the stairs.

Fernanda called, "*Signor!*" and something more in Italian. The door leading into Lady Tameson's bedroom opened and shut.

The doctor?

Lavinia lingered a moment, then was ashamed of her curiosity and went softly downstairs.

Halfway down she heard Lady Tameson give a stifled exclamation, as of disgust. Or fear? After that there was no more sound.

She was closing the last trunk when the footsteps came back down the stairs. If they belonged to the doctor, he would go straight on out the door through which he had apparently admitted himself. If they were Daniel's, he would come in to inspect her progress.

She bent over her work as the door opened.

"Can I help you with that, Miss Hurstmonceaux?"

She stiffened over the trunk fastenings. She would have thought it impossible, in the airless heat, to feel cold, but chills went over her just as they had done in the London courtroom.

It took all her willpower to straighten herself and look around calmly.

"Thank you, Mr. Peate. But I have almost finished. And you have made a mistake with my name."

"I do beg your pardon. Of course. You're Miss Hurst. Flora's new companion." Jonathon Peate was looking at her with his bold impertinence. "In this somewhat dim light you looked exactly like another young lady I saw not long ago. Miss Hurstmonceaux. Lavinia Hurstmonceaux," he added with deliberation.

"It's very easy to make a mistake. I hope you found your aunt well."

"As well as can be expected. And how are you enjoying your new position, Miss Hurst?"

"Very well, thank you."

"Splendid. I'm glad to hear it. I will look forward to renewing our acquaintance at Winterwood."

"At Winterwood!"

"Don't look so surprised, Miss Hurst. Or is it alarm I see in your face? It's too dark in here to see much at all. Why don't you have a shutter open?" He crossed to one of the windows and threw open a shutter. The light streaming on his face seemed to heighten his ruddy color. "There, now I can see you. You really are quite extraordinarily like that other lady."

"What an odd coincidence," Lavinia said coldly.

"It certainly is. And don't admire my good memory. One simply doesn't forget quickly your kind of looks. And hers, of course. But I'm scarcely flattering you by confusing you with her. She wasn't exactly in enviable circumstances." He laughed softly as he added, "Cousin Charlotte has invited me to spend some time at Winterwood. I believe I shall enjoy that." He wrinkled his nose. "I say, these Venetian smells aren't exactly lavender water. I'll have to close this again. Stuffiness is the better of two evils. You will have to try to survive, Miss Hurst. I'm sure my young relative Flora would be most upset if you didn't."

Was that a threat? Why would he threaten her?

When he had gone, shutting the door with a bang and calling in his loud jovial voice for the gondolier, Lavinia tried to reassure herself. She was feeling a little sick. She couldn't be certain that Jonathon Peate knew who she was. He might have been only guessing. He must have seen her on one of the days of that interminable two weeks of the trial. She knew there had been a great number of sightseers, particularly men. Surely it wasn't her bad fortune to meet one of them so quickly. But she did remember the strange searching look he had given her in the hotel yesterday. Some memory had nagged at him then. Later he must have remembered what it was.

So now he was either certain of his knowledge, or bluffing.

But why? Did he think that, scared of his betraying her secret, she would allow him to put her to some future use?

Rather than that, she would let him tell the whole truth.

But it would hurt Flora, who had conceived this sudden ardent affection for her, dreadfully. She didn't yet return Flora's affection, but she was extremely reluctant to have that tragic little figure in her wheelchair hurt.

And Daniel? How would he accept such news? Lavinia clenched her hands, feeling them gritty with dust, and beginning to shudder with revulsion and despair. Daniel mustn't know. She couldn't bear him to know. Her chin lifted and hardened. Perhaps Mr. Jonathon Peate would get a surprise himself when he found that she was not so easy to manipulate after all. He forgot that she had come through an experience not designed to make her easily frightened or to rely on tears. When lies were of value, she would tell them without compunction. Let him find out how little she could be terrorized.

But what exactly was he up to?

It seemed that Jonathon had scarcely gone before the doorbell clanged.

That would be Charlotte coming back to see if her work was finished, and to pay her second visit of the day to Aunt Tameson.

Fernanda flapped across the *sala* in her loose espadrilles.

The door opened. Daniel's voice said, "I have come for Miss Hurst, Fernanda," and Lavinia was hurriedly wiping the moisture off her cheeks.

"Have you finished, Miss Hurst?" Daniel was in the doorway. "My wife has a bad headache, so I have come for you. I'll just go upstairs and pay my respects to the Contessa. We plan to leave Venice next Monday. I have been making all the bookings."

The old house was suddenly alive again. Lavinia sat on a trunk until Daniel came downstairs. She knew in that brief passage of time that nothing could ever make her confess her past. She desired so ardently that he think well of her.

Then he was in the doorway again, not smiling, but looking at her with his too observant eyes.

"You have streaks down your cheeks, Miss Hurst. Is it the heat?"

Lavinia opened her eyes wide, willing the tears to be dry.

"Yes, it's dreadfully hot. I tried opening the shutters, but that made it worse. But I've got everything packed to the last handkerchief, in spite of an interruption by Mr. Peate."

"What did he want?" Daniel's voice had ceased to be friendly.

"He made a call on his aunt."

"Deathbeds become quite a family reunion, had you ever noticed, Miss Hurst?"

"I am not very familiar with deathbeds, Mr. Meryon."

"No. Well—the old lady seems fond of Mr. Peate, or so my wife assures me, so I expect he does no harm. I wonder if I could make Fernanda understand that we would like some lemon tea. You look fatigued."

Lavinia was about to protest, then subsided gratefully.

"That would be very pleasant, Mr. Meryon. I confess I do feel a little tired."

Again, while he was gone, she forgot to tidy herself, but sat waiting passively for him to return. He was gone for a long time and when he returned he was carrying the tea tray himself.

"This isn't a conventional establishment. My wife's aunt seems to be quite eccentric. Apparently she refuses to pay servants. She imagines they rob her. Well, by tomorrow there won't be much to rob her of." He threw the dust sheet off a tapestry-backed chair and sat down. "It's sad, don't you agree, seeing a great house break up."

He knew that the marks on her cheeks had been made by tears. He was giving her the opportunity to attribute them to the air of pervading and haunted melancholy in this old house.

"Yes, I wonder who will live here next. Shall I pour the tea, Mr. Meryon?"

"Please do. A rich American, perhaps. They are beginning to discover Europe and the fascination of living in houses to which centuries have given their individual atmosphere. Winterwood is like that. Each generation has added something to it. My grandfather built the ballroom, my great-grandfather had the gardens landscaped. My father contented himself with bringing back statuary from Greece and Egypt. We have sphinxes on the terrace. My grandfather built the Temple of Virtue in the shrubbery. He was a wonderful old pagan."

"And what is your contribution, Mr. Meryon?"

"So far nothing. But I have plans. My wife calls them grandiose. A new wing was always meant to be added, according to the original plans. Up to this time no one has had enough money."

"And you intend to be the one to do it?"

"I hope to. Then Winterwood will be one of the most beautiful houses in England. My son Simon will inherit, and after him his son. I'll become the ancestor who built the new wing. Which, in its way, is a form of immortality. Do you think that attitude is wrong, Miss Hurst?"

Lavinia roused herself from watching his face and wondering if it ever grew soft like that for a woman.

"No, I don't think it wrong, at all."

"My wife thinks me a little too dedicated to a house. She thinks it a religion. I wonder if that's such a bad thing."

Charlotte must be jealous of his house. She wondered if she would be, too.

"I only look forward to seeing it."

"And I look forward to showing it to you."

Their eyes met across the dim room.

"You must wash your face, Miss Hurst."

"Yes. Yes, it's the dust. And the heat."

His eyes lingered.

Then he said, "Are we working you too hard? Are you sorry you didn't travel with that quiet elderly couple, after all?"

She would have been safe with the Monks. Now she wasn't safe at all. There was Jonathon Peate with his veiled threats, and this man who noticed her or ignored her as he pleased.

"Then I would have missed Winterwood, which you make me think would be a pity."

"You must guard against us, Miss Hurst," he said suddenly.

"What do you mean?"

"We're inclined to use people." He must have thought his remark obscure, for he explained, "Look at you now, dusty and dirty. You've been working like a slave."

Lavinia knew that this wasn't what he had meant at all.

"Dust will wash off. I'm not afraid of work."

"No, I see that," he said slowly, making no more explanation. "Well, then, are you going to wash off the dust before we leave?"

It almost seemed as if he had been trying to warn her about something. But his warning had not been the blatant threat of Jonathon Peate; it had a kind of tenderness and regret that she knew she would keep on remembering. Was he telling her not to fall in love with Winterwood, because her love would inevitably have to include its master?

He kissed her hand meaninglessly; he gave her orders in a brusque way; he ignored her, or he gave her that disturbing intense regard; he used her to satisfy his spoiled daughter's whims; he confided in her his dreams about Winterwood; he noticed her tears; he was an enigma, and she was certain that she was going to fall in love with him. Uselessly, hopelessly, and, she was dismally sure, permanently.

Just as they were leaving, Lavinia heard a movement at the top of the stairs. She turned to see a short, square figure wrapped in a voluminous bedgown.

It was the Contessa.

"You!" she said, pointing at Lavinia. "Have you packed everything? My velvet ball gown?"

"Yes, Contessa."

"My cashmere shawls?"

"Yes, I especially noticed them."

"Good. They cost a mint of money. Venetian shopkeepers are robbers. What about my sables?"

Lavinia had noticed some fur pieces, ancient and dilapidated.

"Yes, Contessa. They're in your trunks."

"You're saying yes to everything, girl. Are you doing this to hide your laziness? I must be properly dressed at Winterwood."

"You can come in rags, my dear lady," said Daniel. He spoke with the indulgence he used toward Flora, and the old lady loved it. She gave a hoarse chuckle and added that although he was still a stranger he seemed trustworthy. She must have had servants who had robbed her, Lavinia thought, to make her so full of suspicion and live such an eccentric shut-away life.

"But I'm not trusting anyone with my jewelry," she said. "I shall have it all about my person when I travel."

Chapter 6

IT was unfortunate that Lady Tameson and Flora took an instant dislike to one another. It was a matter of ego. Each wanted undivided attention. Flora declared Lady Tameson to be an unpleasant old woman with a nasty cross face, and Lady Tameson said quite frankly that Flora was an unmitigated nuisance, and should get herself out of that chair and onto her legs as soon as possible.

They sat in the compartment that Daniel had reserved for them and glared at one another. Lady Tameson was dressed in a dramatic black velvet cloak and a bonnet trimmed lavishly with faded French roses. She had several diamond brooches pinned to the bodice of her dress, and a large flawless emerald on a gold bar in her high lace collar. She was a walking jeweler's shop, Eliza confided to Lavinia. If she were to be let out of sight, some thief would most likely knock her down and rob her.

But she wouldn't be let out of sight. Charlotte would see to that. She had fussed interminably, giving orders to everyone at once. Eliza was to put the footstool under the Contessa's feet and have the smelling salts handy; Flora was to stop whining; Lavinia—"Miss Hurst, this is no time for stargazing!"—was to keep the children occupied with picture books; Edward must sit quietly, and not try to lean out of the window; and had Daniel counted every piece of luggage, for one couldn't trust these Italian porters.

Daniel seemed impervious to the panic Charlotte was creating. Just as the train drew out of the station Lavinia, indulging in another moment of forbidden stargazing, found him at her side.

The lovely islands floating in the heat haze, the lavender sky, the tall campaniles, the serene sea, were slipping away.

"You look as if you were bidding farewell to happiness forever, Miss Hurst."

"Do I? It's true I was happy here."

"And why should it be so difficult to enjoy that state somewhere else?"

She bit her lip, and smiled.

"I hope it won't be difficult, Mr. Meryon."

"It won't, at Winterwood."

Charlotte's voice was sharp and suspicious behind them.

"What are you saying about Winterwood? I believe, Miss Hurst, that my husband never stops for one moment thinking of that place, even in his sleep."

"I was saying, my love, that Miss Hurst would be as happy at Winterwood as she has been in Venice."

"I thought Miss Hurst was engaged for Flora's happiness, not her own."

"Charlotte, Charlotte!" That was Lady Tameson in her high petulant voice. "Did you see anything of Jonathon at the railway station? I thought he was going to come and see us off."

"No, aunt, I didn't. If he had been there, he could scarcely have missed us. We aroused enough interest."

"People always stare at me," Flora said complacently.

"It's because you've got stick legs," said Edward.

"How do people know that? My legs are covered with a rug. It's because of my tragedy that they stare at me."

"Charlotte, you've ruined this child. I find her bad-mannered and vain. People staring at her, indeed. Precisely what they were staring at"—Lady Tameson patted her chest—"was my jewelry. They don't often see someone wearing a fortune in stones."

"That's a little vulgar, Aunt Tameson."

"Nonsense! I will enjoy my possessions while I can. You'd better be careful, Charlotte, or I may give orders in my will to have my jewelry buried with me."

Charlotte laughed, pretending a tolerant amusement.

"It's yours, aunt dear. You must do what you want with it. It's only that Daniel and I don't want you robbed on the journey. You must promise never to get out of our sight."

"Are there robbers on this train?" Edward demanded with the greatest interest. "I wish they would come in here. I would run them through with my sword. Where's my sword, Mamma?"

Lavinia had sat beside Flora, and felt the small cold hand creep into hers.

"I wish they would kill her," Flora whispered ardently.

"Now, there's no danger," Daniel said in his easy voice. "But Charlotte's right about your not wandering out of our sight, Contessa."

"Much chance I have of that," the old lady grumbled. "With so many watchdogs. Jonathon tells me you have invited him to Winterwood, Charlotte, so I shall see him then."

Charlotte stared at her for a moment with a look of unguarded surprise. She flushed deeply, then went pale. For once she seemed at a loss for words.

Daniel was watching her, too. "Is this true, Charlotte?"

"Yes, I suppose it is. Cousin Jonathon was most helpful, and I suggested that Aunt Tameson might like to see him again when she had recovered from her journey. I made no specific date."

"You don't care for my nephew, Daniel?" Lady Tameson's black eyes were very observant.

"I scarcely know him," Daniel answered, still looking at Charlotte.

"I hate him," Flora declared in no uncertain voice. "He laughs when there's nothing funny. I think he laughs at us."

"Flora!" Charlotte seemed glad of the opportunity to turn her attention on her daughter.

There was no doubt that she had been disturbed, and no doubt that Jonathon was coming to Winterwood uninvited.

Daniel's eyes were speculative. But he said nothing more. Charlotte decided to open the hamper and have luncheon end the uneasy conversation. She might have been deliberately creating a diversion.

The long journey passed with no mishap but exhaustion on the part of everyone. Flora and Edward slept through the night, bedded down on the narrow seats. Lady Tameson was propped in her corner with so many rugs and cushions that she looked like a stout Buddha, with a winking emerald at her throat. Charlotte dozed a little, sitting upright, and Eliza, still feeble from her illness, nodded so violently that once she tumbled off her seat. Lavinia didn't believe that Daniel closed his eyes any more than she closed hers. She couldn't know what he was thinking, but for her pictures of her past life seemed to flit by with the passing moon-drenched landscape. There had been so much happiness until Mamma and Papa had died, and then so much gaiety and recklessness, borne on by her wild brother, and unduly influenced by him because he was all she had left. They had become known as the wild Hurstmonceaux twins.

It could be that Jonathon Peate had been at one of Robin's gambling parties. There had always been strangers coming to them, and he looked a gambler.

Perhaps he had been at Lord Rilke's that fatal weekend. But she thought she had met everyone there, in spite of Justin's mad possessiveness.

For a moment it seemed as if Justin's face was silhouetted against the window frame, that dreadful tallow-colored face. She shuddered violently and Daniel noticed.

"Tired, Miss Hurst?"

"A little."

"Can you sleep?"

"I don't think so."

"I never sleep on journeys, either."

He spoke in a whisper so as not to disturb the sleepers. The swaying lamp had been turned down to only a glimmer. His face was as blurred as it had been that night in the gondola. It still suggested great strength and self-will. He was not a man to be opposed. Lavinia doubted if she would want to oppose him, but if she did—her blood tingled. She was wide-awake, and the phantom face outside the window had gone.

"Let us pass the time by talking about ourselves," he suggested. "How many journeys have you gone on, in the past?"

"Only one other abroad. My parents took—me to Paris." She was rigid. She had so nearly said "Robin and me."

"And wasn't it pleasant?"

"Yes, of course."

"You shivered, as if something had happened to you there."

"Oh, no. I was only thinking—we were so happy. Mamma shopped and Papa took me to art galleries. I remember the trees were turning brown and dropping their leaves into the Seine, and Papa made me speak French all the time. It seems a long time ago."

"Perhaps you will go again."

"Oh, I don't imagine so."

"I think it very likely. I would like Flora to speak good French."

"That would be simple enough with a French mademoiselle."

"Yes, that's one way."

"I'm not qualified to teach Flora, if that's what you're thinking, Mr. Meryon."

"I doubt if the person who can teach her exists. She's a demon with governesses. But children are great imitators."

"You wouldn't want her to imitate me!"

"You sound horrified, Miss Hurst." He settled himself more comfortably in his seat. "Actually that's exactly what I did mean."

"But, Mr. Meryon, you scarcely know me."

"I was simply talking about your poise. I hope to get to know you better, of course."

"Mr. Meryon—you will make me think it isn't only Flora who is a demon with governesses!"

He began to laugh.

"Did I deserve that? Perhaps I did. I must say my wife has either deliberately engaged a succession of very uninspiring females, or else that is a characteristic of the genuine governess." He saw the sharp movement of her head. "Don't misunderstand me. Anyone could see you're not the genuine article."

"Please, Mr. Meryon! I am doing you a favor by taking this position and you are doing me a favor by giving it to me. Don't ask too many questions."

"But I can't help being a little inquisitive. Was it an unfortunate love affair?"

"You could call it that."

"Because I refuse to believe that just being penniless could have blighted your life. Something must have happened to force you into traveling with that quite dreadful cousin of yours. But I promise, no more questions. Someday—"

"Someday what?"

"One recovers from a broken heart."

"Oh, my heart—"

"Wasn't broken?"

"Not in the way you mean, Mr. Meryon."

There was a movement opposite, and the waft of violet perfume that followed any stirring of Lady Tameson's clothes drifted over. Lavinia was abruptly aware of sharp black eyes watching her steadily.

She leaned across to whisper, "Are you all right, Lady Tameson?"

"I'm as stiff as a poker. I would like a sip of wine if there's any left."

"I think so. Mr. Meryon—"

"I'll get it," said Daniel. The resultant flurry woke Charlotte, who stirred and said exhaustedly, "What is it? Is Aunt Tameson ill?"

"Merely thirsty, Charlotte," the old lady answered. "Don't fuss. I'm finding the journey quite diverting."

"Diverting! I'm choked with soot and aching in every bone."

"Then go back to your seat and try to rest. Miss Hurst is bringing me some wine."

Charlotte pressed her hands to her temples, a familiar gesture. "Well, if you're sure you're all right, aunt—" She closed her eyes wearily. Her frail white face looked alarmingly delicate with dark stains beneath her eyes.

Lavinia bent over Lady Tameson with the glass of wine. At that moment the old lady looked much stronger than Charlotte, her eyes twinkling vigorously.

"I believe I'm going to find Winterwood diverting, too," she murmured, between sips.

Her eyes sparkled maliciously. She had obviously heard the whole

of the conversation between Lavinia and Daniel. What had she made
of it? What was there to make of it?

On the Channel steamer Flora found that she was to share a
double-berthed cabin with Lady Tameson. She made a great fuss.

"I will not be locked up with an old woman about to die!"

"Flora!" her mother scolded. "Please, no tantrums now that we're
nearly home."

"I am not having tantrums, Mamma. I'm merely stating that I
want to sit up on deck with Miss Hurst and Papa."

"Flora, you are the most exasperating child. Papa and Miss Hurst
will *not* be sitting on the deck."

"Do as you're told, pet," Daniel said. "It's going to be cold and
windy on deck and you need a rest."

"What about Edward?" Flora asked mutinously.

"Edward will be with me," Charlotte said. "Daniel, take her down.
We can't listen to this kind of thing."

"She is very tired," Lavinia said.

"So are we all." Charlotte, indeed, looked the most tired of all. The
contrast between her black hair and her white skin was now more
eerie than attractive. Her great pale eyes dominated her face. She
had not lost her look of intense anxiety during the whole of the
journey. She must have been very nervous that Lady Tameson would
die en route, involving all kinds of difficulties.

"I shall be seasick!" Flora threatened.

"And so shall I, if merely from looking at you," Lady Tameson said
suddenly. She had an uncanny way of seeming sunk in a stupor, and
then rousing herself and being more alert than anybody. "I regard
you as very disagreeable company, but I will do my best not to em-
barrass you by dying before I reach England."

The two stared at each other with implacable hostility. It was
Flora whose eyes dropped first.

"You are not to look at my legs," she muttered.

"Naturally not. One never looks at a lady's legs. One pretends they
don't exist, and she supports herself on air. For my part, I can't support myself at all. Daniel, your arm. Let us proceed to this dungeon
that Flora dreads so much."

Whether from apprehension, the rough sea, or sheer determination, Flora was sick before the shores of France had receded on the
horizon. Eliza, who had been instructed to stay in the cabin with the
two infirm passengers, coped with this emergency and later came up

to report to Charlotte, whom Daniel had tenderly wrapped in rugs on the deck, that both her charges had fallen asleep.

"Thank goodness," said Charlotte faintly. "Eliza, are you all right?"

Poor Eliza, who had scarcely recovered from the indisposition she had had in Venice, was looking green.

"It's just the stuffiness down there, madam. If I can get a breath of air I'll be all right."

"Miss Hurst, are you a good sailor?" Charlotte asked.

"Moderately so, Mrs. Meryon."

"Then will you be so good as to go down and see that Lady Tameson and Flora are all right."

"They were sound asleep, madam," Eliza put in. "Otherwise I wouldn't have left them for a minute."

"I know, Eliza. Oh, dear!" The ship plunged and shuddered, and Charlotte tightened her wraps about her, shivering. Even Edward had decided it might be better to sit on his mother's lap than to explore the slippery decks. Daniel was not in sight.

"I'll go down, Mrs. Meryon," Lavinia said, and made her way toward the companionway, clutching at whatever support she could find.

She had a struggle to open the door of the cabin. Something seemed to be jamming it.

"Be careful!" Flora screamed. "You're crushing me. I'm on the floor."

In the greatest alarm, Lavinia edged her way in, to find Flora had somehow fallen out of her bunk, and was lying across the floor, her face distraught.

"Oh, Miss Hurst! I'm so glad you've come! Great-aunt Tameson was dying. I had to get her medicine for her."

Lavinia leaned quickly over the old woman, who was lying very still, her face a frightening bluish color. But her eyes were open, and not at all lifeless. Indeed, they gleamed with their habitual amusement.

"I'm not dying. I—merely had an attack." She paused, breathing deeply. "This—disagreeable child—somehow got my medicine bottle." She moved a hand, showing the bottle clenched in her fingers, half of its contents spilled on the sheets. "I—dispensed with a spoon." She lay quietly, concentrating on breathing.

"Is she—dead now?" Flora whispered.

"No, she's not dead. I think you may even have saved her life. How did you get out of your bunk?"

"I fell when I was reaching for the medicine bottle. I got a quite dreadful fright. You should have heard Great-aunt Tameson groaning. Will you stay with us, Miss Hurst?"

"Yes, I'll stay." Lavinia had lifted Flora and laid her back on her bunk, covering her with blankets.

"Oh, that's good. This is a most disagreeable ship. I was sick. Did Eliza tell you?"

"Yes. I hope you're better now."

The child was shivering violently, her face pinched, the freckles she had got in the hot sun looking dark against her pallor.

"Has Teddy been sick?"

"No, not yet. I'm going to put another blanket over you. You're cold."

"Thank you, Miss Hurst. Don't go away, will you?"

"I told you I wouldn't." Lavinia had turned to Aunt Tameson, whose face was beginning to lose its look of terrible exhaustion. "Are you better now, Contessa? Would you like me to get the ship's doctor?"

"Certainly not. I know—and Flora knows now—exactly what to do if I have another attack."

Flora shot up. "That doesn't mean I like you any better, Great-aunt Tameson. I simply don't care for people dying."

"And I don't care for people not walking. It's nonsense. You have a perfectly good pair of legs. I saw them. A bit thin. They only need some massage. I'm sure Miss Hurst will see that you get that."

"Will that make them less thin?"

"Certainly."

"I wish I only had to drink some medicine out of a bottle and be well, like you."

"That's just an easy way for the old. The young have to fight. Now will you stop chattering like a monkey and let me sleep."

Quite meekly Flora lay down and pulled the blankets up to her chin.

"Isn't it odd, I don't feel seasick now," she murmured. A little later she whispered guardedly, "I do still hate that old lady. But perhaps not quite so desperately. I hope Edward is being sick."

Then her eyelids fell and she was asleep. Lady Tameson slept, too, or appeared to, the light catching the diamonds glinting on her bosom. Lavinia sat on a stool in the swaying cabin, pondering on personal involvements. Already no one was escaping—herself, Flora, Lady Tameson, Charlotte with that strange Jonathon Peate. Daniel? It seemed likely, simply because he was not a person to remain uninvolved.

Chapter 7

Winterwood at last.

They reached it as dusk was falling. The carriage had met them at Dover, and driven them across the early autumn countryside, through small villages, and down lanes where the hanging branches of oaks and beeches tore at the carriage roof.

At a bend in the road Daniel suddenly called to the coachman to stop.

"What's the matter?" Charlotte asked.

"I want Miss Hurst to get her first glimpse of the house from here. It's a good vantage point. Would you step out, Miss Hurst?"

Charlotte frowned at him in the dusk.

"Really, Daniel, Miss Hurst can walk to this point another day. We are all much too tired to start looking at the scenery."

Daniel held out his arm to Lavinia, who had no choice but to obey. She stood in the cool windy dusk and looked across the fields to the silhouette of the great house, stark and forbidding in this light, a great mass that might almost have been a prison.

There was a moon, not yet grown bright, drifting behind ragged cloud. Its wanness in the colorless sky gave an ineffably melancholy atmosphere.

Lavinia couldn't control a slight shiver. The wind was cold, after the warmth of Italy. She had imagined that Winterwood, by its very name, would be surrounded by gentle woods and shrubberies. She hadn't expected it to stand stark and austere on the crest of the low hill. There were some trees, to be sure, great oaks and elms that were giving up their leaves to the tearing wind, and close to the house dark squat shapes indicated clipped yews along a terrace. But the overwhelming impression was one of bleakness.

Daniel was shouting above the wind.

"I plan to build the new wing on the right-hand side. It will make an enclosed courtyard. We catch the wind from the Channel. On a fine day you can see down to the Goodwin Sands, and hear the sea.

I intend making another trip to Italy to bring back some statuary for the courtyard. What did you say?"

She wanted to ask where the garden was. She had thought there would be a charming formal garden, not this bleakness, with the chilling wind and the faint smell of the sea.

"It's bracing up here," said Daniel. "There are none of the fogs and vapors one gets in low-lying places."

"Daniel! How long are you going to keep us waiting?" came Charlotte's fractious voice.

"Miss Hurst, do you see my room?" cried Flora, putting her head out of the carriage. "It's that one on the second floor at the end. I can see that Phoebe has lit the lamps. Edward's room is on the third floor next to the nursery. He's only a baby still."

Edward's voice protested shrilly. "I am not! You know you were only moved down because you couldn't walk. It isn't because you're grown-up!"

"Children!" Charlotte scolded.

"Please, Mamma! I'm only telling Miss Hurst how to find her way. Which will her room be?"

"The one Miss Brown had, of course."

"Oh, no, Mamma, that's next to Edward's. I want her near me. Let her have the red room. I may need her in the night."

"Be quiet, Flora! What nonsense, a governess having the red room. Miss Hurst, you would oblige us if you would get back in the carriage so that we can continue our journey."

Flora said no more, but later Lavinia noticed the gleam of tears on her cheeks as Daniel lifted her from the carriage at the steps leading up to the great front door. He noticed them, too, and asked what was the matter.

"Nothing, Papa. I am only dreadfully tired." Her voice was far-away and wan. But over her father's shoulder she winked at Lavinia. Lavinia suddenly had to straighten her mouth and keep it stern. It seemed obvious that she was not going to be relegated to the small obscure room recently occupied by Miss Brown. For her age, Flora was the most unscrupulous person she had ever met. One would have to start teaching her honesty.

There was a great bustle as the front door was flung open, and servants appeared to curtsey to Charlotte and Lady Tameson, to help with Flora's chair, to carry baggage. Charlotte presented Lavinia to the housekeeper, Mrs. O'Shaughnessy, and Lavinia felt herself facing a new problem, the approval and acceptance of the maids, from Mrs. O'Shaughnessy down. She knew, remembering her own succession of governesses, the difficulties that could be encountered. Too much favor from the family made one resented, and too little, despised. For instance, they would scarcely have appreciated the master's stopping the carriage to show her his estate. Nor would she be very popular if she was given one of the rooms intended for guests on the first floor.

Charlotte was giving orders in her high, tense voice. The Contessa was to be assisted upstairs. "Go very slowly, Joseph!" Phoebe was to see that Flora got into bed immediately and had her supper there, Lily—where was Lily? A young girl with apple cheeks came forward, bobbed dutifully, and was told to take Edward up and get him into a bath as quickly as possible as he was filthy. "Don't stand any nonsense, Lily. He has been very tiresome all the way from Dover." But this order was softened by a melting smile at Edward, and a promise that she would be up shortly to kiss him good night. Miss Hurst was to be shown her room, "The usual one, Mrs. O'Shaughnessy," and since it was late and no doubt she was tired, perhaps she would prefer a tray in her room to coming down to dinner.

Before Lavinia could make a grateful assent to that, Charlotte was going on restlessly. Were there letters from Master Simon? Where was Sir Timothy? Surely he hadn't forgotten the time of their arrival? Had Doctor Munro been told that he would be required to call in the morning to examine the Contessa, and would Mrs. O'Shaughnessy have dinner put ahead half an hour as they would all like to retire early.

Daniel, after carrying Flora upstairs, had disappeared. As Lavinia waited for the maid who was to take her to her room, she heard his voice from an open doorway off the wide hall, "Well, Uncle Timothy, we're safely back, in spite of your dire predictions."

"And the old lady?"

"The old lady, too, safe and sound."

"Ah ha! I must pay my respects to her. How has she weathered?"

"Not badly. Charlotte worries about her."

"She was a redhead, I remember. Damned handsome woman. We all thought Willie Peate a lucky fellow. But her looks went off after her boy died . . . She finally did well for herself, though. A Contessa, eh? I don't trust foreign titles. I've lost my spectacles again, Daniel. The maids will tidy up . . ."

"This way, miss," said the maid, appearing in front of Lavinia.

Lavinia followed her sprightly little figure up the stairs. She couldn't have been more than twelve years old, and, when asked, said that her name was Mary and she had just been promoted from the kitchen. It was her ambition to be a housekeeper one day, since she never intended to marry.

Lavinia was amused by such an emphatic opinion coming from such a tiny creature.

"Why do you say that, Mary?"

"Well, miss, my dad drinks and treats my mum something awful. And my sister Nellie, her husband has a fair temper and beats her. It seems to me being married isn't a happy thing. There's even the master and mistress here. You'd think living in a big house and everything they'd be—" She stopped abruptly. "I shouldn't have said that, miss. Mrs. O'Shaughnessy said we were never to gossip about the family. If you'll come down here, miss. This is your room."

The little maid opened the door of a small, austere room. It had all the necessary equipment, to be sure, even a writing desk, which Lavinia supposed was a luxury. And who was she to take exception to a neat iron bedstead after the filthy straw pallet that had been her bed for that terrible three months?

"It was Miss Brown's room, miss."

Mary's eyes in her shrewd little face were speculative as she looked at Lavinia.

"And don't ask me why she isn't here now, Mary," Lavinia said cheerfully.

"No, miss. I expect she didn't get on with Miss Flora. I'll bring your supper up, miss."

Lavinia had taken stock of the room, determinedly finding it more pleasant than she had at first thought, with its square of Turkey carpet, its flower-patterned washstand china, its one comfortable chair and even a small watercolor above the dressing table, when Mary returned with her supper tray.

"Oh, miss, there's ructions. Miss Flora is screaming for you and the mistress says she's to behave, she's getting altogether out of hand. I wasn't listening specially, miss, you just couldn't help but hear as you went by. And the master went upstairs looking that angry."

"I'll go down," said Lavinia.

"Oh, miss—don't say I told—it's just I can't bear that poor Miss Flora being scolded. There she is helpless in a chair. Wouldn't you scream?"

"Yes, Mary, I would."

Having begun to understand fairly well the workings of Flora's shrewd and devious mind, Lavinia had thought she would time her scene for the next morning, when the flurry of settling Lady Tameson in was over. Then she would produce some forlorn tears, say she was nervous of sleeping alone, and begging for Miss Hurst to be given the room adjoining hers. If her wish was not granted quickly enough, she would probably faint once or twice and be unable to eat any luncheon.

But something had precipitated the scene.

Lavinia reached the door of the big pleasant room with its thick carpet, its spotlessly white curtains and white frilled bedspread, its leaping fire and cheerful lamplight, to find the room full of people. Flora was sitting very straight in her chair by the fire. Her face was scarlet with fury. Her mother stood over her, an angry unyielding figure, while Edward, in his dressing gown, capered about laughing shrilly. Daniel, his face troubled, looked down at Flora, and Phoebe, the scared maid, tried to be as unobtrusive as possible with a jug of steaming water at the washstand.

"I won't give it to you, Mamma. I won't!"

"Flora, you heard me!"

"Papa! Oh, Miss Hurst! Please, dear Miss Hurst, tell Mamma this is mine."

Charlotte turned a face as angry as her daughter's. She clearly resented Lavinia's appearance and opened her mouth to order her not to interfere, when Daniel intervened in a calm judicial voice, "Yes, perhaps Miss Hurst can throw some light on the matter. Flora has a brooch, Miss Hurst, which she says the Contessa gave her."

"She stole it, she stole it!" Edward chanted, swooping around the room in a mad undirected rush.

"I did not! Edward, you are a liar! Great-aunt Tameson gave it to me for saving her life. I told you, Mamma!"

Lavinia knelt beside Flora and unlocked the clenched fingers, to display the magnificent diamond brooch. The little girl was hot and trembling.

"It is mine, truly! Because I did save her life, didn't I, Miss Hurst?"

"Why did you?" asked Edward. "I thought you hated her."

"I do, too."

"Then you should have let her die."

"Edward! Be quiet, and go to your room." Daniel spoke sternly. "Phoebe! Take that child upstairs. Now, Flora, perhaps we can hear quietly what happened."

"Papa, you believe me, surely?" Flora lifted anguished eyes.

"Of course I believe you. But why didn't you tell us at once about the brooch? It's very valuable, you know."

"Great-aunt Tameson gave it to me the next morning after she nearly died," Flora said rapidly. "She said I had been very resourceful and then she gave me the brooch. It was one she had pinned on her dress. She said it was worth about a thousand pounds and I could have it before the vultures got the rest. What did she mean by vultures?"

"She's a very old sick woman and doesn't know what she's saying or doing," Charlotte said sharply. "Old people always think their things will be stolen."

"I'm not a vulture and I didn't steal this," Flora said. "I'm going to sell it and buy a new horse for Papa to make up for Chloe." Her mouth tightened stubbornly. "So you needn't think I'm going to give it back. Anyway, why don't you ask Great-aunt Tameson about it? She'll tell you she gave it to me."

"She's asleep and not to be disturbed," Charlotte said. "Certainly I intend to ask her in the morning. In the meantime, that brooch must be put away safely. Even if she has given it to you, you can't possibly wear it until you're grown-up. It's a most unsuitable present for a little girl."

"That's why I'm going to sell it," Flora said patiently.

Daniel's mouth twitched suddenly. With great tenderness, he said, "Flora, pet, when you show me that you can walk again I will have the greatest pleasure in buying you a new horse. I certainly don't intend you to sell your jewelry to buy one."

"Then I may keep the brooch, Papa?"

"If Great-aunt Tameson confirms your story in the morning. Now, there's been a great deal too much noise and excitement. I suggest Miss Hurst stay with you and see you to bed."

Flora lifted up both her arms in an impulsive gesture.

"Oh, Papa, I do love you!"

Charlotte's face had gone cold.

"Daniel, this is quite ridiculous, a child being allowed to keep a brooch of that value. I am sure Aunt Tameson's solicitor will take great exception to it."

"I've never heard of a law that prevents a living person disposing of her possessions as she wishes."

Charlotte clicked her tongue impatiently.

"It's the unsuitability of the gift. And anyway Flora shouldn't be rewarded for behaving with sense, for once. Do as your Papa says, Flora, and go to bed."

"Yes, Mamma," Flora said with deceptive submissiveness. Her eyes gleamed beneath their tawny lashes. "And I really don't care so much for the brooch, Mamma. I'll give it back to Great-aunt Tameson if Miss Hurst can have the room next to mine. I beg you, Mamma. Because I know I shall have nightmares and scream. I'm so exhausted after all that traveling."

Daniel suddenly laughed.

"The minx has got round you, my love. In any case, what she says is eminently sensible. Let Miss Hurst move down. If that is agreeable to Miss Hurst, of course."

With elaborate sarcasm, Charlotte said, "Does it suit your convenience, Miss Hurst? I think you will find the room comfortable. We usually give it to our more important guests."

Lavinia refused to meet Daniel's eyes, which she knew were waiting to twinkle at her. How was she to stay here if Charlotte became her enemy? For it would be foolish to think Charlotte defeated.

"I am happy to do what is most suitable, Mrs. Meryon."

"It is not in the least suitable, but the house seems to be temporarily ruled by my daughter. Don't imagine that is a state that exists all the time." Charlotte stood over Flora, her hand held out. "I'll take that brooch, miss. And I want to hear no more from you tonight."

When they were alone, Lavinia said to Flora, "Did you steal the brooch?"

Flora looked acutely hurt. "Don't you trust me, Miss Hurst?"

"No, I don't."

Flora sighed.

"I didn't steal the brooch. Great-aunt Tameson did give it to me. She said I might as well have something before other people took all her things from her. She said she was surrounded by thieves. Who did she mean, Miss Hurst?"

"I really can't imagine. Old people get queer ideas."

"Well, she won't need her brooches and things in heaven," Flora said practically. "She'll have pearly wings then."

Chapter 8

THE next morning Flora, wheeling her chair toward Lavinia, complained, "Mamma wouldn't let me in to Great-aunt Tameson's room. They're writing."

"Writing?"

"Letters, I think. Get Joseph to carry me downstairs and I'll show you the house. Then we'll go out in the garden. I want you to see my blue garden. It is entirely my own. Everything in it is blue. I never let Edward in it. Do come, Miss Hurst."

"I thought it was my place to tell you what to do."

"Tomorrow will do for that. Today I'm going to be the hostess. Pray come, *dear* Miss Hurst. Let me entertain you."

Lavinia allowed herself to be prevailed on sufficiently to ring for Joseph, the stalwart footman, who made nothing of Flora's weight.

"How was Great-aunt Tameson?"

"She looked cross. She has the red room. Did you like the room I got for you, Miss Hurst?"

It was remarkably like her old room at Alford Chase. She had felt sadly at home with the shining mahogany furniture, the velvet-covered chairs drawn invitingly to the fireside, the attractive washstand china and the bed with its huge soft mattress and spotless white coverlet. The bed linen was monogrammed, the carpet thick, the branched candlesticks on the mantelpiece were heavy Georgian silver. There were books at her bedside, a volume of Keats' poems, and Mr. Thackeray's latest novel.

None of this comfort was meant for Lavinia Hurst. But it had come her way, and already she was taking a slightly malicious pleasure in Charlotte's helpless disapproval. Not that she underestimated Charlotte. There would be penalties to pay for this victory Flora had won for her. In the meantime, the lovely room gave her courage. Later she would write a letter to Robin at the elegant Sheraton writing desk, and tell him of her good fortune.

Downstairs they encountered an old man in a velvet smoking jacket who peered at them from watery blue eyes and asked them if they could possibly tell him where he had mislaid his spectacles.

"Oh, Uncle Timothy, have you lost them again?" Flora said. "You are awful! Have you been to see Great-aunt Tameson?"

"How can I see anything without my spectacles? Did those foreign doctors teach you how to walk again?"

"No, Uncle Timothy. They only hurt me a good deal for nothing. They said I must be patient."

"And are you? Who is that with you?"

"It's Miss Hurst, my companion. This is my uncle, Sir Timothy Meryon, Miss Hurst. He's really my great-uncle, but he doesn't like to be called that because it makes him feel too old."

The old man held out a cool-skinned elegant hand.

"How do you do, Miss Hurst. How long have you been with my niece?"

"She's only been since Venice, Uncle Timothy."

"So you've stayed a whole week. That's quite a record! I hope you don't intend to be driven off by a little temperament, like those other ninnies. The child has to let off a bit of steam. Sitting in that damn wheelchair. Where are you off to now?"

"I'm showing Miss Hurst the house, Uncle Timothy."

"Splendid. May I accompany you? Follow me, Miss Hurst. We'll go to the long gallery first. Are you interested in family portraits? We have one or two rather good ones, a Holbein and a pair of Van Dycks."

The long gallery held a portrait of a woman who looked so like Daniel that Lavinia had to linger. She was young, and wore a yellow sash around her high-waisted dress. Sir Timothy noticed Lavinia admiring her.

"That's Grace, my late brother's wife. Daniel's mother. She was beautiful, wasn't she? She died before she was thirty. She hated dying; she wanted to stay here. She loved Winterwood. She was going to make it a wonderful mistress. A house needs a good mistress. It responds to love. Had you ever noticed that?"

"Yes, I had. My mother loved—where we lived."

Even that meager statement gave away too much, for Sir Timothy peered closely at her with his dim eyes. But he shook his head in defeat.

"It's no use, all faces look alike to me without my spectacles. I shall just hope you are decorative, Miss Hurst. I like decorative young women about."

"Uncle Timothy!" Flora scolded. "You know Mamma dislikes you flirting."

The old man shuffled off, tch-tching irritably. Lavinia heard him mutter, "Only amusement a fellow has left. Charlotte has no sense of humor. This is the long gallery, Miss Hurst. It runs the entire length of the house. The windows give fine views over the parkland, as you can see. I can't without my spectacles. But the view is there. Now come and see the Adam drawing room."

The drawing room with its two elegant white marble fireplaces, delicately scrolled, the carved ceiling, the ruby red damask walls, the Aubusson carpet, the French mirrors, and glittering chandelier. The dining room also overlooked the park with its ragged trees, and long slopes that ran away into blue mist. The morning parlor, a pretty cozy room with yellow silk walls, and a set of miniatures over the mantelpiece; the library lined from floor to ceiling with books, and with well-dented leather armchairs and strewn papers, which suggested the master of the house spent a lot of time there; the smoking room, Sir Timothy's own particular haunt; the gun room; another sitting room that looked over the terrace and the flower garden; the ballroom, with pillars and a frescoed ceiling.

Daniel hadn't exaggerated. Winterwood was beautiful. It could become a hobby, or an obsession, or just an overwhelming love. To be happy with Daniel, one would have to share his love. Did Charlotte?

"Do you like it, Miss Hurst? Would you like to be its mistress?"

Flora had a knack of asking awkward questions. To her relief Sir Timothy answered for her.

"The right woman can be set in this house like a jewel. But the wrong one—ah ha, Daniel, I smell your cigar."

Daniel came strolling in from the terrace just outside the ballroom. How long had he been there? Had he been listening to their conversation?

He ruffled Flora's hair and said, "Good morning, Miss Hurst. Well, aren't you going to answer Flora's question?"

He looked young and very alive, his black eyes sparkling, as if Winterwood had already rejuvenated him.

"If we are going to play a game of make-believe," she said, "then of course I would like to be mistress of a house like this. What woman wouldn't?" Then she lost her dignity, and clasped her hands, and said with intensity, "I think it's the most beautiful house I ever saw."

He was pleased.

"What did you like best?"

"I'm not sure. The little yellow parlor perhaps."

"How fortunate. I was going to suggest that you and Flora spend the mornings there, instead of her making the tiresome journey up to the schoolroom. That would be convenient to the garden if you want to take walks."

She believed that idea had come into his head only after her expressing a liking for the yellow parlor.

Flora was exclaiming in some glee, "Oh, Papa, what a very good idea, but Mamma won't approve."

"Mamma has her sitting room upstairs. She scarcely ever uses the parlor. The arrangement will be convenient to everybody."

"And Edward won't be allowed in?"

"Edward's tutor arrives tomorrow. He'll be fully occupied. And Simon will be home, too. Miss Hurst must meet my elder son."

"Splendid," said old Sir Timothy. "We can continue our chess games. I have no opponent when Simon is at school. Young Edward doesn't concentrate. At his age Simon could beat me. When am I going to be permitted to see Tameson Peate, Daniel?"

"The Contessa?"

"Oh, bother that foreign title. I place no belief in it. The only titles I respect are ones like my own, given for services to one's country. Tameson was always Willie Peate's wife to me. But I must first locate my spectacles. I believe the servants hide them, you know. They have a little conspiracy. It amuses them to see me groping about like a blind walrus. I can't even see this new young person of Flora's. How does she look, Daniel? Is she like the others?"

"Not in the least, Uncle Timothy. Is that a matter of importance to you?"

The old man gave a throaty chuckle. "Certainly it is. I'm not in my dotage, you know. I hope you will see that Flora treats her well. None of your pranks, Flora. Always treasure a pretty woman. Isn't that right, Daniel?"

Although Sir Timothy eventually discovered his spectacles, and perched them on his nose when he went upstairs to meet Lady Tameson, he still declared that she bore no resemblance to the pretty redhead he remembered.

"She's a great deal older," Charlotte pointed out. "How can you expect her hair still to be red?"

"She's become vulgar," the old man said disapprovingly. "Showing off her title like a flag. I don't suppose a Count is any more important than a baronet, but she behaved as if I were a sort of superior old servant. That Italian sun, or something, has gone to her head. And suggesting that Winterwood is nothing compared with her damp crumbling *palazzo*. Not to mention wearing jewelry in bed. Really, I wouldn't have believed this of that nice simple girl, Tameson Peate."

"I don't suppose you really remember her at all, Uncle Timothy," Charlotte said.

"She's changed a great deal," Sir Timothy insisted. "She doesn't even seem English."

This seemed to be Aunt Tameson's biggest failing as far as Sir Timothy was concerned. She had turned traitor. He said that as Charlotte's aunt, naturally she was welcome at Winterwood, but expressed the wish that he should not have to be inflicted with her company.

"Of course you won't be," Charlotte said, as if indeed this was the situation for which she had hoped. "I imagine she will keep mostly to her room. The Italian doctor warned her against any kind of exertion."

"Frankly, I'd never take the word of a foreign doctor," Sir Timothy declared. "You might have her for a long spell, Charlotte. I'm a year older than her if I've calculated rightly, and I expect to keep above ground for another ten years. Give old Tameson a new heart and me a new pair of eyes, and we'd give you young people a dance yet." Chuckling, and fumbling for his spectacles, which he had pushed onto the top of his head, Sir Timothy meandered off to the smoking room. He banged the door firmly behind him, as if he expected Aunt Tameson's immediate encroachment on his privacy.

Aunt Tameson's next visitor was Doctor Munro, an elderly man with a drooping white moustache and twinkling blue eyes set beneath grizzled white eyebrows. He, unlike Sir Timothy, had not known Aunt Tameson when she had lived at Croft House as plain Mrs. Willie Peate. He had no comparisons to make, and in any case was interested in her body, not whether she wore a diamond brooch on her nightgown.

It was unfortunate that Lavinia was just taking Flora to the yellow parlor when the doctor came downstairs, talking very audibly.

"Keep her happy, Mrs. Meryon. That's the best advice I can give you."

"You can't say how long, Doctor?"

"One can't, with a case like this. It might be today, or in six months. With care, it might be a year. Her heart's worn out. That's all there is to it."

The voices died away, and Flora said intensely, "She's going to die, isn't she!"

"But you knew that, darling. You saw for yourself on the ship."

"Her medicine kept her alive. Why can't it always?"

"She's old. People wear out."

"Well, I just don't like people dying around me. Why can't she go back to Venice? We don't want corpses!"

"Flora! I thought you hated Aunt Tameson."

"So I do, so I do."

Flora pummeled the arms of her chair, on the verge of one of her hysterical outbursts. Lavinia stood up.

"We've done too much this morning. You're tired. I'll ring for Joseph to take you upstairs."

"I don't want to go upstairs. I want to show you my blue garden."

"Later today, darling."

"Then it might be raining. The flowers will be all withered and spoiled. I want to show you the baby's head."

Flora's conversation sometimes became so ghoulish that Lavinia looked at her sharply.

"A baby's head?"

Flora smiled slyly, thinking she was getting her own way.

"Yes. You'll like it. It smiles although it's broken."

If Lavinia was expected to recognize the same gallant courage in this child with her own damaged body, she refused to be beguiled in this way. She tugged the bell rope.

"Later today, I said. I'm coming up with you to rub your legs. We're going to do this for half an hour every day. After that you're to have luncheon in your room and then rest."

Flora looked at her in fury.

"Miss Hurst, you're to do as I say! That's why I made Papa engage you."

"And do I look so weak? Come now. Here's Joseph." Lavinia turned to the tall young footman. "Take Miss Flora to her room, Joseph. She's going to rest. Don't mind if she struggles. She's simply overtired."

Joseph grinned, his bright young eyes admiring Lavinia.

"I'll manage, miss."

Flora looked as if she were about to scream, instead changed her mind and went limp. She remained like that after Joseph had laid her on her bed and gone. When Lavinia took off her shoes and stockings to rub the pitifully thin legs, Flora said between clenched teeth, "I've made a mistake about you, Miss Hurst. You're worse than Miss Brown. I shall tell Papa to dismiss you."

"Does that hurt?" Lavinia asked clinically, busy with her task.

"Yes, it does."

"Can you move your toes?"

"You know I can't. I've told a thousand doctors I can't."

"Try, all the same."

Flora's thin body went rigid. The skirts of her tartan dress bunched up, hiding her face. Her feet, a child's feet, too small and narrow, stayed limp. Would they ever support that frail body again?

"You're going to try that every day," Lavinia said calmly. "And one day it will happen. Have you got a pink dress?"

Surprise forced a polite answer from Flora.

"No. Mamma says I can't wear pink, I'm too pale."

"I think you could. Say, a white muslin with sprigs of pink roses, and a pink sash. I'll speak to your mother about it."

"She won't pay any attention. She hates me. She thinks I'll never get married and she'll have me forever and ever."

"You certainly won't get a husband if you make this fuss every time I want to make your legs stronger."

There was a long silence. Finally Flora said in a barely audible mutter, "Would it be any use if I said prayers for her?"

"For Lady Tameson? Of course it would. You can pray that she has courage, and you, too."

"Is that what you pray for yourself?"

"Yes."

"Because you haven't got a husband?"

"For a great many reasons."

"Do you mean that about the pink dress?"

"Certainly."

"A pink dress isn't going to stop people dying around me. Is it?"

Lavinia met the unhappy belligerent eyes. A strange sensation took possession of her. She wanted to put her arms around the frail little body, draw it close, protect it. She had done that for that wretched little chimney sweep dying in jail, a child of not more than eight years who had stolen an apple from a plate in some fine dining room. She had wept over him. She mustn't allow herself to weep over Flora or she would be no use at all.

"No, it isn't, lamb. But Lady Tameson might like to see you in it."

"She won't. She called me an unmitigated nuisance."

"Which was true. Now, I'm going to ring for Mary to bring you a tray, and after that you're to sleep."

"Phoebe looks after me, not Mary."

"I thought you might like Mary better. She's not much older than you, and she's pretty."

"Mamma's going to be furious if you order the servants about. That's one thing she won't stand from a governess."

"I'm not a governess," Lavinia said calmly. "I'm in charge of your physical health, which at the moment comes before your education. I'm afraid my orders will have to be obeyed. By you, too. Do you understand?"

"Only if it pleases me," Flora said sulkily. "I'm to be humored. The doctor said so."

"And I don't want any more repetitious remarks. I'm going to tell Mary to draw the curtains as soon as you've eaten your luncheon so that you'll sleep. I don't want to hear any more from you until four o'clock."

Before she went down to luncheon herself, Lavinia heard Flora telling Mary, who had brought her tray, that she was very clumsy and inefficient, and much too small.

"How old are you?"

"Thirteen, miss."

"I'm only eleven, and I'm sure I'm taller. If I could stand up I would prove it. Miss Hurst is going to make my legs strong enough so that I can stand."

"That'll be grand, miss," came Mary's cheerful voice.

"Why do you have to work when you're really no bigger than Edward?"

"Because my dad likes the bottle, and my mum has six smaller'n me at home. And they has awful big appetites."

"Don't they get enough food?" Flora asked in a shocked voice.

"We has plenty of bread and dripping. But I'm going to be a housekeeper one day and then I can help my mum and my brothers and sisters, see?"

"Don't you want to be married?"

"I'd as soon dig my grave."

This macabre statement brought an admiring giggle from Flora.

"Goodness! You must hate men. If I don't get married, either, and I don't suppose I will, you can be my housekeeper. Papa will buy me a house . . ."

Remembering that conversation, Lavinia was able to face Charlotte at luncheon with perfect equanimity.

"I thought it a good idea to make this change, Mrs. Meryon. Mary is such a cheerful little creature. Flora will like having her about."

She didn't at first notice Charlotte's anger. She had learned to look for her petulance, her imperious manner, and her constant dying air, as exhaustion overcame her or a headache was threatened, but she hadn't yet met this hectic look of unreasoning temper. In one moment Charlotte had changed from her languid camellia beauty to something quite distraught.

"Miss Hurst, you are taking altogether too much on yourself. Are you suggesting my daughter make a friend of a servant?"

"Charlotte, my love!" Daniel spoke quickly and placatingly. "Miss Hurst is only doing her best—"

"Oh, yes, you will take her side, of course. I've seen that ever since we left Venice. Miss Hurst is the complete paragon."

"Miss Hurst happens to be the one person Flora has liked since her illness." Daniel still spoke with patience. "If only because of that she is a paragon, I agree."

"Yes!" Charlotte had pushed back her chair and was standing. The rose pinned among the lace ruffles of her bodice trembled violently. "She has already seen that she occupies the best bedroom. You have taken away my favorite yellow parlor for her use. And now she presumes to manage my servants."

"Mrs. Meryon!" Lavinia's heart was beating almost as violently as Charlotte's. "I did come here only on the condition that I had complete charge of Flora."

"And I made a condition, too. That you were engaged on trial only."

Lavinia was standing, also.

"If you wish to terminate my employment, Mrs. Meryon, I am only too happy—"

Daniel would not allow her to finish.

"Don't talk nonsense, Miss Hurst." He went to put his arm round his wife. "Charlotte, I'm going to take you upstairs. I think you should rest."

At first she pushed his arm away violently, but then sank against him. The hectic flush had died from her cheeks, leaving her with an extreme pallor.

"Yes, I must rest. I'm so tired. The journey—having a dying woman in the house—you warned me it would be too much for me."

Daniel led her away. Sir Timothy, who had said nothing during the uncomfortable scene, motioned to Lavinia to resume her seat.

"Your soup's getting cold, my dear. No need to starve. Daniel knows how to manage her."

Lavinia was still inclined to tremble.

"Was it my fault, Sir Timothy?"

"Don't give it a thought, my dear. Charlotte enjoys making a fuss."

"Was that all it was?"

The old man nodded. "And it won't be the first scene you'll see. She's a highly strung creature. She gets overwrought with one thing and another, and then you have it—firecrackers!"

But Daniel didn't seem to dismiss the affair quite so lightly. When he returned to the dining room, his face looked drawn and remote. Nevertheless, he noticed Lavinia's anxiety and said,

"Don't worry, Miss Hurst. You did nothing wrong. The exchange of Phoebe for Mary is an excellent idea. My wife agrees."

"Agrees! But—"

"She has a headache. That makes her a little unreasonable. She wants you to go up and see her after luncheon."

Charlotte lay on a couch in a darkened room. At first Lavinia could see only the pale shape of her face. But presently her eyes adjusted themselves to the gloom and she saw the bed with its ornate headboard and rich satin spread, the multitude of bottles on the bedside table, the bowl of roses scenting the air.

"You wanted to see me, Mrs. Meryon?"

"Come in, Miss Hurst." Charlotte's voice had its familiar languor. "I am quite prostrate. I shouldn't have attempted to go down to luncheon."

"Can I get you anything?"

"Just pass me my smelling salts. The bottle with the crystal stopper. Does life ever become too much for you, Miss Hurst?"

"Occasionally. But I—but you—"

"I know what you're going to say. That I have a beautiful home, a husband, children. That is all true. But one is never free from problems, even so. I have my wretched health. And Flora. What would you do with a crippled daughter all your life, Miss Hurst? And now my poor aunt as well. One gets frightened—" Her voice died away.

"Frightened of what, Mrs. Meryon?"

But Charlotte was following an odd line of thought.

"I had sixteen trunks when I came to Winterwood as a bride. And my dowry. Oh, I didn't come of an ancient or a noble family. But my husband didn't care about that. He said I was so beautiful he couldn't stop looking at me. It was true, too. And I still am, even if the money's all gone, even if Winterwood is such a hungry monster."

Her eyes fluttered shut, then opened again, showing themselves still a little wild from that hysterical scene. Lavinia waited a little, then said, "Why did you want me, Mrs. Meryon?"

"Oh, just to tell you that your duties are entirely with Flora. Don't concern yourself with anything else."

"The business about Mary is concerned with Flora, Mrs. Meryon."

"Yes, yes, I realize that. I will inform Mrs. O'Shaughnessy of the new arrangement. If it makes Flora happy, then I am happy."

But she wasn't happy. She kept staring at Lavinia, until Lavinia was impelled to ask, "Is that all, Mrs. Meryon?"

"Yes, that's all. Just remember your duties are with Flora."

"But have I exceeded—"

Charlotte waved an agitated hand.

"Please, Miss Hurst! I don't want to discuss the matter further. It is only that you haven't the right manner. Miss Brown and the others were meek. They kept their eyes downcast."

"Perhaps that's why they couldn't manage Flora, Mrs. Meryon."

"Perhaps. But I won't have your eyes roving all over the place. Devote them to your charge."

Lavinia returned to her room to continue the letter she had begun to Robin. She read the last sentence, "If only you could see the room I am sitting in you would be happy for me." She went on compulsively, finding the act of writing a relief. "But I am disturbed by Mrs. Meryon's behavior. She is delicate and inclined to be hysterical and she made a quite unprovoked scene at luncheon. I can only think that she has something on her mind. She seems suspicious of me, as if I will see too much. She seems frightened, too, although of what except her aunt's impending death, I can't imagine. Is it that she is jealous of me—how can she be, she is so beautiful herself? Is it that she has moods when her mind becomes slightly deranged? I did think that for a moment today. Mr. Meryon is so tender with her. But there is something hanging over this place . . ."

Lavinia's pen dropped from her hand there, and she stared into space. Charlotte was not the only one who was afraid. Lavinia knew that Jonathon Peate would come to Winterwood. Although she had tried not to think about his threat, it was always at the back of her mind. She didn't know his purpose. She was sure it was not good. But each day was making her more anxious that no one should discover her secret. The scene with Charlotte, for some reason, had intensified her anxiety. Fear was catching.

But perhaps she, like Charlotte, was suffering only from the weariness and strain of the long journey.

She lay down on the sofa at the foot of the bed, and before she knew it was sound asleep. She was awakened by the sound of voices quarreling.

She sprang up and opened her door to find Eliza, who had been given the permanent duties of nurse because the old lady had taken a fancy to her, hurrying along the passage to Lady Tameson.

"Miss Hurst, did you give Miss Flora permission to go in to my lady? I left her having a nice nap, and here I find her sitting up playing cards. Did you ever! Listen!"

Flora's voice, high and shrill, was the loudest, but Lady Tameson was far from inaudible.

"You cheated, Great-aunt Tameson! I saw you! You ought to be ashamed of yourself!"

"I did nothing of the kind, you unpleasant child. My king has taken your queen."

"But you took it from the wrong pack. I saw you cheating. I refuse to play with you any more."

"Then good riddance. I'll be glad if you'll leave me in peace."

Lavinia hurried into the bedroom to find Flora with her wheel-chair drawn close to the bed, Lady Tameson sitting bolt upright, and cards all over the counterpane.

"Flora, what is this? You're supposed to be resting."

Two pairs of guilty eyes turned. Flora began to giggle, and Lady Tameson drew in her mouth, although her hand crept across the counterpane toward Flora's.

"Save your breath scolding her, Miss Hurst. I invited her in. But I regret it now. She has been rude and objectionable."

"Miss Hurst, Great-aunt Tameson cheated. I saw her quite distinctly. She's old enough to know better."

Lady Tameson's mouth tightened into a nutcracker shape. Her black eyes snapped.

"I won the game. My king took your queen. If you're going to play games with me, you'll find that I usually win."

"I'd rather lose than cheat," Flora shouted, her face scarlet. "I wonder you dare to, since you're going to die so soon. What will you say to God?"

It was unfortunate that Charlotte, better for her rest, was just coming downstairs with Edward. Edward raced forward, his face bright with anticipation of trouble.

"What is it, Flora? Have you been rude to Great-aunt Tameson?"

"No, I have not. Telling the truth isn't being rude."

"Flora!" Charlotte's voice was tight with anger. "Go to your room. Miss Hurst, this is exactly what I was warning you about. If

you can't keep Flora in order you are no better than the others. I
can't have my aunt upset by all this noise."

Lady Tameson sat up straighter.

"I'm not upset, Charlotte. I was merely explaining to my great-
niece that when I play games I usually win." Her eyes glinted
strangely. Charlotte saw the look, but before she could say anything,
Flora persisted, "She wanted to play, Mamma. The doctor said she
was to be made happy."

"Flora, you would oblige me by not answering back. Go to your
room immediately. And although you say you're not upset, Aunt
Tameson, you look very flushed. I think you should rest quietly. If
you're feeling dull, Edward will show you how nicely he can read
and write. Teddy darling, I want you to fetch your new reading and
writing books and your pencils."

Edward pouted, caught his mother's eye, and muttered, "Yes,
Mamma."

As he followed Flora out, Flora turned to him contemptuously.
"Are you going to suck up to her? I thought you hated her."

"Mamma says I have to."

"Why are you wearing your velvet suit? It makes you look like a
little angel." Flora's voice was sharply sarcastic. "Are you supposed
to make Great-aunt Tameson think you're her little Tom?"

Edward's anxiety was greater at that moment than his sense of
injury.

"I don't want to read to her. She's too old. I don't like old ladies."

Flora was merciless. "Are you afraid she'll die while you're there?
She might, too. I bet you wouldn't get her her medicine in time. I
bet you'd just scream for Mamma."

Charlotte came out of Lady Tameson's room.

"Children! Do what I told you to at once." It seemed that she
was even angry with her beloved Edward. "Miss Hurst, I cannot
have these children constantly quarreling. They must be kept apart
until Edward's tutor arrives. I suggest you take Flora out for some
air in the garden before the sun goes. Teddy, I told you to fetch
your books." Her voice softened. "Don't be alarmed, my pet.
Mamma will stay with you."

The sun had almost gone. It hung, a red ball, beyond the woods,
and there was mist in the air. Joseph had to help Lavinia with Flora's
chair down the steps of the terrace where the two sphinxes, accustomed to desert vistas, looked over English lawns and fountains with
round, surprised eyes. Flora meant no time to be wasted on dull

lawns and gravel walks. She ordered Lavinia to take her through an opening in the privet hedge, across the archery lawn, past the slope that led down to the shrubbery and the ornamental lake, across the walled kitchen garden with its herb and strawberry beds, its raspberry canes and espaliered peach and apricot trees, and through a door in the brick wall to the little blue garden.

It was an enchanting place. Butterflies drifted about the blue and purple michaelmas daisies; there were late sweet peas, heliotrope and blue phlox. Earlier in the year, Flora said, there was lobelia, gentians, and morning glory. She eagerly wheeled her chair down the uneven paving stones to where the morning glory vine had climbed all over the stone infant's head on its slender plinth. Leaves lay across the rounded brow and the broken nose. Moss had filled the eyes. There was a crack in the stone that distorted the smiling mouth.

Lavinia pulled the vines away and began to scrape the moss out of the eyes. Flora watched her silently. When she had finished and the round-cheeked face was clean and curiously naked, Flora sighed.

"I always used to do that, but I can't now, and I wouldn't allow anyone else to touch it. It's my baby."

"It's a charming garden," Lavinia said.

"My grandmother made it. She put the baby here, too. It was before Papa was born, and she thought a lot about babies. She used to sit here and long for one of her own. And then when Papa was born she died."

"How sad."

"It's not sad in this garden," Flora denied vigorously. "No one is allowed to come here without my permission. If you sit under the fig tree over there no one can see you from the house. It's the best place in Winterwood to be private." Suddenly she added, "You may come here, Miss Hurst, when you want to be private. Only remember to shut the door in the wall so that Edward can't get in."

"Poor Edward."

"He's not poor at all. He's sucking up to Great-aunt Tameson. I expect he wants one of her diamond brooches to give to his future wife. Though I can't imagine who would marry him. Will you sit under the fig tree and long for a baby, Miss Hurst?"

Flora's rapid change of subject took Lavinia unawares. For once she couldn't quickly compose her face. She had been thinking of Daniel's mother sitting idly in the sun, her face peaceful and content, as she dreamed of the birth of her baby. A stone one, charming as it was, had not needed to suffice for her.

It wasn't true that this garden wasn't sad. It was unbearably sad.

"You are too young to talk about things like that, Flora. Let us go in. It's getting chilly."

Flora permitted herself to be wheeled away without protest. But it was too much to hope that she had given up the subject.

Upstairs she said, "What will you wear to dinner tonight, Miss Hurst?"

"My blue silk, I expect."

"Is that your only good dress?"

"If you don't count this brown one I have on."

"Would you like a pink one, like the one you said I could have?"

"Naturally, but I can hardly ask your Mamma for one for myself as well, can I?"

"You looked beautiful at the opera. Papa said so." Flora was thoughtful. Suddenly she said, "Don't be sad, Miss Hurst."

"Sad?"

"About not getting a baby. Your face was sad."

"You imagine things," Lavinia said roughly. "And don't despise my blue silk too much. It's very suitable."

The change in Charlotte at dinner was remarkable. It was because Daniel had brought her a gift, a little Italian greyhound bitch with a red leather collar. He had been calling on the new people at Croft House. It appeared that they bred this fanciful kind of dog.

Charlotte was enchanted with it. She gathered the slim shivering little creature into her arms and said that she would call it Sylvie.

"Thank you, my love," she whispered. She was wearing a red dress, and now that pleasure had brought some color to her cheeks she looked astonishingly lovely. Lavinia, who had come on the tender little scene in the drawing room, for the bell had rung for dinner some minutes before, thought—he loves her.

The greyhound was a charming toy, and Charlotte insisted on having it at her feet during dinner. Her headache had quite disappeared, she said, and she had become very gay.

"Daniel, let's have some amusements. We mustn't let the house get gloomy because of Aunt Tameson. Already the children have been feeling it. Isn't that so, Miss Hurst? Flora has been particularly difficult. Though I must say my darling Teddy, when I finally persuaded him to, got his copybook and showed Aunt Tameson how well he could write. He was perfectly sweet with her, and was very amused when he found her writing very bad and shaky and his so much better. I hope, when Mr. Mallinson comes, her signature won't be quite so undecipherable."

"Witnesses will take care of that," Daniel said. "I'd suggest responsible people like Mrs. O'Shaughnessy and Miss Hurst. Then, if affidavits are required later, they can make them."

"Of course," Charlotte said in a relieved voice. "You understand everything."

"You're quite certain that this is your aunt's wish?"

"But naturally. It's on her mind every minute. She won't be happy until it's done. She said this in Venice, darling."

Daniel was aware of the nervous edge coming back in his wife's voice and said quickly, "Then the sooner the better."

Charlotte gave a little sigh. "Yes. I've written to Mr. Mallinson suggesting Saturday. He may care to stay overnight. Tomorrow, if she is well enough, my aunt insists on going to see little Tom's grave. The doctor said she should take airings, but I trust she won't always show a preference for the churchyard. Let us talk of something more cheerful."

"Then I have the very thing," said Daniel. "The mailbag arrived just before dinner. It contained an invitation to a weekend at Windsor Castle at the end of the month, to attend a ball, and races at Ascot."

Charlotte clapped her hands.

"Oh, how jolly!" Then her face fell. "But I can scarcely leave my aunt."

"Nonsense! With a house full of servants!"

"Yes, but supposing—" she hesitated, and finished with words Lavinia was sure she hadn't been about to say, "supposing she asks for me."

"Personally," said old Sir Timothy, who had been paying absorbed attention to his food, "I find the Queen a monstrously dull creature thinking about nothing but filling the nurseries, and that German husband."

"Nevertheless this is a command," Daniel said. "Unless we are virtually at Lady Tameson's deathbed, we must go. So make your arrangements, my love."

Charlotte fed a tidbit to the little greyhound under the table. She said, "I shall need a new dress," and looked happy. Her eyes, with their curious drowned look, were shining. The harpy of the luncheon table had vanished to give place to this childlike creature. Was this mood completely here, or was she acting one more part? The devoted mother (to Edward only), the dutiful niece, the petulant invalid, the wild-eyed creature torn by temper and anger, and now the child-wife, although she must be quite thirty years or more.

What was she as a lover, Lavinia wondered. How would she be in the bedroom tonight with her new pet betokening her husband's affection, and the promise of a visit to Windsor Castle? What warmth and excitement did she bring to love?

It was difficult to push those painful thoughts out of her mind and listen to Sir Timothy, who had reverted to the interesting subject of Lady Tameson.

"I must say, Charlotte, I found your aunt extraordinarily chipper, considering what old Munro says. But it's a pity she's lost her red hair. The only thing I recognized about her was that abominable violet scent she always used."

"It's a long time since you last saw her, Uncle Timothy," Charlotte said. "And anyway you see so badly now."

"I'm well aware of that. Don't suppose she thought I'd improved, either. I asked her a few things about Willie Peate. I'm glad to say she hasn't forgotten him, in spite of this Count she married. She said she would always remember him with tenderness. He was the father of her child, and, of course, one of the country's heroes. Sometimes one wonders if anyone remembers the heroes of Waterloo except the Duke himself, and he was always a cold fish, anyway. Though they said he had tears in his eyes when he looked across those fields of slaughtered. Daniel, I laid down this claret the year after Waterloo. It's done nicely, don't you agree?"

"Splendidly, Uncle Timothy. I've just ordered a consignment from the Château Margaux vineyards."

"Fine. Simon will thank you for that one day. It's a pity one's lifespan is so short. I'd like to see that mature."

"I expect the ancestor who planted the Lebanon cedar would have liked to see it grow to its present size, too. We must take the appreciation of these things on trust."

"Well, I'll never cease objecting to dying," Sir Timothy said obstinately. "I'll wager that old woman upstairs feels the same."

Chapter 9

Simon, on holiday from school, and Edward's tutor, a fair-haired nervous young man called Mr. Bush, arrived together the next day.

Simon was a grave, quiet boy so like his father that Lavinia loved him on sight. Flora, too, had a great affection for him, though she pretended otherwise.

Edward's reaction to the two arrivals was to disappear for the entire morning, and to be brought home muddy, wet and unrepentant. He flew at once to his mother, muddying her skirts, but Charlotte merely smiled fondly and said that although Mr. Bush was to teach him arithmetic and grammar, he was not to crush his high spirits.

"Poor Mr. Bush," Flora giggled. "He looks completely alarmed already. Do you like his appearance, Miss Hurst?"

"Yes, but I think he looks too young and gentle."

"I fear so, too," Flora sighed.

"Why are you so distressed? For Mr. Bush's sake?"

"No, for yours, Miss Hurst. I had thought he might make a husband for you. Mamma never said he was so young, or so entirely unsuitable."

"Your mamma had Edward's future in mind, not mine."

"Yes, but I had thought you might have a romantic friendship, while Edward was being taught better manners."

"Flora, you're quite incorrigible. Now let us get on with our lesson, and have no more matchmaking. Poor Mr. Bush."

The thought made them both suddenly burst into peals of laughter. A shadow fell across the table. Daniel picked up the book they had been reading.

"The poems of Alfred Tennyson. I hadn't known Mr. Tennyson was a humorist."

"Oh, Papa, he isn't," Flora spluttered. "Miss Hurst and I were having a joke."

"May I not share it?"

Flora refused to see Lavinia's warning glance. "I was hoping to arrange Miss Hurst's marriage to Mr. Bush. But I'm afraid he's un-suitable. Isn't it a great pity? Papa, don't you find it amusing?"

"Not in the least," said Daniel. "Just as I find the part of match-maker very unsuitable to you."

Flora's eyes sparkled.

"Are you angry with me, Papa?"

"With you for being precocious and with Miss Hurst for encour-aging you." He swung on his heel and went out.

Flora stared at Lavinia aghast, then burst into violent sobs. It was some time before Lavinia could calm her. Then she said, "It's be-cause Simon is home. Papa loves him best."

"That's nonsense."

"Then why was he cross with me just because I mentioned your marrying Mr. Bush? And he gave Mamma Sylvie. He knows how dearly I would love a greyhound. And soon they are going to have a gay time at Windsor while I am stuck here in this damn chair."

She stared at Lavinia aggressively, waiting for her exclamation of shock at the unladylike word. In this mood she was very plain. Her mother's delicate beauty had missed her completely. She was a pale little caterpillar of a person, perhaps with a chrysalis to break out of, though at this moment it seemed she was doomed to plainness, and a pathetic endless search for love.

Lavinia quelled her distaste, then wondered if it were not distaste but a heart-wrenching pain. It would be easy to fall into self-pity with Flora. She, too, disliked thinking of the gay royal occasion at Windsor.

"Is everyone to be helpless and unhappy simply because you are? Anyway, your mamma will let you take care of Sylvie while she is away. And perhaps by the time they return you will be able to walk again."

Flora's fingers curled into her palms hard.

"Miss Hurst, you really are the most stupid person. You know very well I am a prisoner in this chair forever."

"That's because you want to be."

Flora was startled out of her bad temper.

"I *want* to be! Do you think I *like* it?"

"You make a great fuss when I want to rub your legs. You say you can't do exercises. So I can only conclude you enjoy your condition."

Flora bit her lip. "Are you going to leave me?"

"Why do you ask?"

"Because you said that as if you hated me."

"I think you talk too much about love and hate. No, I'm not going to leave you, at least not until you can walk again."

And that was a rash thing to say, for suddenly Flora's face blazed with the first look of hope Lavinia had yet seen in it. But all she said was, "Then I suppose I had better try to do those old exercises. Come, Miss Hurst. Take me upstairs."

Now she was committed. Flora had to be made to walk.

The strange woman called that afternoon after Charlotte and Lady Tameson had departed for a drive which was to include a call on the vicar, Mr. Clayton, and a visit to little Tom's grave. Edward had accompanied them and, as usual, Flora was jealous.

"Mamma's making Edward Great-aunt Tameson's pet, too."

"You don't want to go to a graveyard," Lavinia said.

"I do. I love the little angel on Tom's grave. I love it almost as much as the baby in my garden."

"How can you go in your chair?" Edward jeered. "You'd go bump bump over the graves. Anyway, I don't want to sit in the carriage beside Great-aunt Tameson. She smells."

"It's only her violet perfume. I expect she wears it so little Tom will recognize her when she goes to heaven."

"I wish she'd go soon," Edward said. "Mamma is always making me do reading and writing with her. I can write my name better than she can write hers and she's as old as the hills."

"You're showing off," said Flora. "She'd rather play cards with me, and I hate her more than you do."

Edward had gone off unwillingly, dressed in his blue velvet suit, with his black curls shining. And later the stranger had arrived.

She was sitting in the hall when Lavinia took Flora down for her afternoon walk. Joseph said she had been there for half an hour and was waiting to see Lady Tameson. She was a plainly dressed elderly woman, a neat black bonnet framing her pleasant face. She had made a long journey, she had said, and wouldn't leave without seeing Lady Tameson.

Just then Lavinia heard the wheels of the carriage, and pulled Flora's chair aside to allow Lady Tameson, leaning heavily on Charlotte's arm, to enter.

The visitor sprang up and dropped a curtsey.

"Ma'am!" she cried. "Asking your pardon, but I heard about your return and I had to come and see you. After all these years."

Lady Tameson stared.

"Charlotte, who is this? Why should she want to see me?"

"But don't you remember Bessie Jenkins, ma'am? I was with you when the news came from Brussels, about the poor master, and then when your little boy died, bless his heart. You wouldn't forget crying all night in my arms, ma'am?"

Lady Tameson's mouth opened and shut, but no sound came. She seemed bewildered.

"It's a long time ago. Bessie Jenkins? You must have changed."

"Asking your pardon, but so have you, ma'am. Your beautiful hair that I used to be so proud to brush—"

It was Charlotte who interrupted, her voice high and strained.

"Naturally people change in forty years. My aunt is very feeble, Mrs. Jenkins. You haven't chosen a very opportune time to call. It would have been better if you had written first, so that my aunt could have been prepared. Just now she's distressed after seeing her son's grave. I must get her upstairs." Over her shoulder she said, "If you go to the kitchen one of the maids will give you a cup of tea."

The expression on Bessie Jenkins' face was first one of disappointment, then of anger. She stared after the two slowly ascending the stairs, and said clearly, "I won't be taking any tea, thank you. I'll get on my ways."

She was muttering to herself as she made for the door, "That Miss Charlotte always was above herself."

Flora, who had watched and heard everything with the keenest interest, suddenly wheeled her chair rapidly after the disgruntled Mrs. Jenkins.

"You are speaking of my mother," she said haughtily.

"Aye. I spoke the truth."

"Do you remember her, as well as Great-aunt Tameson?"

"She was a wee bit of a thing. She'd not recall me now. But the mistress—aye, her memory's gone, poor thing. She wouldn't have not recollected Bessie Jenkins otherwise. Well, I'll be off, and sorry I made the journey."

"Great-aunt Tameson wouldn't mean to be unkind," Flora said earnestly.

"No, I wouldn't have thought so. I wouldn't have thought her head would be turned by marrying into the foreign nobility. But it's a sad thing she doesn't remember her Bessie. We shed many a tear together once upon a time. Well now, that's life. And you're a poor wee thing sitting in that contraption."

Flora's eyes flashed. "It's not forever. You don't have to be sorry for me."

"I can see that. I like a bit of spirit. You're like my poor mistress used to be. Bless you, lassie. You can tell your mamma I won't trouble to call again since I can see it's no use. Though I'd never have believed the mistress would have forgotten her Bessie."

The next day Mr. Mallinson, the solicitor, came down from London. There was a great deal of solemnity while he took his instructions and prepared Lady Tameson's will, with the ceremony of signing it to follow. Lavinia was called in to take her part in this. She noticed that poor Lady Tameson was quite distressed and nervous. No doubt signing her will did make her see all too clearly the grave yawning. Mr. Mallinson seemed to understand this, for he was as soothing and tactful as a doctor. When she had at last made her laborious signature, "Tameson Barrata," and worried about her handwriting being too shaky he assured her that it was perfectly legible, and in any case the two witnesses had observed her making it, which was their purpose.

"Well, Charlotte. I've kept my word."

"Yes, aunt, dear. Now you must rest."

"Why? I'm not exhausted from signing my name. Don't shut me away now that everything's done neatly. Ask Flora to come and play a game of cards with me."

It seemed that the ceremony of the will had upset Charlotte more than it had Lady Tameson. Her eyes were strained and apprehensive. Had she thought the old lady would die before her estate was made over to the occupants of Winterwood—as undoubtedly it had been?

"Aunt, you know Flora always upsets you. You both quarrel."

"I like quarreling. Send the child in."

Apart from Mr. Mallinson's visit nothing happened that weekend. His business accomplished, Mr. Mallinson proved to be a jolly little man fond of his food and wine. He played chess with Sir Timothy after dinner and reminisced about various episodes in his legal life. He regretted that he had not known Lady Tameson previously. It was his partner, now deceased, who had acted for her at the time of her first husband's death.

Charlotte didn't sing that evening. She reclined on the couch, Sylvie, the little greyhound, curled up beside her. She said she felt quite well, but she wasn't really relaxed. Once she sighed deeply, as if some worry were over.

In the morning Daniel and Simon went riding, and later everyone except Lady Tameson went to church, even Flora, whom her father carried in and propped among cushions in the family pew. The sides were high enough to prevent the curious from staring in, but there were plenty of stares of pity and interest when Daniel carried her out again. Flora was used to this and clearly enjoyed it. She put on her most wan look and drooped against her father's shoulder, her eyes remarkably observant beneath their meekly lowered lashes. A pat on the head from the vicar and a reverent inquiry as to her health completed her satisfaction.

Lavinia was pleased enough to have Flora take all the attention. She wondered how long it would be before she stopped being nervous of the stare of strangers. Supposing someone exclaimed, "Miss Hurstmonceaux!" as Jonathon Peate had done.

But the quiet little village took no more than a passing interest in her. There was much more to take attention, with poor crippled Miss Flora's appearance, and the talk about Mrs. Willie Peate, now a foreign contessa, and the London solicitor down.

Sunday passed and it was Monday and Mr. Mallinson left in the dogcart to catch the train back to London.

That was the morning Edward played truant again from poor Mr. Bush and was found fishing for tadpoles in the village pond, his jacket muddied and his feet soaking wet. Winterwood was a large house, but scarcely large enough for Edward's yells not to be heard all over it when his father punished him. Charlotte retired to her room and Flora gloated over the chastened Edward.

"Did Papa beat you? It was hardly worthwhile for a few silly tadpoles. What do you plan to do with them? Grow them into frogs?"

"No."

"What then?"

"I'm not telling." Edward was tearstained and sulky. "It isn't fair, anyway. You play cards with Great-aunt Tameson and Simon plays chess with Uncle Timothy and I have nobody."

"You're Mamma's pet," Flora pointed out.

"Mamma has Sylvie now."

"Then you have Mr. Bush."

"And you had better go to him at once if you don't want more trouble," Lavinia said. She weakened. She supposed the child was lonely. "Later you may come for a walk with Flora and me."

But Edward hadn't finished with trouble for that day. Suddenly, late in the afternoon, Lady Tameson screamed. When Eliza rushed in, she found the old lady blue in the face and moaning with pain. A draught of her medicine revived her sufficiently to gasp something about a "beast" in the bed and Eliza stripped back the sheets to find two of Edward's tadpoles, expiring more successfully than Lady Tameson.

This time the culprit had the grace to look a little frightened.

"Edward, you could have killed her!" Lavinia exclaimed. "Don't you realize that?"

"Tadpoles don't hurt you!" Edward said sulkily.

"But why did you do it, you little imp?" Eliza was beside herself with fright. "Did you want to kill your poor old auntie? What good would that be doing you?"

"It was only a joke," Edward maintained stoutly. "I only thought the tadpoles would—would—" He had seen his mother coming and burst into loud sobs. "Mamma, I wasn't really trying to kill her."

Charlotte was hurrying, her arms outstretched.

"Who is saying such a terrible thing? Miss Hurst! Eliza! This is frightful. An innocent child!" She gathered the sobbing boy into her arms. "I was resting and I heard the commotion. Whatever is the trouble?"

Eliza's homely face was settled in stern lines. She held up a dead tadpole, almost brandishing it in her mistress' face.

"I found this in my patient's bed, ma'am. The discovery brought on one of her attacks."

"She's—not dead?"

Charlotte's words brought a fresh roar from Edward.

"Hush, Teddy! Eliza! She's not—"

That was when Lavinia knew that Charlotte hoped poor Lady Tameson was dead. The old lady had only needed to be kept alive until her will was made.

Eliza, Lavinia divined, had had something of the same thought, for she shook her head with sour satisfaction.

"No, ma'am. She's recovered as well as possible."

"Then there's no harm done, thank goodness." Charlotte turned to Lady Tameson's door with obvious reluctance. "I'll just have a look at her. Wait for Mamma, Teddy."

Lady Tameson's voice from within the room was weak but quite audible, a rasping accusing voice.

"That spoiled brat of yours has nearly been the end of me, Charlotte."

"It was only an innocent prank, Aunt Tameson. All little boys do these things."

"So even if I lay here dead, you'd be making excuses for him."

"But you're not lying there dead, and of course I intend to speak to Teddy. He didn't mean any harm. He's very fond of you."

"Fond! There's only one person fond of me and that's my own son."

"Aunt Tameson!" Charlotte sounded alarmed. "I'm going to send for Doctor Munro."

Aunt Tameson's voice grew stronger. "Oh, pshaw! I'm no worse than usual. I'll die when my time comes. But not before! Don't count on that!"

Charlotte came out slowly, her face worried. She closed the door carefully, saw the listening women, and said, "She's talking as if Tom, poor little Tom, weren't dead."

"Old people wander a bit, ma'am," Eliza said. "It was the shock, I expect. Usually she's got all her senses. I'll go in to her."

"Yes, please do. And Teddy—come with me. Mamma wants to have a long serious talk."

Chapter 10

IT HAD been only a childish prank of Edward's, and in its way it had
served a purpose, for Edward had obviously frightened himself and
his behavior mended. Young Mr. Bush began to look happier. He
strolled sometimes with Flora and Lavinia on their walks, showing a
deference to Flora that pleased her. Simon's short holiday was over.
Dressed in his school clothes, he said courteous goodbyes. When he
had gone it was time for Charlotte and Daniel to prepare for their
visit to Windsor.

A week was given over to clothes. Charlotte was having a new ball
gown made, and two new tea gowns, each with delicious quantities
of lace ruffles. Eliza, who had, in her slow, cautious way, begun to
like and trust Lavinia, now offered to make a gown for her if she
could buy some material.

"I'm a good seamstress, Miss Hurst. My mother was a mantua-
maker, and she taught me."

"And where will I wear the gown, Eliza?" Lavinia asked, with some
bitterness.

"Now don't you fret, Miss Hurst. There will be plenty of opportunity to wear it. Christmas is coming, and there'll be balls and
parties here. If you'll excuse me saying so, your blue doesn't do you
justice. Mind you, I don't mean anything too fashionable, but something becoming."

This offer was most kind of Eliza, and Lavinia gratefully accepted.
She had been paid her first wages that morning, and decided recklessly to lay them all out on a piece of good silk. She would take
Flora for a day's outing to Dover, and material could also be bought
for Flora's promised pink-sprigged muslin. That had to be arranged
with Charlotte, but Charlotte seemed so excited and stimulated by
the prospect of the coming weekend, that she agreed carelessly to
everything.

"By all means, Miss Hurst. Attend completely to Flora's wardrobe.
Buy her any pretty thing she fancies, poor sweet. Go to Blacketts
and charge everything to my account. Order the brougham, and take

Joseph with you. Don't let Flora overtire herself, though I am sure
I can trust your good sense in that respect."

Daniel came to hear of Flora's and Lavinia's proposed outing, and
made a special visit to the yellow parlor to express his pleasure.

"So Miss Hurst is turning your head," he said to Flora.

"Oh, no, Papa, she only says I may look better when I can put my
hair up. When can I put it up?"

"I should think in about five years' time."

"But that's *forever!* Do I have to wear little girl dresses until
then?"

"You must ask Miss Hurst."

Five years. Did he think she would be here that long? She would
be twenty-seven. And unmarried . . . In an even voice Lavinia said,
"I intend to buy her shoes also, Mr. Meryon."

"Shoes? But—"

"It's a whole year since her accident, and naturally her feet have
grown. She has nothing to fit her, and she can't wear slippers forever. I thought a pair of buttoned kid boots, and a pair of shoes suitable for parties or dancing."

Daniel's first surprise had gone and his eyes didn't flicker.

"Of course. A splendid idea. Get what you think fit, Miss Hurst.
I wish I could come with you."

"Don't be silly, Papa. You'll be kissing the Queen's hand. That's
much more grand."

"But not so enjoyable."

"Papa! You'll be executed for treason."

Daniel was looking at Lavinia. He had that reflective look that
she had never quite interpreted, although she was almost sure it
meant approval. Perhaps admiration. She didn't see how he could be
overwhelmed with admiration for her when she had had to keep her
natural high spirits and vivacity so damped down, so constantly
crushed into the manner of an obedient servant. She must appear
very colorless beside Charlotte's dramatic, haunting beauty. She was
perfectly certain she hadn't misinterpreted the interest in his gaze
that night at the opera in Venice. But her appearance since then in
her dutiful dull gowns must have erased that memory from his mind.
She had an irresistible desire to revive it.

"Are you feeling sorry for me, Miss Hurst?"

"Sorry?"

"That I am to be shot, as Flora suggests?" Flora giggled with delight, but Lavinia remained quite silent, looking at him. "You were
looking sad. It was only a joke, you know."

"Miss Hurst doesn't like jokes like that, Papa. Once, when I mentioned the gallows, she went quite white. Didn't you, Miss Hurst?"

"Because she is more sensitive than you, no doubt. Well, I must be off." Daniel's voice was brisk again, that contemplative note gone. He took Lavinia's hand. "Goodbye, Miss Hurst. I am in your debt. Goodbye, little minx." Flora got a kiss on the forehead, and Lavinia's own forehead tingled strangely, as if his lips had been placed there. "Take care. Don't let anything happen to either of you while I am gone."

Flora was still in a mood of euphoria. "Dear Papa! What could happen to us? He'll only be gone four days."

"I suppose a great deal could happen in four days." Lavinia was feeling tart. The gallows that had threatened Robin . . . Daniel's close regard . . . That kiss that had seemed to be her own. She felt strung-up and tense, and, for some odd reason, apprehensive. The house was going to seem peculiarly empty and unguarded with the master and mistress away.

But everything was all right. The drive into Dover and the morning's shopping with Flora were a great success. Flora was made much of in the shops. A couch was arranged for her to recline on, and everything was brought to her for her inspection and approval, materials, ribbons, dancing shoes tied with satin ribbons, and a ravishing chip straw bonnet trimmed with pink rosebuds. She felt like a grand lady, Lavinia could see. She waved this away and asked for that, then caught Lavinia watching her with amusement and became loftier than ever in sudden embarrassment and defiance. But there was no doubt she had a fugitive prettiness when she was happy like this. It was possible she would even grow into a woman of charm and distinction, if not of positive beauty. Lavinia knew, all at once, that she wanted to watch that happening, and realized that she was letting this very temporary position grow into something much more permanent. Even after a few hours away she knew she was longing for the return to Winterwood, and the first glimpse of the great austere house set on its hill. In so short a time she had let not only the inhabitants, but the house itself grow on her. It was going to stay in her dreams for a long long time.

"And now," Flora was saying in her lofty voice, "show us some materials suitable for an evening gown for my companion, Miss Hurst."

When Lavinia protested, Flora waved an autocratic hand.

"Be silent, Miss Hurst. I wish to choose this."

Lavinia had a moment of panic that her one precious new gown would be of some gaudy material admired only by a child. But Flora proved to have excellent taste. She insisted on a greenish-gray length of taffeta that, she observed, exactly matched dear Miss Hurst's eyes.

The parcel was to be wrapped and put with the others, Flora said, but not to be added to the account. She personally wished to pay for it. Before Lavinia could stop her, she had produced her little bead purse and taken two sovereigns from it.

"It is my gift," she said, and added under her breath, "Pray don't make a scene."

It was ridiculous, this reversal of their positions. Lavinia struggled with hot resentment at the fate that had reduced her to accepting gifts from a child.

They were bowed out of the shop by the manager, Flora managing to retain her hauteur even in Joseph's arms.

"Flora, I really cannot accept a gift like this."

"It is just as important to accept gracefully, as it is to give," Flora said primly. "I don't think you are a very good accepter, Miss Hurst."

"I don't think I am, either."

"Then you must begin to reform," said Flora in her preaching voice. But almost immediately she had reverted to being a child again. "Miss Hurst, do you think I may wear my new shoes this evening? Uncle Timothy always asks Edward and me to have tea with him when Mamma and Papa are away."

"Certainly you may. So long as you're not too tired."

As it happened, Lady Tameson felt well enough to go down to tea, too. It was quite a merry party in the drawing room, for Mr. Bush came down, also, and proved himself an accomplished pianist. His father was a musician, he confided to Lavinia, and this was what he had ambitions of being himself. He kept looking at her in an admiring way, and Lavinia knew he was longing to ask what her private ambitions were.

Lavinia would not let his glances spoil the party. She seized Edward and said that they would dance as Mamma and Papa would be dancing at the palace this evening. While Mr. Bush played a spirited polka, she guided Edward, screaming with merriment, up and down the room, while Flora clapped her hands, and Sir Timothy said, "By Jove, I wish I were younger myself."

It had not grown quite dark enough for the lamps to be lit, and the curtains were still looped back, showing a darkening view of the garden. As Lavinia, out of breath and glowing with warmth, collapsed into a chair, she had a queer impression that the sphinxes on the terrace had moved closer. Indeed, one seemed to be peering with its dead eyes right into the room. What nonsense. It wasn't the sphinx, it was a man, one of the gardeners, passing and pausing to look inquisitively into the forbidden territory of the drawing room. The fire before which Lady Tameson nodded lit the room sufficiently for it to be perfectly clear to him. The white face had given Lavinia quite a shock. It was time the curtains were drawn.

Lady Tameson stirred and awoke. She pointed at the shining toes of Flora's shoes, peeping beneath the hem of her dress.

"Why are you wearing those ridiculous shoes?"

Flora's eyes flashed.

"Because I intend to dance in them one day."

"Then you'd better start doing something about it, hadn't you? Letting yourself being carried about. Ridiculous nonsense! Sheer laziness!"

"It is not laziness, you—"

"Flora!" Lavinia said hastily.

Flora bit her lips and glared balefully. "I'll dance on your grave, you horrid old woman!" Lady Tameson let out her raucous chuckle.

"I'll not let it disturb my rest. Where's Eliza? I want to go to my room. I'm tired. All that jigging about everyone's been doing. I think a short game of cards before supper, Flora."

"I shall beat you!"

"Come and try then, come and try."

Eliza and Mary came, and Phoebe to light the lamps and draw the curtains, and Joseph to carry Flora to her room. Edward was banished protesting to the nursery and Sir Timothy said that he would take a glass of sherry before dressing for dinner. Perhaps Miss Hurst would join him.

But Lavinia excused herself. Even though the lights were lit she felt oddly uneasy. Overheated and restless. She felt a stroll in the garden in the cool dusk imperative. She wanted to escape from the thought that was really the cause of her mood, Daniel dancing with Charlotte in the great ballroom at Windsor Castle, while she had only the admiring glances of a nonentity of a pale-faced, pale-haired schoolmaster. She had to fight one more of the unending battles with her pride.

The sun was sinking, a red ball behind the hill. It was a chilly dusk. Little flurries of leaves were whirled about in sudden winds. The terrace was empty, but Lavinia could see Coombe, the gardener, pottering about the rose garden, cutting off dead heads. It must have been he who had passed the window and peered curiously in.

So far Lavinia had explored only part of the garden. She had not yet had an opportunity to walk down to the shrubbery and the ornamental lake. She saw a wildfowl hover, and then plummet downward to the water. This gave her steps a direction. She would walk down to the lake and back, a pleasant brisk stroll which would refresh her before the long evening which Sir Timothy would expect her to spend with him. He had an unashamed enjoyment in the company of personable young women.

The paved pathway came to an end at the bottom of the rose garden. After that one crossed the lawn to the shrubbery, and broad paths between the rhododendrons led down the gentle slope to the lake. At least this was what Lavinia expected them to do, but she must have taken a wrong turning, for she seemed to go deeper and deeper into the shrubbery. Pushing aside branches, and debating whether to retrace her steps or go on, she came quite unexpectedly on the circular stone building. Its doorway was framed with miniature pillars, giving it a Grecian look. It must be the Temple of Virtue built by one of Daniel's ancestors. What a gloomy place to build what should have been a romantic building. Though perhaps at that time there had been only small newly planted shrubs about it. Now the hoary branching bushes and one weeping willow had grown out of all control, and shut the temple into a green damp darkness. The walls were thick with moss and creeping ivy. The door flapped on a broken hinge, leading into a circular chamber with stone floors littered with dead leaves, pillars supporting the roof, and uninviting mossy stone seats built around the walls. It was a dismal place, hidden and forgotten.

But not entirely forgotten—Lavinia cried out as someone laughed softly in the gloom. A man stepped from behind one of the pillars. Before Lavinia could say anything a match flared, dazzling her. "Ah! Miss Hurstmonceaux! I beg your pardon. I've made that stupid mistake again. Miss Hurst. We meet once more."

She backed away.

"Mr. Peate! What are you doing hiding here? It was you who looked in the window a little while ago!"

"I've come to see my aunt." His voice was quite unperturbed. She knew that he was laughing silently, for she could see his white teeth.

"Here? You didn't expect to find her in a deserted summer house! Have you some objection to ringing the front doorbell and being admitted in the usual way?"

"None at all. I've merely been taking a stroll before presenting myself. Unorthodox? But we are unorthodox people, aren't we, Miss Hurst?"

"Mr. and Mrs. Meryon are away," Lavinia said stiffly.

"Yes, so I hear. Oh, through quite legitimate sources. My bags are at the George and Dragon in the village if you're doubting my honesty. I walked across the fields. Coming in humbly through the back door, so to speak. Now you can take me up and present me."

"I!" Usually she was quick to sum up a situation, but this one baffled her. Had he lurked about hoping for her to come out of the house so that this would look like a deliberate assignation? Or had he not meant to make his presence known, but, knowing that Charlotte and Daniel were away, had been making a private investigation of the estate? If that were so, he must be annoyed that she had stumbled on him. He didn't show any annoyance. Perhaps this unexpected development suited his mysterious purpose.

She was absolutely certain he was up to no good. For why did he insist on calling her Miss Hurstmonceaux, as if he wanted to intimidate her.

If that was what he hoped to do, he had succeeded all too well. She was cold with apprehension.

"Then come," she said briefly.

As she had expected, Sir Timothy was completely perplexed as to why she should have gone out to walk in the dusk and come back with a strange man. He looked from one to the other, blinking, his spectacles mislaid as usual.

"Is Mr. Peate a friend of yours, Miss Hurst?"

"No, Sir Timothy, I thought you had understood. He is a nephew of Lady Tameson and has called to see her."

"A nephew? I hadn't heard about that."

Jonathon Peate stood smiling.

"By marriage, sir."

"You mean on Willie Peate's side? I hadn't heard Willie Peate had a brother."

"That's quite understandable. He emigrated to Australia." Jonathon's cool blue eyes flicked to Lavinia. She knew he was lying, and that the choice of Australia was deliberate.

"That's interesting, upon my word." Dear Sir Timothy was quite unaware of undercurrents. "Did he make a fortune there? I hear some lucky fellows have in the gold diggings."

"I'm afraid my father wasn't so fortunate. He died on an expedition into the interior. My mother returned to England with me. I remember nothing of this, of course. I was a very young child."

"And so you've had to make your own way in the world," Sir Timothy observed.

"That is true." Jonathon shifted his position casually, as if to show off his clothing, which was in impeccable taste. But he still didn't look a gentleman. He was too bold, too brash. He looked as if he had carefully studied gentlemen's fashions, and had himself outfitted in absolutely correct manner. But his true fancy would be for louder, more showy clothes.

His tale about Australia must be deliberate fantasy. He had never left England, Lavinia was certain. She was also beginning to doubt if Willie Peate had ever had a brother.

If that were so, who was this man?

She would have to make Lady Tameson tell her.

She said that she would go upstairs and see if Lady Tameson were well enough to receive a visitor.

"Oh, she'll see me," Jonathon said. "She has quite a soft spot for me, you know."

A great noise had broken out upstairs. Edward came rushing out of Lady Tameson's bedroom blowing a trumpet earsplittingly. Eliza was wringing her hands and exclaiming, "Master Edward! You are a most disobedient little boy." To Lavinia she said, "Really, miss, that boy just can't be controlled. Phoebe is no use with him at all."

"What has he done now?"

"Just blown his trumpet fit to wake the dead in my poor lady's ear. He was jealous of her playing cards with Miss Flora, though goodness knows why, when he says he can't abide the poor lady himself." She lowered her voice. "He'll come to a bad end, that boy."

"Is Lady Tameson all right?"

"Yes, thank goodness. Only cross and put out."

Lavinia went into the room to find Lady Tameson, quite unhurt, sitting up with her black eyes sparkling.

"What is it, Miss Hurst? If you've come to take Flora away, we haven't finished our game yet."

"No, Miss Hurst, Edward interrupted us."

Lavinia silenced Flora. "Well, I am going to interrupt you, too. Your aunt has a visitor."

The briefest surprise—or was it apprehension?—crossed Lady Tameson's face.

"A visitor for me. Who?"

"Your nephew, Lady Tameson. Mr. Jonathon Peate."

One hand moved slightly on the coverlet, the fingers closing. Lady

Tameson said in a perfectly self-possessed voice, "What's Jonathon doing here? I hadn't expected him."

"He says he's staying at the George and Dragon in the village. He walked across the fields. Indeed, I encountered him by chance in the garden."

Lady Tameson's eyes were hooded, unreadable. "Then I suppose I had better see him, after his long walk. Ask him to come up. Flora, we'll finish our game tomorrow."

The door was shut firmly when Jonathon went into Lady Tameson's room.

"That one's up to no good," Eliza muttered. "And if you ask me, the mistress is frightened of him. She used to get all of a twitter in Venice when he was around."

"You mean Mrs. Meryon?"

"Yes. That was before you came, Miss Hurst. There was one night when she couldn't sleep at all; she just kept walking up and down as if she had something desperate on her mind. Wouldn't let the master in at all. Said she had one of her headaches, but it was more than that. I believe it was something to do with that Mr. Peate." Eliza's good earnest face was worried. She looked each way, and lowered her voice. "He's after his aunt's money, you mark my words."

That was a very reasonable assumption, but Lavinia was sure it wasn't the full story. Jonathon Peate wanted more than a legacy.

"Why did he choose to come when the master and mistress was away?" Eliza went on. "Worming his way in, that's what he's doing."

And wandering secretly about the gardens as if he were estimating the value of Winterwood for his own private purposes.

It was extremely tempting to try and listen at the door. Lavinia overcame this temptation and went to supervise Flora's preparation for bed. She did, however, hear raised voices, as if Jonathon and his aunt were having an argument. But shortly afterwards Jonathon gave his loud confident laugh, so the disagreement could not have been serious, although Eliza reported later that Lady Tameson was overexcited and restless and had had to be given a soothing draught. She hoped the mistress would soon be home to forbid upsetting visitors.

To Lavinia's relief, the man had departed when she went downstairs. Sir Timothy spent the evening ruminating on him.

"Extraordinary fellow. Bit of a rough diamond, wouldn't you say, Miss Hurst? What do you think he's after?"

"I expect a share in his aunt's estate," Lavinia said soberly. "I don't think we can blind ourselves to that, Sir Timothy."

"But I thought the old lady had tied the thing up. Didn't Mallinson fix it all when he was down? Still, Peate can't be expected to
know that." Sir Timothy began to laugh. "Ha ha! The fellow would
have been here a bit earlier if he'd known that."

"Wills can be altered," Lavinia pointed out.

"That's so. And I wouldn't put it past Tameson Peate. She's become remarkably secretive. She's not at all the young woman I remember. I wouldn't put it past her to have some sort of macabre joke
at the end. That's what makes entailed estates so much more pleasant. Daniel knew Winterwood would be his, and Simon knows he'll
follow. There's a beautiful simplicity about that."

"But isn't it a little unfair to Flora and Edward?" Lavinia said.

"Flora will marry, and have her own home. That's if she can get
out of that damn wheelchair. Yes, I admit it's a bit hard on the
younger son, but Daniel will make some provision for Edward. He'll
buy him a commission in a good regiment, no doubt. I was a younger
son myself, but I managed. Even had the Queen knight me," he
added with simple pride.

Lavinia supposed Jonathon Peate had gone back to the village. She
was pretty sure he would still be about when Charlotte and Daniel
returned, but it had suited him to see what he could while they were
absent. When she went upstairs later, Eliza reported that Lady Tameson was sleeping, but uneasily.

Lavinia slept uneasily, too. The atmosphere seemed to have
changed so much since Jonathon Peate's arrival. It was scarcely a
surprise when the gentle rapping came at her door in the middle of
the night.

She sprang out of bed, her heart thumping.

"Who is it?"

"It's only me, miss. Eliza. Could you come? My lady is asking for
you."

Lavinia had the door open.

"Is she ill?"

Eliza was dressed in flannel gown and nightcap and held a gutter-
ing candle.

"No, but she's got some bee in her bonnet about her will."

Eliza had lit the lamp at Lady Tameson's bedside, and the old lady
sat bolt upright, her face gaunt and heavily shadowed.

"Miss Hurst! I want your help."

So Jonathon Peate had succeeded so quickly in what he had come
to do. Lavinia went forward.

"What can I do, Lady Tameson?"

"Get a pen and some paper. We don't need any grand solicitor from London. I know how to do this. Quick, girl."

"But—are you sure?" Lavinia couldn't help hesitating.

Lady Tameson clenched her fists and thumped the sheet.

"Would I send for people in the middle of the night if I were not sure? Whose fortune is this, I would like to know?"

Reluctantly and with some apprehension, Lavinia got pen and ink and paper from the writing desk in her own bedroom. The half-finished letter to Robin caught her eye. *But there is something hanging over this place . . .* She closed the desk and locked it, and returned to the large dim room with its curiously melodramatic atmosphere.

"Now," said Lady Tameson, "write that I hereby revoke all previous wills"—she gave a dry chuckle—"You see I learned the jargon from that pompous fellow from London. I Tameson Barrata revoke all previous wills and declare this to be my last one. Arthur Mallinson to be my trustee as before, but I bequeath everything, put a line under everything, there's to be no mistake about it, to my great-niece Flora. There! Write it."

Lavinia's pen stopped dead.

"Write it, write it!" the old lady ordered.

Lavinia wrote, her hand trembling. The surprise was so great. Flora an heiress. It was wonderful. Jonathon Peate was routed.

But so was Charlotte, and so was Daniel, with his plans for Winterwood.

The room seemed stuffy and too hot, the old lady's hand as she impatiently grasped the pen to sign the amateurish document like a claw. She signed her name slowly, in large shaky letters, then leaned back and said triumphantly, "Now, you, Miss Hurst. Write that you are a witness. And Eliza. That makes it legal."

Lavinia obeyed, and Eliza nervously followed her example.

"Now put it in the bureau. Lock it, and give me the key. Not that anyone will be prying. They all think my will's safely in London with Mallinson." She began to chuckle again, and gasped a little for breath.

"That horrible child Edward nearly deafened me with his trumpet tonight. Why should he get all my money?"

"Was Edward to get it previously?" Lavinia asked in surprise.

"It's none of your business, young lady, but I had intended to leave my fortune to my dutiful niece Charlotte." There was a queer note of sarcasm in her voice. "So you could rest assured it would have finally been her darling Teddy's. Why else did she smother me with attention? Now Flora—that child's honest. And brave. And I believe she cares a little for me."

"Your nephew, Mr. Peate?" Lavinia couldn't resist asking the question.

Lady Tameson lay back.

"Him!" she said. Her black eyes had a look of malevolent triumph, as if she enjoyed outwitting that brash young man. But the effort had exhausted her.

She said very wearily, "Stay with me, Miss Hurst, and I will sleep."

Lavinia obediently pulled up a chair and sat at the bedside. Eliza went back to her bed behind the screen. The lamp was turned down, and the old lady seemed to sleep. But she was still restless. She groped with her hand, and Lavinia took it.

"Greed," she muttered. Her eyes opened briefly. "You've found out about people too, Miss Hurst. One sees it in your eyes. Too young for that . . ." At last her breathing became regular and she slept.

Chapter 11

CHARLOTTE arrived home full of extravagant gaiety. She said they had had a wonderful time; the Queen, who looked dumpier than ever after the birth of her last child, had been exceptionally gracious, and they had met a number of interesting people. She had brought gifts for the children. Where was her darling Teddy, and how was Aunt Tameson?

Flora had hoped her mother would notice her new shoes. She had thrown aside her rug, and displayed her feet ostentatiously. But when Charlotte gave her a perfunctory kiss, and hurried on to embrace Edward, Lavinia saw her draw the rug back over her thin legs, and go quite silent.

Next Charlotte demanded Sylvie, and the little creature sprang forward prettily for her caresses.

It was an attractive picture when Daniel, pulling off his gloves, strode in.

"Papa!" Flora shrieked, coming to life.

Daniel stooped over her and swung her out of her chair, her skirts flying.

"So Miss Hurst has kept you well."

"Oh, yes, Papa. We went to Dover and she bought me the shoes she spoke of. And we were all in the drawing room last evening and Miss Hurst danced with Edward. And later Mr. Peate came to see Great-aunt Tameson."

"Mr. Peate!" Charlotte was very still, her eyes grown dark.

"He is staying in the village," Lavinia answered. "Yesterday he walked across the fields and then came up to the house to see Lady Tameson."

"Why did he walk? It's a wonder he wasn't shot for a poacher," Daniel said.

"I suppose he hasn't a horse or a carriage," Edward said pertly.

"If you ask me, the fellow hasn't got anything." That was Sir Timothy, who had come pottering in in his velvet smoking jacket, his spectacles hanging precariously over one ear. "He's a complete blackguard, I believe. All this talk of Australia. Stuff and nonsense. There must have been a bad streak in Willie Peate's family."

"Has he gone?" Charlotte asked in a voice so quiet that one scarcely noticed its panic.

"Out of these parts? Bless my soul, no. He said he wouldn't be leaving without paying his respects to his dear cousin. I imagine he means you, Charlotte. He said something about a promise. I wouldn't have thought that was a word that made much sense to a fellow like that."

Charlotte had picked up Sylvie, and wrapped her arms tightly around the shivering animal.

"Did he see my aunt?"

"Certainly. That's what he professed to have come for."

"How was she afterwards? Miss Hurst?"

The midnight scene was a deep secret. Eliza had been made to understand that, too.

"A little excited and restless, Mrs. Meryon. Eliza gave her some of the draught the doctor left."

Daniel set Flora back in her chair. His eyes fixed on Charlotte, he said, "Ask Mr. Peate to dinner, my love."

"But I thought you didn't like him."

"We must be civil, nevertheless. I believe you said something in Venice about his being welcome at Winterwood."

"I suppose I did say something like that. After all, Aunt Tameson is his aunt, too. If only by marriage. I didn't really think he had enough regard for her to bother to come."

"Perhaps Winterwood interests him as well as his aunt."

"Why do you say that?" Charlotte asked too quickly.

Daniel was watching her, frowning a little.

"I only made a comment, my love. I had a fancy a man like Jonathon Peate would be drawn toward a great house. I scarcely imagine he has the entree to many."

Charlotte made her familiar gesture of pressing her hands to her temples.

"Don't let us talk of it now. I am utterly exhausted. That long drive. I must go up. Edward, bring Sylvie for me. You may stay a little while if you're quiet. Poor Mamma's head—"

She drifted away, the pretty color gone from her cheeks, her head drooping as if the weight of her coiled black hair was too much for her.

Her headaches were not real, Lavinia suddenly knew. They were a form of escape. She had become very adept at using them. Did

Daniel mind? There was nothing in his face but the faint anxiety which Lavinia realized was almost habitual when he looked at Charlotte.

For the rest of the day Charlotte kept to her room, except to make a short visit to Lady Tameson.

"I couldn't help hearing some of what was said, Miss Hurst. The mistress seems upset about Mr. Peate's visit. She said, 'You'll have to send him away,' and my lady just laughed and said 'Try.' 'Try,' she said, several times. Then she said, 'Just let me die in peace, both of you.' I don't like it, Miss Hurst."

"You don't like what?"

Eliza set her lips. Her honest eyes were puzzled.

"I don't like what's happening, yet I can't put my finger on what's wrong. All I know is I'm on that poor old woman's side. And Miss Flora's, if it comes to that. She's the only one showed her aunt a bit of love. My, there'll be a to-do about that secret will."

"Keep the secret, Eliza," Lavinia urged.

That night Jonathon Peate came to dinner. Lavinia didn't know who had invited him, but there he was, handsome in his brash way, paying exaggerated attention to Charlotte, whom he called "pretty cousin." He was also more than a little interested in his surroundings, and Lavinia saw his eyes wandering speculatively. He even tested the thickness of the carpet with his toe, not minding that his action was noticed.

"Are you interested in carpets, Mr. Peate?" Daniel asked dryly.

Not in the least abashed, Jonathon gave his easy laugh and said that he was interested in everything.

"You have a fine place, Mr. Meryon. I'll be frank and admit that I'm not accustomed to luxury."

"You never stayed with your aunt in Venice, then?"

"Goodness me, no. I hadn't seen her for years. Charlotte and I were in the same position in that respect."

Charlotte seemed to wince slightly, as if she disliked his familiarity. Yet she couldn't keep her eyes off him. It was as if she were hypnotized. She could have pleaded her headache and stayed in her room, but it seemed almost as if she were afraid for Jonathon Peate to be there without her, as if she were worried about what he might do or say.

Certainly he was an entertaining guest. He had traveled a great deal, and talked graphically about countries and people and voyages, both on steamships and sailing vessels. He said he intended to go to America after his poor aunt's death.

"I have an ambition to set up business in New York. In my opinion it's a far more thriving city than London."

"What shall you do?" Daniel asked.

"That I haven't entirely decided. It will depend on my capital." His gaze went around the room again, musingly and deliberately. It came to rest on Lavinia. "I shall also marry." He laughed, showing his fine white teeth. "It's time I settled down."

"You have an attachment, Jonathon?" Charlotte asked merrily.

"I believe so."

"You're not sure? Come, Jonathon, I thought you of all people knew your own mind." Charlotte seemed to be possessed of an uncontrollable gaiety that almost bordered on hysteria. Her eyes were so bright, so wild. "What is it you look for in a woman? Beauty? Domesticity? Fortune?"

"Spirit," said Jonathon, looking at Lavinia. "A bit of devilishness, if you like. Temper and spirit. Like a blood horse." He gave his long laugh. "If that comes with looks as well, I'll count myself lucky."

"You seem very sure of yourself, young man," put in Sir Timothy. "This high-spirited young woman may be having none of you."

"I think she will," said Jonathon, smiling. "I think she will."

Lavinia made a sharp movement, just controlling herself in time. She believed she might have thrown her glass of wine in that abominable man's face. She knew that she was never going to feel safe until he had left Winterwood.

The evening seemed never-ending. Jonathon turned the sheets of music while Charlotte sang. Then he came to sit beside Lavinia, who kept her eyes fixed on her embroidery.

"Where did you learn to do that stuff?" he asked. His expression was so impertinent, so mocking, that Lavinia, in her state of tension, pricked her finger and had to dab at the blood with her handkerchief.

Jonathon gave his loud ha-ha-ha. "It's not a natural occupation to you, I can see. Charlotte, how did you come to employ a governess who doesn't excel at the womanly occupations? Perhaps Miss Hurst is better at arithmetic."

Stung to lifting her head and looking at him, Lavinia caught Daniel's gaze instead. Her heart sank. For the first time she saw a question in it.

"Miss Hurst is not a governess," he said quietly. "Neither is she on trial at this moment."

The unfortunate word sent a flood of color into Lavinia's cheeks, but luckily Charlotte, in her quite unpredictable way, had disliked even that doubtful kind of attention which Lavinia was getting, and came sweeping across the room saying that perhaps Jonathon would like to play a hand of bezique. Sir Timothy enjoyed a game, and so did she.

Lavinia took the opportunity to murmur excuses and slip out of the room. She didn't go upstairs. She was too agitated and restless. She went to the long gallery, lit only by moonlight, and paced up and down, trying to compose herself. One day she would not be able to control her hot temper, and then everything would be finished— Flora with the new shoes she was to walk in, poor dying Lady Tameson, the luxury of the house, the charming blue garden with its uninterrupted quiet . . .

It was only when she thought of losing these things that she realized how much they meant to her, even Flora with her mixture of disagreeable manners, pathos and fugitive charm.

The moonlight lay in pale swathes across the floor. In the darker areas she had to avoid furniture and the two suits of armor that stood near the door. They were like figures watching her silent perambulation. On her return journey, one of them spoke.

"What is the trouble, Miss Hurst? Why are you so agitated?"

She would have noticed him before if she hadn't been so wrapped in her thoughts. His white shirtfront was perfectly visible and not at all like the rigid armor-plated chest she had thought it.

"You shouldn't startle me like that, Mr. Meryon."

"I'm sorry. Shall we ring for lights?"

"Oh no, no. I only came here for a moment, to be alone."

"Does Mr. Peate worry you?"

He had said she was not on trial. Was he now going to put her on trial and conduct a cross-examination?

"He is a little too familiar, perhaps. But it's not for me to criticize your guests."

Daniel made a violent exclamation, as abruptly bitten off.

"Being meek doesn't suit you. Why the devil do you have to be meek?"

She looked at him in astonishment.

"What else could I be?"

"I don't know. I'm only wondering how long you can keep up this charade."

"If you mean I'm not suited—"

"Oh, you are too well suited. You have warmth and heart. So we use you. Mercilessly."

"Mercilessly?"

"Perhaps. I should tell you to go, Miss Hurst. But I can't because Flora needs you. You see that I put my daughter's good above yours. That's what I mean by being merciless."

"I don't think I understand you. Am I to come to some dreadful harm by staying here?" When he didn't answer, she laughed uneasily. "I am quite accustomed to coping with unwanted attentions if you are thinking of Mr. Peate."

"I wasn't thinking of Mr. Peate."

"Then—"

"Your eyes are shining in the moonlight, did you know?"

She did, because his were shining also. She was astonished at how much they had progressed in intimacy since that afternoon in the Contessa's *palazzo*. And yet this had happened without intimate conversations, with nothing more than an occasional meeting and a few formal remarks. In Venice it had been instinctive only; now it was palpable, unmistakable. For one giddy moment she thought he was going to kiss her. She almost willed him to. She stood motionless, aching with the desire to have his arms about her.

But a vestige of common sense remained. She found the logical center of her brain telling her that at least Jonathon Peate's attentions were honest. Daniel had a wife for whom he showed a constant anxious tenderness; he bought her extravagant and charming gifts, he loved her. So what was this scene but another version of the quick fumble in the dark by the master with the servant?

She made herself move away, saying, "I think I find this conversation quite unintelligible, Mr. Meryon. Will you excuse me if I retire?"

He followed her into the lighted corridor. Out of the treacherous moonlight and the shadows sanity had come back to him, too. His voice was as formal as hers.

"Certainly, Miss Hurst. I hope you sleep well."

It was a mistake to turn and say good night. For then she saw the torment in his face.

You should leave Winterwood . . . But you can't desert Flora. Her young life is more important than yours . . . You know you can't leave Daniel, but how long will you be able to keep out of his arms. How long?

"I hope you sleep well, Miss Hurst," he had said. Mockery. Hypocrisy. For he loved his wife. How could he not? She was so beautiful, so gay, but poised so uncertainly on the edge of happiness, retreating into headaches and collapses, needing his tenderness and understanding.

Lavinia did at last fall asleep, but only to be wakened by Charlotte laughing. She thought the card party must have only now broken up, and that they were going upstairs to bed.

When the laughter continued, she fumbled for the candlestick at her bedside, and struck a match. The light fell on the face of the little bedside clock, showing that it was four o'clock. Then why was Charlotte still walking about?

The laughter died, then began again, so close that it seemed to be just outside her door. There was a whispering; then Charlotte said quite clearly, "No, it isn't my cousin who has upset me. I find him amusing and pleasant and I have no intention of sending him away." Abruptly she broke into another peal of laughter. For no reason at all Lavinia found herself shivering. She heard Daniel's voice, "Hush!" and Charlotte saying, "Don't stop me. If I didn't laugh I would go mad."

Daniel must have taken her arm then, for there was a murmur of something about "Bertha" and "one of your pills" and the voices died away. Presently a door shut. The strange early-morning promenade was over.

The next morning Flora couldn't eat her breakfast. She said she was perfectly well, but not hungry. When Lavinia began the massage of her legs, which was now routine, she said, "Why do you *pretend*, Miss Hurst? You know I will never walk again."

Lavinia suddenly guessed the reason for this mood. Flora must have heard the disturbance in the corridor last night.

"Did you sleep well?" she asked. "I don't suppose you did. People were walking about awfully late. Mr. Peate kept your mamma and papa up playing cards."

Flora lifted a tearstreaked face.

"If I don't marry, Mamma will have me for*ever!*"

"Not necessarily. You may have your own establishment."

"How? Papa isn't rich enough. He says Winterwood takes all his income."

Lavinia wished she could tell Flora how rich she was going to be.

"Don't let's be so gloomy."

Flora leaned forward, her face sharpened into an uncomfortable intensity. "How can I help being gloomy, when Mamma says she will go mad? It's because of me, I know."

"Mamma exaggerates. And so do you. The sun's shining today, had you noticed? I thought we might take an airing into the village later. I have some small purchases to make, and perhaps you have, too."

"What should I need?" Flora said sulkily.

"I don't know. A new face, perhaps. I don't much care for the look of this one this morning."

"When Mamma laughs like that, Papa gets upset," Flora said rapidly as if telling a long-suppressed secret. "He looks worried and says she must take her pills. He never laughs, too. Because there isn't anything funny to laugh at, except privately in Mamma's head."

So Flora was touched by the chill of that laughter, too. It was perplexing, especially since Charlotte was so gay when she came in to say good morning. She was dressed in a pale gray hiding habit and looked very elegant.

"What's this? Your breakfast not eaten? Are you ill, dearest?"

"No, Mamma."

"What is it, Miss Hurst? She looks pale."

Flora's passionate glance toward Lavinia meant that nothing was to be said.

"I think she just needs some fresh air, Mrs. Meryon. I thought if the sun stays out we would go for a walk into the village."

"What a good idea. I am going out, too. Sylvie needs exercise, and so do I. We ate such large meals at Windsor. Course after course. I was telling Teddy about Prince Edward's toy soldiers. He has not only the British army but the French, too. I have promised Teddy some similar ones. What would you like, Flora dear? I am not sure what were the little princesses' favorite toys. They are allowed to look at but not touch their mamma's collection of dolls."

"I am too old for dolls," Flora said ungraciously.

"Naturally, darling. But there must be something you would like."

"I want nothing but a new horse."

Charlotte's brow puckered anxiously. Did she realize her uncontrolled laughter last night must have disturbed the house, and now was she trying to make amends by being the perfect mother, the perfect wife?

"Someday, my darling. But I can't buy that in the village, can I? Now cheer up. I hope that walk will put some roses in your cheeks."

Fortunately the day stayed fine enough for the walk into the village. Lavinia asked Mary to come, too, thinking the perky little creature would chatter enough to amuse Flora. They took it in turns to push the chair down the rutted lane, and finally Flora was giggling wildly at the bumps and skids. In the village she plainly enjoyed the deference paid her, the doffed caps and the bobs, and the anxious inquiries about her health.

Lavinia left her with Mary on the village green while she went into the tiny dark apothecary's shop to make some purchases. Perhaps, in her position, it wasn't wise to be asking for her favorite rose-perfumed soap, and rice powder, but there was a limit to the sacrifices that she could make.

"Good morning, miss," said the chemist. "I hope the young lady is better. I'd advise a warm scarf against the wind."

"But she isn't ill," Lavinia said, in surprise.

"No, I suppose toothache isn't exactly an illness. But it's painful enough, for all that. I hope the laudanum was an effective remedy."

Lavinia was about to tell him that he was making a mistake, he must be confusing Flora with some other child. Some instinct stopped her, and she listened to him saying, "Now there's a lovely lady, Mrs. Meryon. So upset about Miss Flora that she came herself to fetch the medicine for her. I advise care in its use, though. It's dangerous stuff."

"Yes, I'm aware of that." Lavinia took her purchases, and paid for them.

Had Charlotte wanted the laudanum for herself? Did that explain her erratic moods?

Chapter 12

WHEN they got home, Jonathon Peate was standing warming himself at the fire in the library. He looked as much at home as if he had been a constant guest at Winterwood for the whole of his life. He saw their arrival, and came strolling to the door, giving his jovial laugh.

"Hullo, princess. Have you been taking an airing? And the fair Miss Hurst!" He bowed low. "If I had known, I would have accompanied you."

"But you would not have been invited," Flora said in her clear, merciless voice. "Call Joseph, Miss Hurst. I wish to go up immediately."

Charlotte came hurrying down the stairs at that moment, saying, "I'm sorry, Jonathon, but Aunt Tameson isn't feeling well enough to see anyone at present. She's had another attack, and is resting."

"I'll wait," said Jonathon smiling. "I have plenty of time."

"By all means have some sherry with me. But it's no use expecting to see Aunt Tameson tonight. Miss Hurst, what are you doing standing there?"

"Waiting for Joseph to take Flora up," Lavinia answered calmly. She wondered why Charlotte's voice had that edge of hysteria. Was she so upset because Aunt Tameson had had another attack?

Flora's hands were tight on the arms of her chair. When Joseph came she clung to him, looking over his shoulder at Lavinia.

"I hate Mr. Peate! I expect Great-aunt Tameson heard his voice and that's why she is ill again."

But, strangely enough, Lady Tameson wasn't exhausted from another attack. She heard their approach and rang her bell violently. When they went in, she said, "I've been waiting for you, Flora. I have the cards dealt."

Flora's face brightened.

"Mamma said you were not well enough to see anybody. Was she just telling a lie to that horrid Mr. Peate?"

Propped against the pillows, Lady Tameson looked remarkably

alert. At Flora's words she first of all looked startled; then a curious, sly look came over her face.

"I've got them all running," she said obscurely. She gave her dry cackle. "So Jonathon's downstairs, is he? Well, let Charlotte entertain him. Now, miss. Get your outdoor things off. Hurry up. I have a feeling I'm going to give you a sound trouncing today."

"If you cheat, Great-aunt Tameson, I'll refuse to play with you again."

"Oh, get along with you. Everyone has to cheat at some time. The important thing is not to be caught at it."

So Charlotte had not even looked in to see if her aunt were well enough for visitors. For reasons of her own she was keeping Jonathon away. Lavinia thought about the laudanum she had purchased and was suddenly cold. Surely Charlotte could not be planning to hasten the old lady's death—because it was dangerous to her interests to have Jonathon using his persuasions on a gullible old woman . . .

Anything seemed possible that evening, for although Jonathon had departed before dinner, Charlotte was terribly restless. At first she talked too much, then was completely silent. She toyed with her food, and paid no attention to the conversation of Daniel and Sir Timothy. Almost before dessert was finished she sprang up to leave the table, and Lavinia had to follow her.

In the drawing room she turned her strange intense gaze on Lavinia and exclaimed, "Don't stare at me, Miss Hurst. You did nothing through the whole of dinner but stare at me."

"I'm sorry, Mrs. Meryon. I hadn't meant to."

"You're wondering why I didn't allow Mr. Peate to see my aunt. It was only because he isn't an ideal sickroom visitor, as even you must admit. He means well, no doubt. But all that virility—" Charlotte shuddered, as if the virility disturbed her as much as it must an old sick woman. Yet Lavinia was certain it wasn't the real reason for keeping Jonathon away. And could she continue to do so? Jonathon wasn't a man to be prevented from doing what he wished. "I can wait," he had said.

As it happened, there was no need for Charlotte to worry. For Lady Tameson died that night.

Only Eliza was with her.

Hours later, after Doctor Munro had been and gone, the funeral arrangements made, and the bedroom door shut, and the little silver bell on the bedside table stood silent, Eliza was still incoherent.

She had grown fond of the old lady she said. She would miss her terribly.

"She had just said her prayers, Miss Hurst. I'd never heard her say them before. She must have had a feeling she was going. She said, 'You've been good to me, Eliza.'" Eliza's apron went to her eyes. "And then she kept groping at her neck. I don't know whether she couldn't get her breath, or whether she was feeling for a crucifix. I once nursed a Roman Catholic lady who held her crucifix all the time, and that put it in my mind. But my lady wasn't a Roman Catholic, was she? She can't be, if she's to be buried with her little boy."

Eliza looked a little calmer, as she made her recital of the night's drama.

"I might have just fancied it. It was ever so queer in the half dark. I'd only had time to light one candle and I really couldn't see properly. Poor lady. She's to be buried with her rings on, the mistress says, because they're too tight to get off. I always wondered at her not having had them cut off before they got so tight. But she was so fond of her jewelry, poor soul. She'll be happy to take some of it with her."

Two ladies attired entirely in black arrived from London to measure Charlotte and Flora for mourning clothes. Daniel and Jonathon Peate, who was there more than ever, wore crepe armbands, but Flora was turned into a little black crow, and even Edward had to wear a black bow tie and an armband. Charlotte planned to go to the funeral swathed in black veils—perhaps to hide her expression, Lavinia thought, for try as she would she couldn't show grief. Her eyes literally shone with relief. It was as if poor Lady Tameson had died in the nick of time.

Yet Jonathon, whatever his hopes might have been, seemed in no way perturbed. He put on a long face when he remembered, but most of the time he was as loud-voiced and smiling as ever, and was always about somewhere, sitting over the library fire, walking up and down the long gallery, or prowling about the gun room, or the gardens.

He would be leaving after the funeral, Charlotte said. Lavinia was in the library when Charlotte and Daniel came in. She had been looking for books for Flora's history lesson, and was on her knees behind the high leather couch, searching for titles. She intended to announce her presence at once, but her intense anxiety to know the future of Jonathon Peate kept her silent.

"We must extend hospitality to him until then," Charlotte was saying. "How would it look if we didn't?"

"Because he is some sort of cousin of yours, don't let him assume he has permanent rights on our hospitality," Daniel replied. "I don't like the fellow. I don't like his effrontery. I believe he hadn't the faintest degree of feeling for his aunt. He seems to me to be quite callous."

"Oh, no, he isn't," Charlotte said. "Haven't you seen the way he looks at Miss Hurst?"

"I'm not blind," Daniel said curtly.

"Could that be why you don't like poor Jonathon?"

"If you mean that I don't like lasciviousness, yes."

"Miss Hurst hasn't complained."

"Perhaps she is in no position to complain."

"Perhaps she doesn't feel it a cause for complaint. There is something about her that deliberately attracts men. Haven't you observed it, my love?"

Charlotte's voice was sly, insinuating. "Perhaps, if Jonathon is to go, she should go, too."

"She will go when her usefulness is at an end." Daniel's voice was so hard and final that Lavinia began to wonder if she had imagined that tender scene in the long gallery. But he had used the word "merciless" then, she remembered. Now he was merely illustrating what he had meant.

"Let us say no more about it," she heard him conclude. "This is hardly the time, with a funeral on our hands. How long, pray, are you going to wear those excessively gloomy clothes?"

Charlotte gave a little rippling laugh.

"Do you not like me in them? Then I promise not for long. Aunt Tameson wouldn't have expected it. She was a very worldly woman. I have ordered some more pleasant gowns in gray, if that pleases you. I would have liked lavender, but that color will always remind me too painfully of my poor darling aunt. Perhaps we might have some festivity for Christmas, not too much, of course, but all this gloom is bad for the children. A very small party on Christmas Eve?" Charlotte's voice had become light and gay, with one of her mercurial changes of mood. They were going out of the room, Charlotte saying, "And I should like to give you a new hunter for a gift. I remember hearing you say you needed one. And I promise I shall not object if you have architects down in the new year . . ."

Lavinia laid down the books she had selected, and rubbed her stiff hands. She wished she hadn't listened. Overhearing other people's conversations was wretched. Daniel's words had sounded so hard and cold, and now the apprehension she had had ever since Lady Tameson's death settled more heavily on her. Charlotte was gaily planning how to spend a fortune. She had still to learn that it was not hers.

"How are we going to tell them?" Eliza had said, shivering.

"That is my task," Lavinia had answered. "I will do it when Mr. Mallinson comes down from London. And don't worry, Eliza. There is no blame to be attached to us. A dying woman's request must be respected."

Jonathon Peate looking at her with his unconcealed desire; Daniel planning to keep her until her usefulness, like an aged horse or dog, ended; the secret will to be confessed to; Flora silent and white-faced since Lady Tameson's death . . . The prospect was scarcely pleasing.

Flora sat patiently in her chair while the long-faced dressmaker, Miss Toole, clucked over her sympathetically.

"What a little mouse she is, to be sure. Not a word out of her."

Lavinia agreed. She even wished that Flora would indulge in one of her fits of temper and hysteria. She had scarcely spoken since the news had been broken to her of her great-aunt's death.

She had simply said in a muffled voice, "I'm glad. She was a disagreeable old woman," and her eyes had gone dark, almost black, with shock. After that, even Edward couldn't rouse her to a spark of life. She was pale and listless, paid no attention to her lessons, and refused to do the simple exercises Lavinia had devised to keep her body supple. She let everything be done for her without protest. She seemed to have lost her anger. That, Lavinia was afraid, was the worst thing of all.

But she insisted on going to Lady Tameson's funeral. She wanted her mourning clothes made, and submitted with that meek lifelessness to the fittings. The only time she objected was when Lavinia suggested she should wear her new shoes.

"Oh, no, Miss Hurst. You said they were for dancing. That makes them quite unsuitable for a funeral. Just put them back in the cupboard."

And there, Lavinia was afraid, they would now stay. But it would all soon be over, the melodramatic panoply of grief, the hearse with its four black horses with nodding black plumes, the black-clad attendants, the day into night atmosphere. Jonathon Peate forebore, for once, to smile. Charlotte looked frail and lovely behind her black veil; Daniel's face was composed into the correct sober lines. Daniel had refused to have Simon brought home from school, and had decreed that Edward was too young to attend such a mournful ceremony. He disapproved strongly of Flora's presence, but had not forbidden it.

Mr. Mallinson had arrived from London and was there, and Eliza, her eyes red-rimmed from crying. Otherwise no one knew or cared about the burial of one elderly woman brought back from a foreign country to be laid beside her long-dead son.

There was no one to speak a eulogy on the dead woman, for no one had really known her. Only Flora made any comment at all. She said in a tight, resentful voice, "She shouldn't have gone to little Tom. I needed her more." Then, almost immediately a strange look came over her face, her eyes blazed.

"What's the matter?" Lavinia whispered anxiously. Was the child going to have one of her fits of hysteria here, in the churchyard?

"I want to go home. Quickly."

There was food and wine laid out in the dining room, and a huge comforting fire burning.

But no one was much interested in it, for as they returned to the house, Flora announced the reason for her odd behavior.

"I moved my toes, Miss Hurst. While we were beside the grave. The crows were squabbling in the trees and they sounded just like Great-aunt Tameson laughing. As I thought that, my toes moved."

"Show me," said Lavinia, whipping off the rugs.

But now, with everyone gathered around, nothing happened. Flora's face was sharpened to an eerie thinness with her effort. She began to cry, her fingers dug into her eyes.

"But it did happen. Truly it did. I didn't imagine it."

"Then it will happen again," said Daniel. He lifted her in his arms, ready to take her upstairs. "Cry as much as you like, my darling. You should have cried days ago."

"Papa, Great-aunt Tameson told me I could move my toes if I tried. She said I was just lazy. I wish I had been nicer to her."

"I think she loved you as you were. Isn't that so, Miss Hurst?"

Lavinia nodded, knowing that to be more true than even Daniel suspected. Flora was put on her bed, but refused to be comforted. At last Charlotte, who could not now control her impatience for the more important ceremony of the day, the reading of the will, said that she had the very thing with which to quiet Flora's distress.

She hurried away, and came back with a dark blue bottle.

"Now, dearest, swallow just a spoonful of this, and you will have a lovely sleep."

Flora's anguished eyes sought her mother's.

"Aren't you happy, Mamma, that I moved my toes? It means that I will walk again, doesn't it?"

"I expect it does." Charlotte had poured the colorless liquid into a spoon. "Open your mouth."

"It means I won't be a burden on you forever, doesn't it? Aren't you glad?"

"Darling, you were never a burden. There. Now you will rest."

Flora made a face at the disagreeable taste of the liquid. Charlotte put the bottle on the bedside table, and looked at Lavinia.

"It's quite harmless, Miss Hurst. It only has sedative properties."

"And pain-killing ones?" Lavinia asked. "It's laudanum, isn't it? I believe some people use it for a bad toothache."

Charlotte's eyes flickered.

"Yes, I have heard that. But I keep it for my headaches. I find it quite efficacious. In the smallest quantities, of course. To take too much would be dangerous."

Daniel was watching her.

"My love, you never told me this."

Charlotte shrugged. "Details of illness are much too tiresome. Of course I don't bore you with them. Flora will sleep now. Miss Hurst will stay with her. We must go down. Mr. Mallinson will be waiting."

Flora watched them go, her eyelids already heavy.

"Why is Mr. Mallinson waiting for them? Is it to tell them who is to have Great-aunt Tameson's diamond brooches? I hope Edward isn't to have one for his future wife. He was much too horrid to Great-aunt Tameson. Even more horrid than I was. Miss Hurst . . ."

"Yes, Flora."

"Even if I walk again, you are not to leave me . . . I would be very grieved . . . you must stay . . ."

She was asleep.

Lavinia rang for Mary to come and sit with her. Contrary to Charlotte's orders she had to leave her charge. She had to join the group in the library and produce that amateur but authentic document, the indisputably last will and testament of Tameson Barrata.

Chapter 13

LAVINIA knew that to the end of her life she would never forget that scene. They were sitting around the table in the library, Daniel, Charlotte, Jonathon, Sir Timothy, and Mr. Mallinson. Charlotte's face was startlingly pale against the unrelieved black of her dress, and her smoothly piled black hair. Mr. Mallinson's cheeks were rosy in the lamplight. He had not brought back any of the churchyard gloom with him. Scenes like this were no doubt too familiar in his life. But he did raise a surprised eyebrow when Lavinia handed him the folded sheet of paper.

Charlotte, beginning to reprimand Lavinia for her unceremonious entrance, was abruptly silent. And now they all stared at her.

There was fear in Charlotte's eyes. It was as blatant as if she had cried out. Her face could go no paler, but it seemed to sharpen and be drained of blood.

Lavinia searched the other faces. Who else was afraid?

With thankfulness she saw that Daniel was not. He only looked surprised and interested. Sir Timothy, too, merely looked exasperated because, as usual, he had mislaid his spectacles and he could not see her clearly, nor guess what was going on.

Jonathon? He stared at Lavinia with a peculiar bold aggressiveness. For once he was not smiling. She was quite unable to guess his feelings.

It seemed as if those few minutes, while Mr. Mallinson studied the document she had handed him, went on for an unconscionable time.

Then Mr. Mallinson said, slowly, "This is an entirely new development. But this document appears to be in order."

Charlotte said in a voice that died away, "What—is it?"

Mr. Mallinson cleared his throat and said ceremoniously, "I have in my hands a document that appears to render null and void the will I drew up for the deceased. This young lady will no doubt tell us more about the circumstances relating to it later, but in the meantime perhaps you would like to know its contents."

Sir Timothy said with relish, "The old lady's played a last trick, has she? Can't say I'm surprised. In my opinion she had been corrupted by foreigners. She had learned their devious ways. Well, go on, Mallinson, tell us what she says."

Mr. Mallinson cleared his throat again, pompously.

"The testatrix states that she wishes her entire estate to go to her great-niece Flora 'who appeared to be fond of me.'" Mr. Mallinson frowned testily. "This is a most incomplete document, but it seems to have the vital factors. I am named as executor and trustee as in the previous will, and it appears to be correctly signed, witnessed and dated. So we must accept it as legal."

Charlotte was leaning forward, her eyes disbelieving.

"It can't be!"

But Daniel smiled in pleasure. "Flora an heiress! That is a surprise. What an extraordinarily thoughtful and perceptive thing for your aunt to do, Charlotte. She saw Flora as permanently an invalid, no doubt. Isn't that so, Miss Hurst? Why don't you sit down and tell us about it?"

"That thing must be torn up!" The words burst from Charlotte. "It can't be legal. Written on a piece of notepaper like that! Why, it's like something a child might do. Mr. Mallinson, you can't agree that that trifling nonsense can stand up in a court of law."

Mr. Mallinson narrowed his eyes, watching Charlotte.

"The document is amateurish, I agree. Indeed, for an estate the size of the Contessa's, it is ludicrous. It dispenses very prettily with all my fine clauses. But it is, I fear, incontestable. You are perfectly at liberty, Mrs. Meryon," his voice had become a trifle chilly, "to consult another opinion."

"I will," Charlotte promised. "You may be sure of that. I don't believe my aunt ever signed that. How can you swear it's her signature?"

Here Jonathon made his first sound, and it sounded remarkably like a suppressed laugh, an abruptly cut-off satirical chuckle. But then he laughed at everything because he had no tears. Laughter had to serve even for the bitter disappointment of not sharing in his aunt's fortune. For it must have been a disappointment after his assiduous attendance on her.

"What are you suggesting, my love?" Daniel was not laughing. His voice had an edge. "That this document is forged?"

"Yes," said Charlotte. "We all know Miss Hurst's feelings for Flora. Or are her feelings genuinely for Flora? Isn't she perhaps seeing herself at Flora's side for the rest of her life, nicely sheltered from all the problems of a penniless woman?"

"Charlotte! Be silent!"

"What other interpretation do you put on it?" Charlotte cried furiously. "We are away at Windsor, safely out of the house—and my poor aunt, weak and feeble, is got round in this way. I can see it all. She is encouraged to dislike my darling Teddy, and constantly told how sweet and brave and helpless Flora is. And then this happens!" She pointed a quivering finger at the startled Mr. Mallinson. "Perhaps it is not a forgery, but it is the result of undue persuasion, and I shall prove it."

"Charlotte," said Daniel heavily, "they are both your children. Flora and Edward. If it comes to that, why are you not concerned for Simon, who has never been mentioned?"

"Because Simon will have Winterwood! Isn't that enough for him? Flora will marry. But what about Teddy? Why is he to be penniless? Is this all the reward I get for bringing that tiresome old woman here? After the promises she made to me—"

Mr. Mallinson was rapping the table.

"I beg your pardon, Mrs. Meryon. But I must ask you to be silent. Then perhaps Miss Hurst will tell us how this all came about."

Charlotte sank back in her chair. Suddenly she seemed at the point of collapse, her face alarmingly white, her wild eyes fixed with a frightening hatred on Lavinia.

Lavinia had had difficulty enough in keeping silent herself. Her hands were clenched hard with controlled anger. How dare Charlotte speak to her like that!

"There is very little to tell. Lady Tameson rang her bell in the middle of the night and demanded that Eliza and I come to her and do this for her. I don't know how long the idea had been in her mind. It was certainly not because Flora had been endeavoring to get into her good graces. Indeed, I was constantly scolding Flora for her rudeness. I think she was struggling against growing fond of Lady Tameson because she knew the old lady must die."

"Spare us your philosophy, Miss Hurst," Charlotte said waspishly.

"I am only explaining how the affection grew between Lady Tameson and Flora," Lavinia said, keeping her voice calm. "I am afraid Lady Tameson didn't feel at all the same about Edward. Indeed, there had been an unfortunate episode earlier that evening. This was perhaps in her mind when she insisted on her old will being revoked. She said that Edward was to have benefited in that."

"Edward and his mother," Mr. Mallinson corrected. "Half was to be in trust for the boy, while Mrs. Meryon—but that is now past history. Go on, Miss Hurst. This dramatic scene took place at midnight? But why did you say nothing about it? Why was the new will not sent to me for safekeeping?"

"By Lady Tameson's request it was to be kept a secret. She asked both Eliza and me to say nothing. Let me say that no blame must be attached to Eliza, and as for me, I merely fulfilled the request of a dying woman, which I naturally considered sacred." Lavinia's chin went up. She looked around the table, thanking heaven that in her agitation the faces were now a blur. Her nerves were stretched to breaking. "I won't deny that I am delighted for Flora's sake. But I assure you Lady Tameson's decision was completely her own. It had nothing whatever to do with me. I only hope the money brings Flora happiness. And now, if you will excuse me, I must go and pack. I will be leaving first thing in the morning. I would regard it as a favor if I could have a conveyance to the railway station, but if that isn't convenient I can walk to the village, and hire something there."

Daniel sprang up.

"Miss Hurst, what damned nonsense is this?"

She couldn't take any more emotion. She couldn't read the dismay, the disbelief, the pain, in his face. Pain! She answered coolly, "I don't think you would expect me to stay in a house where I am suspect, Mr. Meryon. Please give me that consideration."

With that, she turned and left the room, her head still high, her cheeks hot with anger. Her departure was as hasty as she could make it without losing her dignity, but not hasty enough to escape Jonathon Peate's unwanted admiration. "Bravo, Miss Hurst! Bravo!"

Eliza was waiting anxiously upstairs.

"Was it awful, miss?"

"It was terrible, Eliza, but it's over now. And you won't be blamed. Mr. Mallinson says the will is in order, so Flora has her fortune. We must just be glad about that."

"But you look so upset. What did they say to you?"

"Never mind that, Eliza. Would you come and help me pack my things?"

"They haven't dismissed you!" Eliza cried.

"No, but I have given my notice. Now don't look so distressed, you silly creature. It was to be expected."

Eliza wrung her hands.

"You only did what you was asked. How can they blame you for that? If they was sane—"

"Sane?" said Lavinia sharply. "Of course they are."

"I've sometimes had fears about the mistress. For years now—she has these tantrums—far worse than Miss Flora's. The master looks so worried at times, my heart bleeds for him. Bertha says"—Eliza looked around quickly, lowering her voice—"she locks her door against him. Ever since Master Edward was born—"

"Come and help me pack," Lavinia said quickly. Only by action could she stop herself listening too avidly, asking questions, behaving no better than a gossiping servant.

"Oh, miss!" Eliza came back to the immediate problem. "Miss Flora will break her heart. And her so much better since you've been here. You've no idea. Bertha and me used to say we hadn't heard her laugh for a twelve-month. All the money in the world isn't going to make up to her for losing people she loves. Both you and my lady in one week! I don't know, miss. Couldn't you consider it?"

"And be called a thief, or worse!"

"We all know you're a lady, miss. But this'll put Miss Flora right back. And after her moving her toes and all." Eliza was too gentle to accuse Lavinia of cowardice or selfishness. "It's not my business, of course. I only know I'll miss you, too."

Lavinia abruptly silenced her.

"Don't flatter me, Eliza. It's no use. You don't understand half the situation. I must go."

Halfway through packing her meager belongings—her simple shifts and petticoats, not much more trimmed than a servant's so that there would be no remarks by laundry maids, her Sunday buttoned shoes, and the despised blue gown, her diary, whose key she wore round her neck, although its entries, made from an overcharged heart, were few and far between—Eliza came in with the half-finished silk gown.

She held it up against Lavinia saying, "The color does suit you, miss. It's clever. Miss Flora does have taste. She'll be ever so disappointed not to see you wear this, seeing she gave it to you."

"Eliza, *stop* it!"

Eliza stared, round-eyed.

"I didn't mean to upset you, miss."

"No, you only meant to drive the nail farther into my heart."

"I'm sorry, miss. Truly. It isn't as if I'll be here long myself, probably."

Lavinia was startled out of her own self-pity.

"Are you planning to leave? Have you another situation?"

"No, but after this—what with one thing and another—"

"You won't be blamed, Eliza. I saw to that."

"No, but—there's other things. I declare I don't know what to do."

"Are you frightened of something, Eliza?"

Eliza gave her a quick look, and lowered her eyes.

"I've done nothing to be frightened of. It's just—" Suddenly she began to cry, her apron to her face. "I miss my lady, that's the truth of it."

That was how Mrs. O'Shaughnessy found them, Eliza still sniffing, and Lavinia, set-faced, closing her trunk.

"The master wants you in the yellow parlor, Miss Hurst. Will you come down at once?"

"Certainly, Mrs. O'Shaughnessy. It was good of you to come and tell me yourself."

Mrs. O'Shaughnessy had never declared herself either for or against Lavinia. She had maintained a remote, dignified silence. But now there was the slightest hint of sympathy in her voice.

"The fewer servants who know about this the better. It will be easier for you after."

"After what?"

"After you continue your duties, I don't doubt."

Lavinia made no comment on that assumption. She asked politely how Mrs. Meryon was now, since she had been somewhat distressed and agitated. Had she developed one of her headaches?

Mrs. O'Shaughnessy looked grave.

"The doctor has been sent for. She was in a state of prostration, I hear. Bertha's sitting with her now. It's natural for her to break down, of course. She had been too calm since poor Lady Tameson's death. But a will reading is always the hardest to be borne. That's what my mother used to say. The dead speak again and it's a terrible shock. But I mustn't stand here chattering. The master is waiting."

It was clever of Daniel to choose the yellow parlor in which to see her. He knew it was her favorite room. In this cosy and intimate atmosphere they might perhaps be able to part without ill will.

He was standing with his back to the fire. She thought he might have been angry, or persuasive, or cool and distant. She hadn't expected this quiet sadness. At first he just looked at her without telling her to sit down. Then he gave a faint sigh and said, "I had thought we were friends."

It was an unfair attempt to weaken her resolution. She refused to be touched by it.

"Your wife said intolerable things. How can I stay after that?"

"Is pride so important, Miss Hurst?"

"Are you suggesting a person in my position can't afford that in-dulgence?"

"Don't twist my words. You know I didn't mean that."

Lavinia was gripping the edge of the table. She mustn't tremble. She mustn't let her color grow too high and show her agitation.

"Then perhaps you will tell me what you did mean."

"Miss Hurst, I can't keep you here against your will. Much as I would like to. But let us get two things clear. What are you going to do if you leave? And what is Flora to do without you?"

She had no answer to either of those things, and he knew she hadn't. Yet he didn't look triumphant. He continued to give her that quiet, melancholy look.

"If Flora didn't imagine that movement in her feet today, then there is a very good chance that she will recover. But her condition, as you probably realize, is a nervous one. The doctors call it a hysteri-cal one. She seems to be slowly coming out of it—due entirely to you, Miss Hurst."

He waved aside her disclaimer.

"I am not trying to influence you. I am merely stating the posi-tion. If Flora has a setback now, her recovery will be postponed for a long time, perhaps forever. And all her great-aunt's money won't compensate for that."

"You're suggesting that if I go, Flora will have this setback?" Lavinia asked stiffly.

"I'm not making a suggestion, I'm making a statement. It's sad, but true. I realize the unfairness of putting this burden on your shoulders, but tell me, Miss Hurst"—his dark serious gaze was in-escapable—"is your pride more important than Flora's chance of re-covery?"

"If you put it like that," Lavinia said angrily, "of course it isn't. Aren't you exaggerating?"

"No."

"Put yourself in my position, Mr. Meryon. How could you stay in the house of someone who hated and resented you?"

"If you mean Charlotte, that isn't strictly true. She's very angry with you now, I admit. I don't know exactly what her aunt led her to believe when we visited her in Venice, but she had apparently built great hopes on obtaining a fortune for Edward. It's not as if the boy will ever be penniless, but he won't inherit Winterwood, and that rankles with my wife. It's perhaps unfortunate that Edward is so much her favorite child. However, when she is in a calmer state she will realize that none of this is your fault. She has these—emotional storms."

He had expressed Charlotte's condition politely, but from the darkness of his face Lavinia suspected his anxiety was much deeper. The mistress locked her door, Eliza had said. She laughed in the night. She collapsed from the violence of her emotions . . .

"I myself am delighted for Flora. The old lady couldn't have done a better thing. Although I confess I hope the fortune isn't too large. That could be as much a burden for a young girl as if it were too little."

"What about the new wing you hoped to build?" Lavinia couldn't help asking.

Daniel shrugged. "That must wait." He looked at Lavinia quizzically. "Did you think I had made a bargain in Venice, too?"

"It is only natural to plan."

"Well, thank you for giving me the benefit of the doubt. But we are getting away from the point. If you still intend to leave us, I will order the brougham to take you to Dover in the morning. But where will you go? What will you do?"

"Isn't that also getting away from the point?"

"By no means. It is the point."

"Mr. Meryon, you have enough concerns of your own not to worry about mine."

He regarded her thoughtfully.

"Your parents are dead, you have no fortune, you are alone in the world. Now you intend to throw yourself on the mercy of whatever strangers might offer you a living. I can't allow this to happen."

"*You* can't allow it to happen!"

"No, Miss Hurst. Did you misunderstand me?"

Lavinia felt the color creeping in her cheeks.

"I thought it was—you were—entirely concerned for Flora."

"Not entirely."

She had no answer now. She could only look at him.

"In other circumstances—" he began, then checked himself. Walking across to the window he said aloofly, "Naturally I would be following your welfare, Miss Hurst. Or at least I would like to be doing so. If you remain at Winterwood, that makes it so much easier for me. But I won't persuade you. And I won't remind you of Flora's state when she finds you gone."

"You won't persuade me!" Lavinia exclaimed in a choked voice. "When not one word you have said has been other than persuading me. You are unfair! Bitterly unfair! You use soft words, which you know are far more effective than anger. You know that you are tying me here. Every day—"

Now he was watching her closely, his eyes brilliantly dark.

"Every day?"

"The ties grow harder to break. What eventually am I to do? Tell me that."

"Shall we take each day as it comes, Miss Hurst? Let us concentrate on small essential things. First you go upstairs and unpack your trunk. Then you make your peace with my wife. You will find her quite rational and reasonable now. I know the course of these emotional crises. She will admit her unfairness. Then, after that"—he looked whimsical now; he really seemed to be cheering up rapidly—"you will quietly see if my daughter can repeat her *tour de force* at the graveside. If it really does seem that she has some movement in her toes, then we will make an excursion to London to see the specialists interested in her case. This by no means needs to be a visit confined to doctors' rooms. We can do shopping for Christmas, and see the sights. Flora will find that amusing, and so, I hope, will you. Have you seen all the sights in London in your past, Miss Hurst?"

Lavinia had one moment of apprehension that Daniel might guess too much about her past before she let the growing pleasure show in her face.

"I am not as worldly as that, Mr. Meryon. But this excursion—"

"We will take Eliza. Or Mary. My wife won't consider coming. She has a nervous horror of doctors' rooms, and indeed of traveling in the cold dark weather. Oh, don't look like that, Miss Hurst! This isn't a bribe designed to persuade you to stay. You have already made that decision. Haven't you?"

"You know I have," Lavinia said in a low voice.

He took her hand.

"Just take each day as it comes, Miss Hurst."

And now she knew that he wasn't using her, for Flora's sake or anyone's. He never had been using her, except in the sense that he did not want to be without her. She almost believed that he loved her. She did know that they both knew how to embrace pain. And that, accepted like this, pain was almost a wild, violent happiness.

Chapter 14

THE servants were whispering about the mistress. She had been shut in her room since yesterday, and no one but Bertha had been allowed to see her. Bertha was not one to talk. She went about with a dour face, saying no more than that the mistress had been ordered complete quiet by the doctor. She would be confined to her room for several days. She was to have a strengthening diet, and no worries.

Nevertheless, the stories were spreading. Phoebe had whispered to Lily, and Lily had told Mary. Mary, who was not one to keep secrets, related all the confused stories to Lavinia. The mistress had been raving, she had screamed if the master came near her, and had said that if that Mr. Peate came to the house again she would send for the police and have him arrested.

Doctor Munro had had to give her a draught that made her sleep for twelve hours without stirring, and when she had come to she had weakly asked for Master Edward, but would see no one else. The little greyhound slept beside her. Master Edward had stayed with her for ten minutes, and then had fidgeted and whimpered, and said he didn't like his mamma sick in bed, he wanted to go and play with his new toy soldiers. So the mistress, poor thing, was quite alone, except for her dog, and Bertha going in and out. She was a poor mazed creature . . .

That was Mary's story. Lavinia suspected it was highly embroidered. (Why should Charlotte want to have Jonathon arrested?) She forbade a word of it to be told to Flora. But Flora's sensitive mind had picked up enough. She woke the morning after Lady Tameson's funeral in a quiet, and seemingly indifferent mood. Lavinia knew her well enough not to coax her out of it. It was better that she stay quiet, conserving her strength. When this strange heavy atmosphere left the house, she would get back her spirits. In the meantime the daily exercises and massage must be kept up, and perhaps the miracle would occur again and Flora would find she could move her toes.

At least she knew nothing about Lavinia's near desertion of her. In the light of a new day Lavinia realized how selfish and impossible that scheme had been. She was committed to Flora until she walked again. That was the truth of it. All other considerations were of minor importance.

Daniel had given orders that at present Flora was not to be told about the fortune her great-aunt had left her. He was afraid that emotion at Lady Tameson's last gesture would be too much for her. It was better to let her grief grow less acute. Not that she could be expected to understand the significance of owning a palace in Venice, a fortune in stocks and shares, and a great deal of very valuable jewelry. She was too young to realize that, crippled or not, she would now be a prey to fortune hunters, and that if she did succeed in walking again she would be able to choose among the most eligible young men in England.

The servants, who were whispering about this great news as well as about the condition of the mistress, were loyal enough. Even Mary, for once, held her tongue. It was someone else who was less loyal.

It was a sunny afternoon and Lavinia had left Flora sitting in the blue garden while she returned to the house to get sketching materials. When she came back, Jonathon Peate was prowling about the grassy walks, and talking to Flora in his loud, carrying voice.

"So you're a rich little girl now. How are you enjoying that?"

Flora answered angrily. "What are you doing in my garden? You were not invited. Do you go everywhere uninvited?"

"By no means. I find most people more civil than the rich and beautiful Miss Meryon. Ah, here is Miss Hurst. Miss Hurst, your young lady's manners are still sadly lacking."

"Miss Hurst, tell him this garden's a private place. He has no right to be here."

"That is true, Mr. Peate," Lavinia said.

Jonathon gave his infuriating laugh.

"For such a rich young woman, Miss Meryon is very ungenerous."

"Why don't you go away from Winterwood?" Flora demanded. "Great-aunt Tameson is dead. There's nothing for you to stay for."

"But I might enjoy staying. There might be people I enjoy looking at." Jonathon wagged his finger. "You mustn't pretend to know all my motives, princess."

Lavinia looked at Flora's white and furious face.

"You had better leave us, Mr. Peate. Otherwise we will have to go indoors."

The merest flicker of something that wasn't perpetual good humor crossed his face. But at once he was smiling, and saying, "Your wishes are mine, Miss Hurst. After all, we must remember to take the greatest care of little Miss Meryon. Even though she is so sadly a cripple and seems to have inherited her mother's mad—sorry, her mother's emotional instability, she is a very valuable personage. Perhaps one day I may succeed in persuading her to like me a little. Anyway, she may depend on it, we will be seeing a great deal of one another in the future. I am to be a guest at Christmas. Isn't that extremely kind of my cousin Charlotte?"

He bowed and swaggered away, his head in the air.

Flora turned on Lavinia in panic.

"Miss Hurst, how could Mamma have asked him to stay? It can't be true! And what does he mean by my being mad like Mamma. Mamma isn't mad. *Is* she, Miss Hurst?"

Lavinia didn't know how to keep the fury out of her voice.

"That Mr. Peate! You mustn't believe a word he says. He is some kind of monster. He calls you a cripple and your mother mad. I would like to kill him!"

Flora began to giggle unsteadily. "If you look like that, Miss Hurst, I believe you could!"

"Your mamma isn't mad; she simply has a very high-strung nervous system. And so have you. You must always try to keep calm."

Flora was growing calmer now.

"So I would, if people were not so exasperating. Mr. Peate, Edward, Great-aunt Tameson. But she is dead. What did Mr. Peate mean about me being rich? Is that another of his horrid jokes?"

The quiet charm of the late autumn afternoon had vanished. Jonathon Peate had a way of turning any peace into discord. He was a menace—and now Lavinia saw that his menace extended to more than her. His pointed remarks about Flora's wealth had some disturbing significance. Surely it couldn't be true that he would be at Winterwood for Christmas. Why did Daniel tolerate it?

Lavinia remembered the conversation Eliza had related between Charlotte and Lady Tameson. "You'll have to send him away," Charlotte had said, and Lady Tameson had answered, "Try."

Lady Tameson was no longer here to explain what it was she knew about her peculiarly stubborn and thick-skinned nephew.

"I expect it's all a mistake," was all Lavinia could say to Flora. "I am sure your mamma hasn't really invited Mr. Peate for Christmas. And as for your being rich, your papa had decided not to tell you just yet, but Lady Tameson left you some money in her will. You are to get it when you are of age. So you see, you have no need to worry about the future. You can have your own establishment as you planned."

"And horses?"

"As many as you want, I expect."

The sudden eager light in Flora's eyes died almost at once.

"But what will be the use if I can't ride? Mr. Peate said I was a cripple."

"Mr. Peate has a way of underestimating people. He doesn't know your determination. You must show him that he is wrong."

She appeared to have hit upon the exactly right thing to say, for Flora's eyes narrowed to fierce slits.

"I will, Miss Hurst! I will!"

Lavinia was certain that Charlotte was afraid of Jonathon; yet it turned out to be true that she had invited him to stay over Christmas. Sir Timothy was astonished.

"I don't know what Charlotte sees in the fellow. He's only some sort of a cousin. She owes no courtesy to him. He's not incapacitated, or penniless, either, by the look of him. I think he's a complete blackguard. Why does Daniel allow Charlotte to have him about?"

The servants all knew the reason Daniel allowed it. It was rather alarming how much the servants did know. Rumors became exaggerated, of course, but Eliza said it was perfectly true that Mr. Peate had visited the mistress. He had just walked in, Bertha had said. The mistress had cried out in shock to see him standing there. But then she had sent Bertha out of the room.

It was quite half an hour before she had rung her bell and asked Bertha to show Mr. Peate out, and he had bent over her and kissed her hand, and said that he adored her. "My exquisite Charlotte," had been his exact words, and supposing the master had heard them!

"So he got round her," Lavinia said.

"Oh, more than that, miss. She was all of a twitter. Said wouldn't it be gay to have Mr. Peate as a Christmas guest. The house needed some gaiety after all this melancholy. Mr. Peate was always so cheerful, never low in spirits. Anyway, she wasn't one of those gloomy people who thought mourning should go on and on. It was so bad for the children. Then she asked for the master to come and see her, and if you realize, miss, it's the first time she's wanted him since she was took so poorly."

Lavinia wanted to reproach Eliza for gossiping, but couldn't. She was hanging on her words.

"And what happened?"

"Well, miss, it was a bit of an upset. He hadn't been with her more than five minutes before she began crying and laughing both at once, the way she does when she has those turns. Bertha could hear her from away down the passage. Then the master came out, calling for Bertha to know where the soothing draught was that the doctor had left. He kept saying, 'Very well, you may have your way this time, but not again. Don't do it again.' You see, he had to give way, or she'd have been worse."

"She finds her attacks convenient," Lavinia said cynically.

Eliza looked shocked and serious. "Oh, no, miss. Bertha could tell you some tales. Oh no, miss, her attacks are real, and to be avoided at all costs. The master knows, poor man. Haven't you seen him looking as if he carries all the cares of the world on his shoulders? That's when he's worried about her. And it's often enough. Too often."

"It's hard to see someone you love suffering."

"That it is, miss. And her so beautiful. You haven't really seen her dressed for a party and all laughing and excited, have you, miss?"

"No," said Lavinia shortly.

"Well, you will, miss, and then you'll see why the master can't resist her."

Flora had left her book and her cashmere shawl in the blue garden. In their agitation after Jonathon Peate's intrusion they had come away without gathering up their things.

Lavinia went down to get them and Jonathon followed her. It was quite obvious that he must have been lurking about waiting for an opportunity to find her alone, just as he had that day when they had encountered one another in the Temple of Virtue.

It was dusk, and she didn't realize he was there until she heard a twig snap behind her. She turned sharply, and found herself in his arms.

She struggled fiercely, pushing away his hateful smiling face with her clenched fists.

"Ah, come now, Miss Hurstmonceaux. A little kiss won't kill you. Or would you kill me?"

"Yes, I would!" she said. "Let me go at once, you monster!"

He released her so suddenly that she almost fell. He was still laughing, but his eyes had that gray, chilling look.

"They say it's easy to kill," he drawled.

Lavinia had picked up Flora's belongings and made to go. He firmly blocked her path.

"By Jove, you're lovely with that color in your cheeks. My cousin Charlotte's celebrated beauty simply fades in comparison."

"Mr. Peate, will you kindly let me pass."

"I'll forgive you for your little tantrum. I expect you're finding the responsibility of looking after an heiress rather trying."

"Mr. Peate—"

He caught her wrist.

"I will let you go when you have promised to marry me."

Lavinia stopped struggling. She stared in complete amazement.

"You'd dare!"

"Why shouldn't I? Are you so unapproachable? So pure? Do I have to refresh your memory, Miss Hurstmonceaux?"

"Will you kindly stop calling me by another name."

"But it's your real name, isn't it? How do I know? Shall I tell you? Have you forgotten the house in Albemarle Street? I know you didn't stay in it long. Just for the season, I believe. Then your brother wanted—or found it necessary—to move on. But during that time there were quite a lot of callers. You must have known about the gambling sessions that went on while you were getting your beauty sleep. I only saw you once then. You were coming downstairs to go shopping. I can tell you exactly what you were wearing. A green velvet cloak and a charming hat with a little green ostrich feather curling round its brim. I had been sleeping off the effects of your brother's excellent port in his study—to the left of the stairs, do you remember? Oh, you didn't see me. But I saw you."

His face came closer.

"And I saw you again exactly a year later in the witness box. You were more quietly dressed. You were paler and thinner. But just as beautiful."

"You came to stare!" Lavinia whispered.

"To admire. You were so loyal to your brother. I didn't expect to see you again after that. I thought you would disappear quietly to live your life in obscurity, and what a catastrophe that would have been. But fate took a hand. You must admit the ways of fate are very strange."

"Deplorably strange," Lavinia said curtly.

"And destined. We were meant to meet again and fall in love."

"Mr. Peate, your fancies are even stranger than fate."

He laughed softly. "Dear Lavinia! You never disappoint me. Your wit, your spirit. What a pair we will make!"

"You can't be assuming—" She stopped, unable to say the incredible words, and he finished them for her.

"But don't you see, you will be compelled to marry me if your secret is to be kept. Naturally I would never betray my wife."

"Mr. Peate, you must be mad! You are mad!"

He shook his head smilingly. "Far from it. Exceptionally sane. And very clever at getting my own way. Marry me, Lavinia, and we'll get on in the world. We'll sail for New York. No one there knows, or cares about, anybody's past. We'll set up a fine establishment. Come now, you must admit that will be better than this half-life you're living. Who else in England is going to offer you marriage? Tell me!"

"There are worse things than being unmarried." Lavinia's eyes raked him with scorn. "Aren't you aware of that?"

She believed she had pricked his assurance a little, for his tone changed. He said softly, "You make a big mistake. What is that dear sweet crippled child, the little bitch, to say when she knows about her adored Miss Hurst's past? Her brother tried for murder; the whole affair very unsavory. What is my high-minded cousin-in-law, Daniel, to think about the admirable young woman he's been defending so strenuously, and secretly wanting to go to bed with?"

Lavinia thought she would like to attack him with her bare hands. She had only felt like this once before—the tallow-yellow face swam before her, its open eyes staring . . . The garden seemed to have become dark. She could scarcely see the last withering flowers, the fallen leaves.

Jonathon Peate had spoiled this charming garden. He had laid his filthy finger on it, and it had been smirched.

"Don't swoon, Miss Hurst. I wouldn't have thought you were the swooning kind."

"Just—let me go."

"I'm not keeping you. You may go when you please. But think about what I have said. I won't hurry you. I'll be quite fair and give you until Christmas to decide. Since it suits me to stay here until then. But I'll expect an answer by the new year. So think carefully, my dear. And remember that I don't make idle threats."

"Miss Hurst, you look awfully sad," Flora said.

"I'm not sad. I was just thinking."

"What were you thinking about?"

"A hat I had once, with a green ostrich feather. It was very pretty."

"Then don't look so sad. I'll buy you another just like it. I can, now I have all this money. I mean to buy gifts for everybody, even Edward. Papa says we are to go to London to shop for Christmas, and Mr. Mallinson, my Trustee, will allow me some money to spend."

Flora's cheeks were pink, her eyes bright. It had been wise for her to know about her fortune after all. She looked so recovered in spirits that Lavinia had to brush aside her own intense depression.

"That is very kind of you. But you have already given me the silk for a new gown."

"And you have never worn it yet! But you can wear it in London. Papa will like to see you in it. And we are to go and see more doctors, but I won't be afraid this time if you are with me."

On the pretext of asking about the visit to London, Lavinia sought out Daniel in his study that evening.

"May I have a word with you, Mr. Meryon?"

"Certainly, as long as it is no more nonsense about leaving Winterwood."

"No. I will stay until you ask me to go," Lavinia replied. And that may be sooner than he expected it to be, she reflected soberly.

He asked her to sit down, and offered her a glass of Madeira. He had been riding, and was still in riding clothes. He looked a little fatigued, the lines deepened in his cheeks, his jaw hard. But otherwise he did not bear the look of someone with the cares of the world on his shoulders, as Eliza had described him.

"Then what is it you wish to discuss with me?"

It was difficult to remain calm.

"You have probably heard that Mr. Peate has told Flora about her fortune."

"Yes, I did hear. But fortunately she has taken it the right way, and thinks only of money to spend for Christmas. So perhaps I was wrong and he right."

"He is never right about anything!" Lavinia said passionately.

Daniel looked at her with raised brows.

"You say that very feelingly, Miss Hurst. Is there any particular reason?"

"Only that he is a most unlikable person, sly, untrustworthy, dangerous."

"Dangerous?"

She nodded vehemently.

"I believe so. Don't let him stay here, Mr. Meryon. Persuade your wife he is here only to do harm."

Daniel's eyes had hardened.

"Explain yourself, Miss Hurst."

"Why, he came into the blue garden, Flora's precious blue garden, quite uninvited, and told Flora she would always be a cripple. He called her a little—" But she could not say the word. She must not go too far or Daniel would recognize her intense personal hatred for Jonathon. "I believe he is one of those people who want to do harm. How can he remain a welcome guest after that?"

Daniel had turned away so that she couldn't see his face.

"You must address your appeal to my wife, Miss Hurst. It is she who wants the fellow here."

"But does she, Mr. Meryon? Or is he intimidating her in some way?"

"Intimidating?" He turned sharply. "Oh, come, Miss Hurst, that's a little unlikely. I believe he is playing heavily on their being kin, if only by marriage, and merely wants free lodgings for a time. So he flatters my wife outrageously, and she listens."

"Flatters?"

The inquisitive brow went up again.

"That is a more likely explanation than yours, Miss Hurst. Anyway, I have heard him at it. And Charlotte appears to find him an amusing and entertaining guest. Which is a rather important consideration at this particular time. To tell the truth, Miss Hurst, I abominate having Peate in the house, and so does my uncle, but if it helps Charlotte we can put up with him until after Christmas."

"How can it help her? That man!"

Now she believed what Eliza had said. For his face had grown careworn, with a deep look of sadness and perplexity.

"My wife, as perhaps you have realized, Miss Hurst, has these breakdowns, when she must not be crossed in the smallest way. Her aunt's will has precipitated one of the worst she has had. Now she is recovering, but her well-being, for some curious reason, seems to depend on having Peate about. She says that the house would be too melancholy without guests, her aunt would have wished this, and anyway he amuses her."

"I believe he frightens rather than amuses her."

Daniel looked at her closely.

"Do you say that because he frightens you?"

"Yes, he does, because of his small cruelties," Lavinia said intensely. "Reminding Flora that she was a cripple, and laughing. Nothing you can say in his favor will impress me."

"I don't intend saying anything in his favor. But we can surely come to little harm with a few more weeks of his company. I believe he came here for pickings in his aunt's will, but now those haven't materialized, he intends to get as much free hospitality as he can for compensation. I'll send him packing in January, I promise you, Miss Hurst." He was laughing. "You do look as if you are afraid of him. Why, the fellow hasn't a subtle brain in his head. And he's vulgar as well, as my uncle would say. Can't you just quietly despise him?"

"I do that already."

"Then—" A new thought struck Daniel. "Is he worrying you with attentions? Miss Hurst! I want the truth."

"No, Mr. Meryon. He isn't worrying me. If it is so important to humor Mrs. Meryon, then of course we must do so. I only think that we should all be on our guard."

"Did you think I was not?" came the quiet answer.

She gave a little sigh of relief.

"You should stop me, Mr. Meryon, when I start pursuing dragons."

"But I like to watch you. You pursue them with such intensity. Now perhaps you will consent to sit down and have that glass of Madeira."

Chapter 15

LATER that day Charlotte gave orders for her horse to be saddled and brought to the door. Dressed in her pale gray riding suit, she ran down the stairs saying she must get some fresh air, the house was suffocating. Sylvie was at her heels. They looked like wraiths disappearing out of the front door, the slender woman and the slip of a dog.

Bertha had followed Charlotte down the stairs and said uneasily that when the mistress was in one of those moods nothing would stop her. Ride she must, as fast as her horse would take her. Goodness knows what she was riding from, but she would come back calm, that was the important thing.

She came back an hour later, when it was completely dark. She had lost her bowler hat, and her hair had come down. It streamed in a dark fall over one shoulder. Although she looked like a witch, she was, as Bertha had predicted, quite calm. She would change quickly and then say good night to the children. It was the first time she had gone to them in their bedrooms since the disastrous day of the funeral and the will reading.

It was remarkable how the atmosphere in the house changed now that the mistress' strange malaise seemed to have passed.

Phoebe was singing at her work and little Mary, with more energy than strength, was filling the porcelain tub in front of the fire for Flora's bath, and twittering like a sparrow about the events of the day.

"Eliza says she can't get used to the bell not ringing in my lady's room. I remember when my own grandma died, we cried because she lay so quiet. She never stopped scolding when she was alive, and it was awful queer seeing her mouth shut. It never was shut before. I wanted her to come back and start belting us again, even though it hurt something cruel."

"Did she leave you anything?" Flora asked.

Mary stared, then gave a derisive laugh.

"What had she got to leave except old clothes? There was her good buttoned boots that fitted Linda, and Ma had her Sunday bonnet."

"Great-aunt Tameson has left me her fortune," Flora said with dignity. "I don't really know what to do with it all. I expect there's quite a hundred pounds. I intend to buy Christmas presents for everybody. Would you like to come to London with us to shop?"

Mary's diminutive figure stood arrested, the copper jug in her hands.

"Me! Do you mean that, miss?"

"Of course," said Flora graciously. "Miss Hurst, we will take Mary to London with us, won't we?"

"Yes. Actually your papa mentioned that we would," Lavinia answered.

"Lor!" Mary ejaculated, her face full of terror and excitement. Flora began to giggle.

"It's not that wonderful, you silly creature. It's not like Paris or Geneva or Venice. But it's well enough. We must make a list of suitable gifts. I intend to buy Simon a cricket bat, but what that spoiled Edward—"

"Who is talking about Edward being spoiled?" came Charlotte's warm gay voice. "Flora, dearest, how are you? Have those lazy toes moved again?"

She came sweeping into the room dressed now in one of her graceful ruffled tea gowns, and smelling of some fragrant scent.

"Oh, Mamma! You're better!"

"Much better, darling. I've been for a long ride and blown all the cobwebs away."

"Then you don't still hate me?"

"Hate you, beloved?"

"For getting all Great-aunt Tameson's money. You may have the jewels, Mamma. I don't care much for diamond brooches. But I really do need a good deal of money for the gifts I want to buy."

"Sweetheart!" Charlotte laughed and held out her arms in an extravagant gesture of affection. "There will be plenty of money for several Christmases. And to tell the truth, I don't care for diamond brooches either. They must be put in the bank until you are older. Papa will arrange it."

"Then I really am rich? Mr. Peate said I was."

A flicker crossed Charlotte's face.

"It's none of Mr. Peate's business, but yes, my funny little daughter, you are rich. And isn't that a lucky thing, since—"

The half-finished sentence took all the light out of Flora's face. In

one second it had lost its delight and grown shut-in, controlled.
"You think Great-aunt Tameson only did this because I am a
cripple. That's what Mr. Peate said."

"I tell you, it's none of Mr. Peate's business."

"Then why must he stay here, Mamma? Why don't you tell him
he's not wanted?"

Charlotte's gaiety was only on the surface after all. Underneath,
the tensions were still there, making her frown, giving her voice a
quick, brittle quality.

"But he *is* wanted, darling. *I* want him to amuse me. Is that so
strange? I can't bear a quiet house, and since we're in mourning we
can't have a large party. Don't look so sulky. You know I can't endure you to be in a pet. Silly child. As if you're not thoroughly
spoiled already—an heiress at your age! Why, you'll be able to marry
anybody—if you grow pretty and walk again." Charlotte's pitying
gaze suggested that neither of these things would happen. She em-
braced Flora again, and said, as if generosity overcame her, "I'm going to spoil you even more. I'm going to give you Sylvie."

"Oh, Mamma!" Flora was incredulous. "But you love her!"

"I shall still exercise her, of course. But she may spend the day in
your room."

"Every day?"

"Of course. Have I made you happy? Then I am glad. You see,
everyone thinks of you, Papa, Mamma—Miss Hurst. Miss Hurst, I
would like a word with you if you can spare a moment."

Lavinia followed Charlotte out. Charlotte walked to the window
seat at the end of the corridor and, sitting down, pressed her hands
to her face.

"That poor creature! Helpless! Plain! Condemned to a wheelchair!
And now she will be at the mercy of fortune hunters. Some man will
marry her for her money and then persecute her, hope she will die."
Charlotte must have realized that those words might just possibly
have described her own wishes. She said brusquely, "Don't look so
horrified, Miss Hurst. That is human nature. Why didn't I have a
normal daughter!"

"Flora is normal!" Lavinia said emphatically.

"Normal! That pathetic creature!" Charlotte gave a short laugh.
"And now burdened by all that money. Three hundred thousand
pounds or more. A great fortune. You may have meant well, Miss
Hurst, but you did *not* do her a service when you encouraged my
aunt to pity her."

"But, Mrs. Meryon, I did nothing of the kind. Pity is the last thing I have ever given Flora."

Charlotte made an impatient gesture.

"Oh, spare me your protestations of innocence. Perhaps you meant well. My husband persuades me you did."

"Mrs. Meryon, I have said I had no influence—"

"On the contrary, Miss Hurst, you have a great deal. Especially on the opposite sex. I am not permitted to malign you at all. In my own house! They say I wrong you—"

"They?"

"My husband and Mr. Peate. They won't believe—"

"Do you listen to Mr. Peate?" Lavinia interrupted, her voice tight with shock. How far did Jonathon Peate think he could interfere? Why was he listened to?

"He is not an easy man to ignore, as you must admit. He is quite —persuasive. But let us keep to the point. Neither my husband nor Mr. Peate will believe that you bring disaster—"

"Disaster!" Lavinia whispered.

"Perhaps unintentionally. Some people have this aura of danger. I see it around you. I have an ability to sense things."

The curious cloud that oppressed Charlotte touched Lavinia, too. Charlotte was right. She did, unintentionally, bring danger. Justin had known that—briefly . . .

"There, you look frightened too, Miss Hurst."

"I don't understand what you are talking about, Mrs. Meryon." Charlotte made an effort to be practical.

"No, of course not. Daniel says I have fancies. I have always had a too vivid imagination. Flora takes after me in that way. You must control Flora's hysterics, Miss Hurst. If mine had been controlled when I was young, I think I would have been stronger now, and perhaps not have these shattering headaches." She pressed her fingers to her temples again, and Lavinia remembered, with a chill, Jonathon's cruel words about Flora inheriting her mother's madness.

"That's why a few drops of laudanum are to be recommended when Flora is overexcited. You will remember that, Miss Hurst, won't you?"

"They certainly did her good after the funeral," Lavinia admitted.

"That's what I say." Charlotte stood up, her animation returning. "And I will send Sylvie down. My adored little dog. Does that make me less of an unnatural mother?"

Lavinia wished she could accept that gesture as a genuine one.

But was Charlotte, too, thinking of her daughter as an heiress, someone who had, belatedly, to be loved?

The uneasy conversation weighed on Lavinia as she returned to Flora's room. Apart from her skepticism, in a strange way she had fancied Charlotte was appealing to her for help. She was frightened —perhaps only of the dark clouds in her head or of her unruly passionate love for Edward and the equally uncontrolled dislike for Flora. Flora was plain, crippled, offending to her fastidious eye, unmarriageable, but now had to be loved because of her fortune.

The tingle of apprehension Lavinia felt was not imaginary. She was privately resolving to keep a close watch over her charge. For as long as she was permitted to. After Christmas, if Jonathon Peate kept his threat, she would have to forget Winterwood and its inhabitants.

"Miss Hurst, people who give you the thing they love best must really care about you, mustn't they?" Flora was clamoring.

"Yes, that's true."

"Then Mamma's giving me Sylvie must mean she really loves me, after all. I am so happy, because now I have a great many people to love me. You, Papa, Mamma, Great-aunt Tameson in heaven, perhaps even Edward. Miss Hurst, may I put up my hair for Christmas?"

"What a frivolous idea! Who are you planning to impress?"

"Well—Simon will be home. He imagines himself so grand. And" —Flora blushed violently, "I had thought Mr. Bush looked at me with a little admiration. If I could look older—" Flora saw Lavinia's smile and finished in her old belligerent style, "Well, he is too young and bashful for you, but for me—he could be a *beginning!*"

"Why, Flora, what secrets! By all means let us have Mr. Bush expiring of love for you. It will be good for you both."

"Miss Hurst! I only meant to practice on him. One must have some experience with the opposite sex."

"That is very true."

"He had wanted to see my sketches. Perhaps tomorrow, if the sun is shining, we could go down to the lake with our sketchbooks."

"By all means. Let us plan how to ravish Mr. Bush!"

Although Flora had not again had any movement in her toes, and no one was certain whether or not she had imagined it, her father still decided that she was to go and see the London specialists.

The journey was made just three weeks before Christmas. Eliza came to give assistance in lifting Flora, and Mary because it pleased Flora to take her.

Mary had never been on a train in her life. She squealed with apprehension and excitement. She thought she would be sick and then she thought she would not. Eliza scolded her, and Flora smiled indulgently, as if she were twenty years Mary's senior.

"You'll be no use to me if you're going to jump about like this all the time we're in London," she said severely.

Mary subsided, trying to be meek.

"Yes, miss. I'll keep still." She caught Daniel's eye, was not sure whether he was angry or not, and whispered abashedly, "I do declare I never went so fast in my life."

Daniel had not caught the prevailing high spirits. He was aloof and unsmiling. Lavinia supposed he was thinking of Charlotte left behind, insisting that London tired her too much and she would be perfectly happy with Edward for company. Or perhaps he was thinking how sad it was that Mary, the daughter of one of his farm laborers, should be able to skip from window to window while his own daughter was a prisoner in her chair. Or was he wondering how often Jonathon Peate would call on his "dear cousin" while they were away?

The visit to the doctor, an eminent bone specialist in Harley Street, was reasonably hopeful. He pronounced a great improvement in Flora's general health and spirits, and was sure that this was the most important factor toward her recovery.

Daniel insisted that Lavinia be there while the doctor gave his verdict since the care of Flora was hers.

"She's a different child, Mr. Meryon. I warned you that the shock of the accident, or perhaps the state of mind of the patient before she had the accident—I don't pretend to know what that was—would take a long time to pass. But now that seems to have happened. I find your daughter much less nervous and much less inclined to hysterical behavior. I don't know what has effected this change—time, her travels abroad, which must have proved an agreeable diversion, the right companionship. Whatever the reason, my prognostications for the future are hopeful. Keep her happy and calm, Mr. Meryon. The trauma will pass. I believe I can promise you that she will be leading an active life before too long." His eyes twinkled kindly. "At least before the time comes for her to put her hair up and go to her first ball. Take a positive line with her, Mr. Meryon. Don't allow her to believe anything but what I have said."

Daniel looked at Lavinia.

"It is Miss Hurst who does that. I think there you find the reason for Flora's improvement."

The doctor regarded Lavinia keenly.

"Then you have been fortunate, Mr. Meryon. My advice would be to hold on to your good fortune."

"Thank you, doctor. But the advice is not needed."

Daniel had at last caught the high spirits of his little party, and insisted on a long shopping excursion that afternoon to the shops that had the most beguiling window displays. And that was when a highly embarrassing situation arose.

It began with Flora insisting on buying Lavinia another gown as her Christmas present. It was no use for Lavinia to protest that she already had the one Eliza had made. Flora dismissed that with a shrug.

"It is very well in its way, but still it is homemade. Things are different now that I have so much money. Besides, you must have more than one good gown. Mamma has more than she can count."

"I am not in your mamma's position. When am I to wear such an elegant gown?"

"If you have it, you will find opportunities to wear it. Please don't argue with me, Miss Hurst. I find you very tiresome when you argue."

Daniel, with a sober face, said, "Remember what the doctor said, Miss Hurst. Flora is to be kept calm. So I think we must go on this shopping expedition. You look disturbed, Miss Hurst. Do you find it so hard to accept things?"

"That is quite irrelevant, Mr. Meryon. The practical aspect is that it will be money wasted."

Flora continued to be infuriatingly smug. "Come, Miss Hurst. Mary is not complaining about having a new bonnet, nor Eliza a shawl. I even intend to take poor Mr. Bush a gift, so why must you be so stubborn and spoil my enjoyment?"

So there was nothing to do but capitulate, with as much grace as possible. In the shop she allowed herself to be whisked away to a fitting room by a black-clad impressively busted shopwoman while Daniel sat on a couch, his expression impassive, and Flora, in her chair, showed a tendency to giggle with pleasure and excitement.

The sea-green or the brown velvet or the yellow taffeta? Lavinia let herself be laced into the different gowns, the efficient saleswoman prodding and twitching and coaxing the snug waists and full skirts into place. She made sounds of extravagant admiration; then, before Lavinia was aware what was happening, she had propelled Lavinia out into the little salon where Daniel and Flora sat.

"Madam, let your husband decide. Now, sir! Have you ever seen your wife look more beautiful? Observe the way the lace falls here."

She flicked the fichu that delicately concealed the low-cut bodice. "Observe the tiny waist, the way the neckline is cut to display the shoulders to best advantage."

In her enthusiasm she failed to notice Lavinia's embarrassment. She went on busily, "If I may take the liberty to express my opinion, your wife looks extremely well in everything she has tried on, but the yellow taffeta, which you have not yet seen, is the *pièce de résistance.*" The woman's French accent was peculiarly her own. "So few can wear that lovely color. But with a skin like madam's, it is quite ravishing. Come and put it on, madam."

Lavinia had managed to find her voice.

"No. This was not— You are making a mistake—"

"Let me be the judge of that," said Daniel with deliberate misunderstanding. "Pray put on the yellow taffeta, my dear."

"Yes, do, Mamma," said Flora, eagerly playing the infuriating game.

Lavinia could have slapped both their faces. Hopelessly caught in the misunderstanding, scarlet in the face, she had to submit to being hooked into the new dress.

"Madam has such a sympathetic husband. You would scarcely believe how few of my customers have their husbands accompany them to buy a new gown."

"He is not—" Lavinia began, stopped, and amended her remark, "often able to be with me." Would she have this woman think Daniel her lover instead? And what was Daniel up to, encouraging her to be paraded in yet more gowns? It seemed to be amusing him. He knew she was trapped and must play this absurd charade to its end.

Yet the yellow taffeta did look well. The shopwoman guided her into the salon like a sleepwalker.

"That's the one," said Daniel in a sure voice. "Don't you agree, Flora?"

"Oh, yes, Papa!" Flora was proving to be a diabolically good actress. "Mamma looks quite exquisite in that. Really you do, Mamma. So make up your mind at once that it is to be the yellow."

Out in the street, walking beside Daniel as he pushed Flora's chair, Lavinia exploded.

"Of all the things to do! Did you *enjoy* embarrassing me?"

"Oh, Miss Hurst!" Flora was still enjoying herself immensely. "If you could have seen your face! You were so angry. You looked as if you might catch fire. Didn't she, Papa?"

"And still does," said Daniel with a sidelong glance. "Perhaps the situation didn't amuse Miss Hurst as much as it did us, my pet."

"It certainly didn't!" Lavinia exclaimed. "And when will I ever wear that most extravagant and beautiful gown? It's quite nonsense spending your money like that, Flora. I *am* angry." She was indeed brushing away tears. She almost collided with a stout gentleman, and felt Daniel's steadying hand on her arm.

"You will wear the gown this evening," he said imperturbably. "If Flora isn't too tired, we are going out to dinner and the theater. That was intended to be a surprise, but since your thrifty soul needs reassuring, Miss Hurst—" He was still laughing at her. Even in the murky light of a London street at dusk she could see how bright his eyes were. "Don't tell me you're not the kind of person who feels that a gown for one occasion only is well justified."

He must be thinking of that night at the opera in Venice. Then she had worn borrowed finery. Tonight she would wear what she was compelled to accept from charity. Yes, charity, even though it was Flora's.

"Once—" she began impulsively, then had to stop. Of what use relating hers and Robin's happy improvidence which had had so sad an end?

Ever since Daniel had broached the question of the trip to London, Lavinia had cherished one desire—to find the opportunity to visit Robin in Pentonville prison. She had not known what kind of excuse to make for being absent for several hours, but as it happened everything was very simple. The morning's excursion had exhausted Flora. She fell sound asleep after luncheon and looked as if she would not stir for hours. Daniel had gone out on business and Mary promised solemnly not to leave Flora's side.

"I'd be scairt to go out alone," she said. "You go and do your shopping, miss."

Even that was easy, for Mary had assumed she had no other intention than to stroll about the shops.

A hansom cab would take her to Pentonville in an hour or less. Then she must persuade the governor to allow her to see Robin. She must say she had come a long journey and would not be in London again for many months.

The scheme worked. She could not believe her good fortune—except that the governor had a certain susceptibility to good-looking young women, for there had been a look in his eye that was not entirely paternal.

Robin was brought from his cell. She had to talk to him through bars, it was true, and a warder watched from the end of the dismal room. But Robin was there, thin, emaciated, overjoyed to see her.

"Lavinia! You look so well. Are you happy? You must be to look as you do."

"Yes, I am happy. I have a very good position. Have you had my letters?"

"Yes. I'm glad you came because they're moving me to Dartmoor next week."

"Oh, Robin! Is it terrible in here?"

He gave his old careless shrug, infinitely pitiable because his shoulders were so thin.

"It's not a picnic. I suppose it could be worse. At least I haven't had jail fever. But you, Lavinia. Have I harmed your whole life? I can take imprisonment. When I come out, I'll emigrate. A man can start again. But you, your chances of marriage—are they ruined forever?"

She had to reassure him. He was so gaunt, so anxious.

"Goodness me, no. I have already had one offer."

"Really! A suitable offer? Do you love him?"

"No, and that's why I refused him. I don't intend to be in a hurry. You wouldn't want me to marry someone I didn't love, would you?"

He winced, remembering what he had done to her.

"Have you ever forgiven me?"

"But of course. We were both to blame. We had lived too recklessly."

His fingers came through the bars to grip hers. The warder was approaching, rattling his keys. The precious interview was almost over.

"Lavinia, promise me! Marry only for love."

"I promise. Even if I have to wait forever."

The length of Charlotte's life . . . And that would be forever.

Although he was thin and gaunt, Robin's health had not appeared to be too bad. That had been reassuring. But the whole visit had been so harrowing that all the way back in the cab Lavinia had had to set her face rigidly against tears. If Daniel were to see her come in weeping and distressed, the secret would be out. As it was, she wondered how she could restore her spirits sufficiently to dress and enjoy the theater.

But again, perhaps fortunately, things were made easy for her. Although Flora had aroused herself, she had found the exciting day too arduous for her and could scarcely hold her head upright. She only wanted to rest, but Miss Hurst was not to spoil her own evening.

Lavinia said that she would be glad to rest, too. Naturally she would not go out without Flora.

"Oh, yes, you are too," Flora insisted. "Papa said the theater could be postponed, but you and he would dine quietly, and you were to wear your new gown."

"He can't have said that!"

Flora's eyes dropped. "Well, not exactly, perhaps. He said you were to dine, but I added the piece about the new gown. Because I want to see you in it, and Papa will be disappointed if you don't look well."

There was a tap at the door, and Daniel, obviously having overheard Flora's remark, walked in.

"That is true, Miss Hurst. But don't look so alarmed. I am only proposing that we eat downstairs. I suggest seven o'clock. That will give you a little time to rest beforehand. You look as if your expedition this afternoon has tired you."

She flushed guiltily.

"I only went—to window gaze."

"I hope you found that a pleasant diversion," he replied imperturbably, and she was sure he did not believe her. The visit to Robin had brought back the past so vividly that it must be written on her face.

In spite of this all her good sense could not bring her to make the excuse of a headache or weariness to evade the meal this evening. She could not change, and become resigned to fate, as Robin seemed to have done. She was still wildly impetuous, running headlong to disaster.

Yet nothing could have been more correct than the dinner, sitting at a table in the corner of the hotel restaurant which specialized in good food rather than exotic decorations. They made formal conversation. They talked of Simon's school, of the possibilities of a good hunting season, of Flora's future as an heiress, of Edward's progress with Mr. Bush.

Then Daniel, in his polite voice, hoped she had not been offended by the misunderstanding in the dress shop.

She said "offended" was scarcely the word, "distressed" was a better one, and that was not so much because of the misunderstanding as the purchase of that unsuitable, extravagant gown.

"Flora must understand I can't accept gifts like that, Mr. Meryon. Your wife would be very disapproving, and for Mr. Peate to see me dressed like that would be fatal."

It must be the wine she had drunk that had made her speak so impulsively. She had never meant to show any sign of her private worry about Jonathon Peate. She might have known Daniel would seize on the scrap of information and demand to know the whole story.

"Fatal! That's a curious word to use."

"Yes. It was a little extravagant. It is only that—Mr. Peate admires me a little too much."

"I was aware of that, but I hadn't known his admiration gave you such apprehension. Does he persecute you? I asked you that once before, and you denied it. Were you telling the truth?"

She was about to say that Jonathon Peate's attentions were becoming intolerable when caution stopped the words. Supposing Daniel interfered and Jonathon carried out his threat to expose her?

"No, he doesn't persecute me, of course. I am really very good at discouraging unwanted attentions."

"You have had too many of these in your life?"

"It is not an asset, in my position, to have good looks," she said wearily. "Flora is very kind and generous, but that is something she doesn't realize. I should conceal my looks, not accentuate them. You realize that, Mr. Meryon. And yet you amuse yourself with things like that absurd charade in the shop today."

She hadn't meant to say that either. She certainly didn't anticipate his violent reaction to her words.

"*Amuse* myself! Is that what you think I was doing? Is a woman of your intelligence so blind? Come!" He pushed back his chair and stood up. "Let us go before I say more than I ever meant to."

He could scarcely restrain himself sufficiently to walk decorously behind her as they left the restaurant. He seemed to want to stride fast and furiously. His whole being was full of contained violence. On the stairs he said that he would see her to her room, then take a turn outdoors before retiring.

"And tear up that gown, Miss Hurst. Or give it to the poor. You're entirely right about not wearing it. Though don't think I lo—admire you less in poplin or whatever you term suitable attire."

"Love?" She had seized on the forbidden word, and turned so sharply that she stumbled on the turn of the stairs and was instantly caught in his arms. His kiss was inevitable. It seemed that no power on earth could have prevented their lips coming together.

But it was only for a moment.

Then he had held her away, his fingers bruising her shoulders.

"Don't make me say the words, Miss Hurst, or they will be forever between us."

"Lavinia," she said in a daze. "Lavinia is my name."

He dropped his hands.

"And this is what we are doomed to, Lavinia. Kissing on stairways. Can you bear it? Can you be content with such small things as being in the same room, eating at the same table, saying a formal good morning and good night? Because that is all we can have. Can you bear never to talk like this again? To embrace?"

"Yes," she said steadily.

"It will not drive you away?"

"It should. But no, it won't."

"And I can't even tell you—explain—about my marriage." His eyes were black with emotion. She had to bite her nails into her palms to stop herself from taking his face between her hands, saying that nothing mattered so long as they were under the same roof . . .

"You look so radiantly happy," he said.

"You told me yourself to take each day as it came."

"Yes, I did. And I told you we would use you, myself, Charlotte, Flora, Winterwood itself. You must have known it wasn't only for Flora that I begged you to stay."

"Perhaps that's why I look so happy."

"In spite of knowing that we must never talk like this again?"

"In spite of that."

"It's madness," he muttered. "When Flora walks again— You must think of your own future. Not my selfishness."

She did risk touching his face very briefly.

"I seem suddenly to have a great deal of courage," she said.

Chapter 16

THE barriers between them were too great to be overcome.

She had said that just to be under the same roof was enough, and for the present it was. But she knew that she was not going to be content always with crumbs. Sooner or later her passions would rebel. What then? Charlotte had said she brought an aura of disaster. And what was to happen after Christmas when Jonathon Peate demanded his answer? It seemed certain that her happiness was to be limited to a few weeks. She would try to live every minute of that time. If Flora could be got to walk, that achievement would be worth all the pain she and Daniel would eventually suffer.

Whether it were Lavinia's fault or not, there was another disaster when the little party returned to Winterwood. This time it struck Eliza. A diamond brooch belonging to Lady Tameson had been found among Eliza's belongings. It had been pinned inside one of her flannel petticoats and the petticoat rolled up and pushed to the back of her drawer. Its very manner of concealment was guilty. Obviously Eliza had stolen it.

Eliza swore passionately that she had not, that Lady Tameson had given it to her.

"She wanted me to have it, madam," she told Charlotte, her plain middle-aged face alight with earnestness and indignation. She had never before, in her life of honest service, been called a thief. "She said I had been kind to her, and begged me to have the brooch. It was for a keepsake. I didn't want to take it, madam. I swear I'm telling the truth, but she was that upset if I didn't."

Charlotte's face was cold and unforgiving.

"I suppose Miss Hurst got one, too. Did you, Miss Hurst? In gratitude for helping my aunt to make that disgraceful will?"

Lavinia's face flamed.

"Of course I did not. There was no question of bribery."

"Then what did Eliza's gift represent? Love? How can I possibly believe such a story? If my aunt gave her such a valuable gift it could only have been because she was persuaded into doing so. She was old and her mind was growing weak. She could have been easily persuaded, I don't doubt. But that is virtually the same as stealing."

Eliza, long-trained in meekness, proved to be a fiery opponent when aroused. She held her white-capped head high as the indignant words tumbled from her.

"If you must know, madam, my lady said she didn't suppose my wages were much, so I could sell the brooch. It would make a nice nest egg. That's the whole truth of it. But seeing as madam will never believe me, and my poor lady isn't here to say I'm telling the truth, I'll give in my notice. I won't stay in any house where I'm called a thief."

Lavinia made a dismayed protest, but Charlotte motioned her to be silent.

"That's very wise of you, Eliza. You have saved me the trouble of dismissing you. You can count yourself lucky I haven't called the police."

Eliza put out her hand for the brooch that lay on the table between them. With her new boldness she said, "Then I'll be taking my property, madam."

"You'll do nothing of the kind."

"Then I must be seeing the master. I fancy he'll believe me. Perhaps he might wonder how my private things came to be searched while I was absent. I'm not accustomed to working in houses where that sort of thing happens."

For a moment it looked as if Charlotte were going to have one of her wild turns. She pushed the brooch violently toward Eliza, saying, "Oh, take the wretched thing. Your drawers were searched because in making an inventory of my aunt's things one brooch was found to be missing. The search was made on Mr. Mallinson's instructions. If the brooch hadn't been found among your belongings, Miss Hurst's would have been searched also. Does that convince you?" She pressed her fingers to her temples in her familiar expression of weariness. "I'm sick and tired of the whole thing. There has been nothing but trouble since my aunt came here. I wish she had died in Venice. Alone in her palace. Why are you looking at me like that, Miss Hurst? She was dying anyway. Would a few weeks earlier have made so much difference? Only a fortune for my daughter, you are going to say. And the old lady lying in a grave where she doesn't belong."

"What are you saying, Mrs. Meryon?" Lavinia cried. "Lady Tameson does belong with her son."

Charlotte gave her a quick, startled glance, as if she had just realized clearly what she had said.

"I was only thinking that she had grown too foreign. She didn't belong in England anymore. She might have been happier under cypresses. Well, I did my best, and what thanks did I get?" Her voice went hard and cold. "Why are you standing there gaping at me, Eliza? I want you out of the house today."

Lavinia was more upset than Eliza. Indeed, now that she had calmed down, Eliza seemed almost happy to be going.

"Don't fret about me, Miss Hurst. I thought somehow it would come to this. The mistress was bound to find out about the brooch and I knew she'd never believe it was given to me. Not that I wanted it. It was only that my lady begged me to have it. It was the only way she knew to repay me, she said." Eliza's apron was lifted to her eyes. "My poor lady. I miss her too much, and that's the truth. I keep listening for her bell and it never rings. I'm better to go, Miss Hurst."

"But how will you get another position?" Lavinia refrained from saying that she knew all too well the difficulties of making a new start with a cloud over one's past.

But again Eliza was surprisingly calm and philosophical.

"Don't you worry, I'm going to take a short holiday first. I haven't had one since I was a girl. But I'll be sorry to say goodbye to you and Miss Flora. I don't suppose you'll be here forever, either, but I hope you'll be seeing Miss Flora through these troubles."

"Troubles?"

"Her not walking, and all," Eliza said, too quickly. Lavinia had a queer feeling that that was not what she had meant at all. Suddenly Eliza, too, had become a mystery. For she would say no more, and she was packed and gone within an hour. She said she had a sister in Norfolk where she would go and stay. She insisted on walking to the village. Lavinia watched her small square figure, laden with her wicker traveling bag, plodding away down the drive and out of sight. She was reminded suddenly of the strange woman who had called to see Lady Tameson, professing to be an old servant. She had almost forgotten that episode. But now it came back to her mind, and she was puzzled. Puzzled and uneasy. She didn't suppose she would ever see Eliza again.

She didn't know Jonathon Peate was standing behind her until she heard his familiar softly derisive laughter. She didn't know how long he had been there.

"Are you afraid that is going to happen to you one day, Miss Hurst?"

She looked into his mocking eyes.

"You did this!" she exclaimed. "You told Mrs. Meryon to have Eliza's things searched!"

"I gave my cousin advice, certainly. After all, the bauble is worth a few hundreds. Too much for a servant to get away with. Pity she has, after all. Charlotte is too soft."

"What do you *want* in this house, Mr. Peate?"

He enjoyed the direct attack. His eyes glinted.

"Mr. Peate? Still so distant? My name is Jonathon. And what do I want? Your answer, my little love. Among other things." He whistled between his teeth. "Among other things."

Lavinia was certain, now, that he had a personal interest in the missing brooch—as well as in more of Lady Tameson's possessions. He and Charlotte. Was that their conspiracy?

Daniel must have known about Eliza's dismissal, but Lavinia had no way of knowing what he thought. She only knew that a bank messenger was sent for from Dover, and he and Mr. Mallinson took away all Lady Tameson's jewelry in a locked box. It was to be put into safe custody until Flora's coming of age. Flora was a little regretful, as she had imagined herself doing what her great-aunt had done, occasionally bestowing a valuable piece of jewelry on someone who had pleased her. But she soon forgot the incident in the excitement of unwrapping her London purchases and inviting Edward to come and witness her munificence.

Edward was unusually subdued, and played quietly in Flora's room. He only set up a noisy protest when Bertha came to take him to his mother.

"I don't want to go. Tell Mamma that I'm busy."

Bertha was shocked. "As if I could do that. You come at once, you naughty boy."

Edward's lower lip was stuck out. "It's too hot in her room and she's always crying. I don't care about Great-aunt Tameson being dead. Do you, Flora?"

"Yes, I do," said Flora, as shocked as Bertha. "It's wicked not to care about people dying. How would you like it if no one cried over you?"

"I wouldn't care. And I wouldn't cry over you, or Mamma, or anybody. I especially wouldn't cry over you."

"You won't have to, because I'm never going to die," said Flora loftily.

"Now stop this nonsense and come, Master Edward," Bertha said impatiently.

"If Mr. Peate's with Mamma I won't come."

Bertha's face tightened.

"Mr. Peate isn't there. So come *along*."

Edward reluctantly followed her, his complaining voice coming back. "It isn't fair, Flora goes to London, and all I do is sit with Mamma. I find it exceedingly tiresome."

Flora watched his departure with brooding intensity. "Serves him right for being Mamma's pet. Why does Mamma never send for us? Why is it always Edward and that abominable Mr. Peate?"

"Flora! She gave you Sylvie. Didn't that show she loved you?"

"It was only a pretense," Flora said.

"Oh, come now—"

"I always knew it was a pretense. Crying for Great-aunt Tameson is only a pretense, too. It's to make people believe she's good when she's not. She's bad."

"Flora!"

"Bad, bad, bad!" Flora shouted, and began to cry so violently that Lavinia was alarmed. The child was overtired, overexcited. The trip to London had been too much for her. Perhaps Eliza's dismissal had been a shock for her, too. She must be quieted before she exhausted herself. The laudanum. This was the time for a drop in her hot milk before she was undressed and put to bed.

Lavinia rang the bell for Mary, and dispatched her for Flora's milk. The laudanum bottle was on the top shelf of the cupboard where Charlotte had left it after its last administration to Flora. She measured out the smallest quantity, corked the bottle and put it back. She intended to mention this remedy to Doctor Munro the next time he came, and ask if he approved of it.

It certainly worked wonders for Flora, for shortly after drinking it she was asleep, and there wasn't a sound from her until morning, when she woke in an alert and energetic frame of mind. She wanted to dress immediately and go downstairs. She no longer intended to be an invalid. Hadn't the doctor in London said that she would be walking in no time? So she would begin by having breakfast downstairs, only coming up at midmorning for her usual glass of milk and a rest if she was absolutely compelled to by exhaustion.

As it happened, this plan suited very well, for Mrs. O'Shaughnessy had arranged for the chimneys to be swept in readiness for Christmas, and Miss Flora's could be done among the first while she was out of the way.

Everyone was up and out early that morning. Daniel had had his horse brought round immediately after breakfast, and had gone off with his steward on an inspection of his tenant farms. A little later Charlotte, in her immaculate gray riding habit, had ridden off with a groom. She had lost the groom somewhere, perhaps conveniently, and come back in the company of Mr. Peate.

Flora, watching them through the window, seeing their animated conversation, Jonathon's head tilted toward Charlotte and her looking as if she were hanging on his words, exclaimed indignantly, "How dare Mr. Peate ride Neptune? Who gave him permission? I shall tell Papa."

"I don't think I would do that, since your mamma already knows." And approves, thought Lavinia.

"Does he think everything belongs to him?" Flora demanded. But her attention was diverted by Mary tapping at the door of the yellow parlor and asking where Miss Flora would have the hot chocolate she always drank in the morning.

She hadn't noticed Charlotte come up behind her, and started at the mistress' voice.

"She will have it in her room as usual, Mary. She is not to miss her rest before luncheon."

Flora scowled over her painting. She was not going to be lured by her mother's affectionate concern.

"I am not tired, Mamma. I prefer to stay down here."

The ride had brought a high color to Charlotte's cheeks. Her eyes were overbright, and curiously dilated, as if her conversation with Jonathon had excited or disturbed her.

"You will do as I tell you, Flora. We want you perfectly well for Christmas. Don't we, Jonathon?"

"Everyone must be bright and merry for Christmas," said Jonathon with his great laugh. "The wassailing season, what?"

"Miss Hurst, do I have to do what *he* says?" Flora demanded, as Charlotte went toward the stairs and Jonathon sauntered after her, his head held arrogantly, as if he owned the house and everything in it.

"No, but you must do as your mamma says. Very well, you may finish your painting first, if it doesn't take too long."

A little later they were interrupted again by a man with a very sooty face who put his head in the door and asked if they had seen his boy.

"The little varmint's vanished. I reckon he must be stuck up a flue. These be terrible treacherous chimbleys, all narrow bends. I know them, of old. And Willie's grown that much in the last year, drat him. I should have brought Percy. I would have if he didn't scare so bad. He comes out all a-tremble as if the chimbleys were full of ghosties. I declare I don't know what I'll make of Percy. Willie's a clever lad, a real bold one. But he will grow, the little varmint."

Flora was horrified. "Could that poor boy be stuck up a chimney? Would he starve there without anyone ever knowing?"

The sweep grinned, showing rotting teeth almost as black as his face.

"Reckon everyone would know, miss. Willie's got lungs like a pair of bellows. He'd be hollering plenty. I expect he's taken a wrong turning and come down in the wrong room, that's all there is to it."

As it happened, the sweep's guess was substantially correct. Willie had come down in the wrong room, Flora's. He had also decided, probably from sheer weariness, to curl up on the fur hearthrug beside the soot-spattered fireplace and go sound asleep.

He was only a very little boy. At first Flora screamed. He looked so black and ragged. Then, as Lavinia bent over him, she overcame her alarm and was full of pity.

"Oh, the poor little boy, Miss Hurst. He must have thought my hearthrug was soft and warm. Must we wake him up?"

"I'm afraid so, or his father will be angrier than ever." Lavinia gently shook the bony shoulder, scarcely covered by the ragged shirt, and as black as the sooty face and head. The child didn't stir. Even when she pulled him upright, his body merely sagged against her and slid to the floor again. She stared in surprise. If she hadn't known it to be impossible, she would have thought the boy in a drunken stupor. Had he had access to a decanter of port or some such thing in any of the rooms? But it was highly unlikely so small a child—he looked no more than six years old—would have a taste for wine.

She went quickly to the bell rope.

"What's the matter with him, Miss Hurst?" Flora asked in alarm. "Is he ill?"

"I think he must be. Or just quite worn out, poor baby."

"Couldn't we wash him and put him to bed?"

Flora was eager, and Lavinia had to say sharply that the little chimney sweep was not a new toy. He must be taken home by his father to whatever poor hovel they lived in. Certainly Flora might find an old jacket of Edward's for him later.

Mary came hastening to answer the bell, and Lavinia sent her for Mrs. O'Shaughnessy. Mrs. O'Shaughnessy was indifferent to the strange unconscious condition of the boy. "Lazy wretch," she said, and showed concern only for the soot streaked all over the hearthrug. The sweep was sent for to carry the boy downstairs. He would revive in the warm kitchen with some good hot soup put into him.

By this time Flora regarded the boy as her special concern. She demanded to be told what happened to him, and where he lived. She intended to call on his family, if he had one apart from his callous father, who thought it natural to send so small a child burrowing up the terrifying tunnels of numberless chimneys. She would take warm clothes and nourishing soups and some of Edward's old toys, if he could be persuaded to part with them.

"He should be playing with toys instead of climbing chimneys," she said heatedly.

"I know, but that's the way of the world," said Lavinia. "You can't cure it all by yourself."

"Now I am rich I can do many many things."

"You can drink your chocolate, to begin with. Oh, I see you have." Lavinia picked up the empty glass. "When did you drink it?"

"But I didn't, Miss Hurst. I haven't touched it."

"Then who has?" Lavinia frowned. "Why, I believe that bad boy must have."

Flora clapped her hands delightedly.

"That's what he did, and that's why he fell asleep. I expect he was hungry and thirsty and tired. I'm *glad* he had my milk."

"You're only glad because you didn't want it yourself. Never mind." Secretly Lavinia was glad, too. "Mary can bring some more."

She pulled the bell rope again, but when Mary came the chocolate was forgotten.

"Willie Jones can't be woken, miss! Cook has slapped and pinched him, and his father's terribly wild. He says he's shamming, the lazy little varmint. But cook says he's sick and they ought to get the doctor. And really, his head do fall sideways awful queer."

"He must have Doctor Munro," Flora declared. "Where's Papa? I want to see Papa."

By the time Daniel had returned from his morning inspection of the farms, Will Jones had carried his son off, still in that profound sleep. Daniel, however, on being told the story by Flora, agreed that Doctor Munro must call at the Joneses' cottage, and attend the boy. If he had been overcome by some strange sickness it must be diagnosed. But Daniel was inclined to the sweep's belief that his son had turned mutinous, and was cleverly shamming. Flora must put the incident out of her mind. Later today Doctor Munro would report, and if the boy were really ill she could call on him tomorrow. But only if his disease was not infectious. Flora, in her delicate state, would be just the person to be vulnerable to a fever.

Luncheon was a silent meal. Jonathon had returned to his lodgings in the village, which was a rare enough thing for him to do, as he was spending more and more time with his "beloved cousin," and Charlotte had sent a message that she had a headache and would be keeping to her room.

But halfway through luncheon she changed her mind and came down after all. She was suddenly standing in the doorway, her eyes sweeping over the people at luncheon, Daniel, Lavinia, Flora, Sir Timothy, and the quiet Mr. Bush. Then, without warning, she sank to the floor in a faint.

She recovered only when she lay on her bed, to which Daniel had carried her. Then she opened her eyes, the pupils so dilated that instead of having their habitual shining colorlessness they seemed black.

"You shouldn't have attempted to come down," Daniel was saying. Because of his alarm, his voice sounded harsh.

"Don't scold me," Charlotte said faintly. "I was only—lonely—up here."

Her eyes went past Daniel to Lavinia. And it was then that Lavinia had the certain knowledge that Charlotte was afraid of something. Deadly afraid. She couldn't bear to be alone even with Bertha in the next room. She was even seeking reassurance from Lavinia, whom she hated.

"I shall send for Doctor Munro," Daniel was saying.

"No, no. I don't need him. I'm not ill. I only—rode too far this morning. It was foolish of me. But Jonathon—persuaded me." She raised herself on an elbow, her ashen face entreating. It seemed as if she might be afraid of shrewd old Doctor Munro, too, as if he might read her secrets. "See, I am better already. If I could have just a teaspoonful of brandy." Tears suddenly ran down her cheeks. "I'm sorry to be so weak. I hate it so much."

Daniel administered the brandy, and straightened himself. He had used no word of endearment, Lavinia had noticed. He had been kind, capable, but remote. It was as if, all at once, he had given up his unequal struggle with his wife's temperament and vapors.

"I'll ring for Bertha," he said.

"No, let me stay with her," Lavinia said. "Flora will be all right for a little while."

"Will she?" Charlotte's eyes were still dark with her secret thoughts.

"Perhaps Mr. Bush might take her and Edward for a walk," Lavinia suggested. "She would enjoy that."

"I'll give orders," said Daniel. "Thank you, Miss Hurst." He stooped briefly over Charlotte. "Try to rest, my dear."

Lavinia hardly knew why she had offered to stay in the darkened room with the fragile figure lying so quietly in the bed. She had had the vaguely hopeful idea that alone with her Charlotte might talk. However, the minutes went by and there was no sound from the bed. Lavinia thought Charlotte had fallen asleep, but a little later she stirred and said that she was cold. Even when Lavinia had put another blanket over her, she shivered.

"It must be very cold to be dead." The words were only a whisper. Afterwards Lavinia wondered if she had heard them correctly, although she was beginning to shiver herself.

Chapter 17

FLORA, Edward and Mr. Bush came back from their walk in high spirits. Flora's cheeks were pink, and her hands full of the leaves and berries Mr. Bush had gathered for her.

"We went down to the lake, Miss Hurst. In the summer Mr. Bush says he will row us out to the island. Oh, and what do you think, Miss Hurst? Willie Jones has had to be put in the cottage hospital. Doctor Munro says he nearly died. He was poisoned!"

Lavinia, still oppressed by the afternoon in Charlotte's darkened room, began to shiver again; she didn't know why. Flora was only being melodramatic, as usual.

"He couldn't have been poisoned. That's a tale."

"No, it isn't, Miss Hurst. He'd been eating berries he'd picked from the hedges. Doctor Munro said it was a very dangerous habit. And I want to go and visit Willie in the hospital. May I, Miss Hurst?"

"Well—tomorrow, perhaps. Why?"

"Because I think his father is cruel to him, making him go up all those dark chimneys, and then starving him so that he has to eat poisonous berries. I want to tell him that I'm not cross with him for drinking my chocolate. And Edward has promised to give him some of his toys."

"Only my old ones," Edward said definitely.

"Oh, you're a selfish pig. You have so many toys you could spare a new one."

"I have not so many, and I'm not rich like you so that I can buy all I want."

"Who told you I was rich?"

"Mamma did. She said it wasn't fair of Great-aunt Tameson to leave you all her money, and she would have to see that it was made up to me in other ways."

"Spoiled little beast," said Flora. "Mamma's pet! But you could give Willie some of your French soldiers."

"What does a chimney sweep want with soldiers? He wouldn't know how to play with them."

"He would so. Anyway, I would show him."

Their voices continued to wrangle as Lavinia sat silently, wondering about her vague alarm, and why she could not identify the thing that alarmed her.

Flora insisted on visiting Willie the next day. He was wide-awake now and sitting up in bed looking important. His face, without its coating of soot, was pale and perky, with a squirrel brightness. He seemed pleased rather than otherwise about his brush with death.

"The doctor had to pump out me stomach, so he did. I'd been eating them berries. I didn't know as they were poisonous. They never did poison me before. Now I'm to stay here for a week and have nourishing foods. Pa's mad as anything. He says if I stay here and eat too much I'll get too fat and then I'll be no use. But reckon I can find another job."

"What sort of job do you want, Willie?" Flora asked earnestly.

"I'll do anything, miss," Willie said cheerfully. He tensed his skinny arm. "I'm strong as a horse."

"Then I shall ask Papa to give you a position. You can be gardener's boy for the present, and later, when I get my own establishment, you can come to that."

Flora was doing her grand-lady act, and the little bundle of bones sitting up in the hospital nightshirt was suitably impressed.

"Oh, miss, that'll be a rare treat. Then you're not cross with me for drinking that stuff in your room. It tasted fine and I was fair starving, although I'd been eating all them berries. But I'm sorry I did it. I didn't know you was so kind."

"There will be plenty of milk for you to drink in my house. I'll never allow one of my servants to be hungry. Miss Hurst, where are the toys Edward sent?"

Lavinia produced them, and Flora tumbled them onto the bed. But Willie was much more interested in his youthful benefactor.

"Ain't you got no legs, miss? Do you have to sit in that chair forever?"

Flora abruptly tumbled from her magnanimous lady-of-the-manor pose to that of an indignant child.

"Indeed I do not, Willie Jones! Don't you ever say that to me again or I'll tell Papa about you drinking my chocolate. That was stealing. You could be put in jail for it. I'd never be able to employ anyone who had been in jail."

"I never bin in jail, miss!" Willie was losing the thread of the conversation, and so was Flora, who began a discourse on the evils and corruption of the unfortunates who had served prison sentences.

"You're talking too much and foolishly, Flora," Lavinia said sharply. "Come, we must go."

"But it's true, Miss Hurst. I could never trust anyone who had been in jail to be near me. Papa would never never allow it. Do you believe he would, Miss Hurst?"

"No," said Lavinia quietly. "No, I don't."

At first, when she found the laudanum bottle in Flora's room two-thirds empty, she blamed the servants. One of them must have been helping herself for some reason, perhaps toothache or some other trouble. Though to take such a lethal dose just for toothache would be mad.

But Mary, when Lavinia questioned her, said in her shrewd way, "Lor, if anyone was to take that much, Miss Hurst, they would be dead asleep for hours, and Mrs. O'Shaughnessy would be bound to know."

Dead asleep. Willie Jones had been dead asleep . . .

Willie Jones had drunk Flora's chocolate, left prepared by Mary. No one had known he would come down the chimney and drink it. The chocolate had been Flora's usual midmorning drink, and naturally it was assumed—by whom?—that she would drink it. But Willie Jones had been hungry and thirsty and had found the steaming cup of refreshment irresistible. And he might later have died had he not had prompt medical attention and a tough constitution.

Flora had not a tough constitution . . .

Lavinia put down the bottle very carefully to conceal the fact that her hand was shaking. She had to see Daniel at once. There were a thousand monstrous thoughts crowding into her head. Charlotte had bought the laudanum from the apothecary in the village. She had said that Flora had toothache, which had not been true. She had insisted that Flora be given a dose whenever she was in a tense and overwrought condition. For that purpose the bottle had been left conveniently at hand.

Charlotte had come in from riding that morning with Jonathon Peate. They had been talking earnestly.

She had immediately enquired whether Flora had had her morning chocolate, and insisted that she do so.

Later, when she had looked in at luncheon and had seen Flora sitting at the table, perfectly normal, she had fainted.

She had said, "It must be very cold to be dead."

She had bitterly resented Flora, her own daughter, being an heiress.

If Flora were to die, her parents, as her next of kin, would automatically inherit her fortune.

If it were to be found that Flora had died from an overdose of a drug, Charlotte would insist that Lavinia had been careless in administering it. It would be little use for Lavinia to deny that, for, with the ensuing notoriety, her past would inevitably come out. She would be blackened before she was heard.

Lavinia tried to compose herself. Surely all those wild imaginings were untrue, merely pieces of a nightmare.

But Daniel must be told.

Daniel was out, and when he came in, he was occupied with his steward. It seemed as if he would never be free.

When Lavinia at last was able to see him, she had worked herself into such a state of agitation that she could scarcely speak coherently.

At first he misunderstood her and demanded twice, "Is Flora all right?"

"Yes, Mr. Meryon. I have told you that it was the chimney sweep's boy who—had the accident. But it was intended to have been Flora, I am sure."

She hadn't thought his face could go so cold, so hard.

"Did Doctor Munro say the boy had had a dose of laudanum?"

"No, Doctor Munro attributed the cause to the berries Willie had eaten. Some of them must have been poisonous. But there was the bottle almost empty. The last time I used it—"

"*You* used it, Miss Hurst?" He might have been speaking to a stranger, and a stranger he distrusted at that.

"Yes, I gave Flora a few drops the other night when she was hysterical."

"Did you often do this?"

"Only once or twice. Mrs. Meryon had told me to do so. I admit it did work wonders."

"It was only a small bottle?"

"Quite a small one. I can show it to you."

"Then if you had used it several times, wouldn't it have been nearly empty? Are you sure you remember just how full it was?"

"I am not blind."

He looked at her, his distrustful gaze suggesting that if she were not blind her memory might be unreliable.

"Was the cupboard the bottle was in locked?"

"No."

"Then anyone could have had access, any servant who might have a secret taste for opium. Oh, these things, as I am sure you must know, do happen. A habitual opium drinker doesn't necessarily fall asleep. When, apart from today, did you look at the bottle to see how empty it was?"

He flung the questions at her as if he were cross-examining her in a court of justice. The echoes of other questions were so vivid— "Will the witness tell the court on what terms she was with the deceased. Friendly? Intimate? Did she, earlier in the evening, invite him to her room? Was the game of cards a pretext for that midnight meeting?" Lavinia began to feel dizzy. She could hardly believe that this inquisitor's face before her was Daniel's, that it was Daniel's cruel unrelenting voice to which she was listening.

"You see, Miss Hurst, you can't swear to any of these things, yet you seem to be suggesting that my wife may have had something to do with this. How *dare* you!"

She wouldn't let herself realize that he had the grim look of a man whose heart was breaking. She only knew that she could be as angry as he.

"I do dare because I care about your daughter's well-being. Yes, I do care, little as I wanted to when I first came. And I am not accusing anyone in particular. I am only telling you the facts. Before you completely discredit what I say, you must at least discuss this with Doctor Munro. And with your wife, and her cousin. I have told you that it was your wife who encouraged the use of laudanum in the first place. She had got it by telling the chemist she wanted it for Flora's toothache, but Flora didn't have toothache. Why should she have told a lie?"

As quick as a flash he had seized on that weakness in her story.

"At that time her aunt was alive?"

"Yes."

"She hadn't made the new will? At least Charlotte didn't know about it."

"No, she didn't."

"Then what fantastic story did your mind invent, Miss Hurst, as the reason for my wife's obtaining a deadly poison? That she had plans to hasten her aunt's death in case she should change her mind about her will?"

"You can't be making jokes!"

"No. I am not making jokes. I have no motives for doing so." She seemed to shrivel before his accusing eyes. Could he think she was trying deliberately to destroy Charlotte? "You had better go back to your charge."

"And you?" she got out.

"I will do as I think fit."

There was nothing to do but go and leave him there. This was no time to think of her own feelings. If she had blackened herself in his eyes forever, at least she had the wry satisfaction of having acted purely for Flora. Had she been wild and impulsive? Did her mind run too much on disaster? Perhaps it did. Perhaps her own tragic experience had deprived her of the ability to reason calmly. Perhaps she had imagined the lethal reduction in the contents of the laudanum bottle. Perhaps Charlotte had taken a dose herself, as probably she often did, and her addiction to it had been her sole reason for buying it.

There must be a simple answer. She was sure she could find it if she were to reflect calmly.

But all she could wonder, with frozen disbelief, was that that man downstairs with his hard eyes and cruel words could ever have said he loved her.

When Flora had her supper later, Lavinia had Mary bring an extra tray. She didn't feel like going down to dinner, she said. Flora had to be reassured that she was not ill, but later the child was doubly intrigued by the activity that went on.

"Miss Hurst, what *are* you doing?"

Lavinia was carrying in blankets and directing Mary and Lily, who were panting with the weight of the mattress they carried.

"Put it there, by the window. I intend to sleep in here, Flora. Now that you're getting so strong I have the fear you might fall out of bed in the night. I have never thought you should sleep alone."

Flora was instantly suspicious.

"Am I worse?"

"No, you're much better. That's what I'm telling you."

"Are you telling me the truth?"

"Of course I am. When do I not tell you the truth?"

"Then why are you looking so angry? I don't need you to sleep in my room if you hate it."

For once Lavinia couldn't keep her patience.

"Don't be so aggravating, pray. You must allow me to use my discretion."

The servants were puzzled, too. She knew they would start gossiping. All the better. The sooner—someone—knew that Flora was never to be alone at any moment of the day or night the better it would be.

The mistress had gone down to dinner, Mary reported. Her face had looked as pale as a ghost's, and she had worn her black mourning again. Then she had been upset because the master wasn't there, but he had come in late, when they had reached the third course. He said he had had late business out of doors. Mr. Peate was there, of course, and he, for once, was in a bad temper and hardly spoke at all. But he drank a great deal (this report had come from Joseph, who had been waiting on table) and smoked the master's cigars. He had sat over the port alone after the master and Sir Timothy had retired to the library. Sir Timothy had been saying something about the plans for the new wing arriving, but the master had said he was no longer interested in them, at least not at this particular time. He had too many other things to worry about.

Daniel, as well as Charlotte, would have benefited from Flora's death. He could have gone ahead with his cherished plans for Winterwood, which had had to be put aside when Lady Tameson had made her new will. He could have attempted to console himself for the loss of his dearly loved daughter by making an historic addition to his equally beloved house.

The twisted thoughts would not leave Lavinia. At last she sat down to write to Eliza, whom she missed sadly. Eliza had begged for news from time to time, especially news of Flora. She had left her sister's address in Norfolk with Lavinia.

It was a great relief to pour all her deadly worries onto paper. Eliza, at a distance from the events, would be able to reason calmly, and draw conclusions. Lavinia sealed the letter, and sent it down to the mailbag in the hall, and wondered impatiently how long she would have to wait for an answer.

Then she began to prepare for bed, her pallet on the floor, where she would sleep uneasily, if at all. Never had she felt as alone as this.

She had just begun to remove her dress, however, when there was a tap at the door and Phoebe was there saying that the master wanted to see her downstairs. She, Phoebe, was to sit with Flora until Lavinia came back.

He was in the library alone. He told her brusquely to shut the door and then to come and sit by the fire. She said, childishly, that she preferred to stand and hear what he had to say, but he said curtly that he was tired, and how could he sit down if she were standing.

So the scene became warm and intimate against her will. What blandishments was he going to use on her now? The hard look had gone from his face, and he did look tired, as he had said.

"Why were you not down to dinner, Miss Hurst?"

"I preferred to eat with Flora."

"Yes. Yes, I see. Has Phoebe remained with her now?"

"Yes, Mr. Meryon."

"Good. Well, then, you will want to hear what Doctor Munro had to say."

Lavinia could not help leaning forward eagerly.

"You saw him?"

"I saw him and discussed the type of poison from which Willie Jones was suffering."

"And what did he say?"

"He's an old fool. Half-blind, too. I can't think why we still use him except that he has always been our family doctor. Still, one can't go on employing a doctor who has the beginnings of cataract in both eyes. I didn't realize how bad his sight was until this evening. He dropped his pipe and couldn't see where it had fallen although it was right in front of his eyes."

"But what did he say about Willie, Mr. Meryon?"

"He said the boy admitted to eating wild berries which had never previously harmed him, but this time he had obviously got hold of one of the more deadly varieties, white bryony most likely, since its red berries would attract him. Or it may have been black nightshade, which looks exactly like black currants. The stomach wash proved that he had eaten berries, and also drunk milk. Doctor Munro hadn't thought to suspect the milk since the evidence of the berries was there before him, but he did admit the boy's symptoms of extreme drowsiness and inertia could come from other forms of poison, such as opium. The main thing was that the patient was recovering and had no doubt learned his lesson about eating or drinking rashly."

"Is that all?" said Lavinia. "Then there is nothing conclusive?"

"Nothing. Unlike you, Miss Hurst, I have no intention of declaring that Willie Jones has nearly died of a drink intended for my daughter."

"You don't believe it!"

"Do you?"

"I'm—not sure."

"Will it comfort you to hear that my wife admits to having taken laudanum on two occasions recently, one only last night. She said she couldn't sleep. You yourself know her nervous state, so I don't think you can deny the truth of her story."

"No," Lavinia admitted reluctantly.

"I want the contents of that bottle emptied."

"Is that all you are going to do?"

"I want also to apologize to you for the way I spoke this afternoon. You had given me a very unpleasant shock."

"I know."

"I think you may have to go, Miss Hurst."

"Go!"

She met his bleak eyes.

"The situation is—untenable. I had thought—but it isn't possible. How do you find Flora since her visit to London?"

"Stronger."

"Yes. I thought so myself. I believe she will recover. After Christmas Edward will go to school with Simon and I intend to take Flora abroad for an indefinite time. If you would be good enough to stay until then"—he put out his hand—"if it isn't asking too much. I am sure you understand."

"The situation is the same as it was when we were in London," Lavinia burst out.

"No, it is worse. Much worse." He seemed about to explain more, then changed his mind, and gave her instructions in his impersonal voice. "Until then I don't want Flora left alone at any time. I believe you have been making plans about this yourself. I appreciate your caution, and though I am sure it isn't necessary, we'll take no risks. Does that satisfy you?"

She had forgotten her own pain in the realization of his.

"Mr. Meryon, this situation can't go on forever!"

"Oh, it is most unlikely to. Strangely enough, the world doesn't come to an end. In the meantime, it is going to be the festive season and I want the children happy. That is your task, Miss Hurst. Can you manage it?"

She said yes because there was nothing else to say.

Chapter 18

Jonathon Peate watched her come out of the library. She gave a violent start as he laughed behind her. He had been standing in the shadows, a glass in his hand, swaying a little. The ruddy color in his cheeks was heightened, his hair disheveled.

"The pretty watchdog, eh?" he observed genially.

Had he been at the keyhole listening to hers and Daniel's conversation? She didn't think he was capable of doing so. He looked too drunk.

But he had known she was in the library, and must have been waiting for her to come out.

"I don't know what you mean."

"Oh, come now, my sweet little darling, when were you unintelligent? You're too bloody intelligent for a woman. But I like you in spite of that. When are you going to give me your answer?"

She backed away in distaste, one eye on the library door lest Daniel should come out and hear this revealing conversation.

"You couldn't think you would endear yourself to me by this behavior!"

"My dearest high and mighty young lady, I have given up trying to endear myself to you. From now on I use other methods." He began to laugh again, his soft drunken laughter much worse than his usual hearty shout.

"The same as you use with Mrs. Meryon?" she retorted swiftly. It was a shot at random, and rather disturbingly found its mark.

For one moment his bold eyes slid from hers. Then he laughed again and said, "I adore my beautiful cousin. But she's a high-strung creature, and far too greedy. In spite of all that she already has. Winterwood, a good-looking husband"—he paused significantly—"even that pasty-faced cripple you are trying so hard to protect."

"What do you know about that?"

He ignored that question and went on, "You and I are the outsiders here. Isn't it the logical thing for us to join up? Stop wasting your time casting languishing glances at Daniel. He's married. You'll never get him. Anyway, he's a dull stick. I can give you a great deal more fun and excitement than Daniel Meryon ever could. And you like excitement, don't you, my lovely Lavinia?"

Lavinia twitched her skirts about her to pass him. He began to laugh again at her white-faced anger.

"Don't look so murderous! I believe I'll scarcely be safe here until after Christmas. Do you remember—that's the date for your answer. We start the new year together."

Again her question came without her apparent volition.

"Why do you wait until then? Why don't you demand an answer now, if you are as impatient as you say? What is to be gained by waiting?"

He had spilled a little of the brandy out of his glass. He stood staring at the small pool on the parquet floor with a suddenly very drunken look.

"Go back to your watchdog duties," he said thickly. "Mind your own business and I'll mind mine."

What was his business? To get what pickings he could, since he must have been as disappointed as Charlotte by his aunt's will? But how was he planning to get them, and how could she expose him without him exposing her?

She stood in the bedroom holding the candle over Flora's sleeping face. The child was growing so much prettier. Her cheeks were quite round, and gently flushed. Her mouth had a soft curve. She looked happy. She was dreaming of Christmas, or perhaps her romantic attachment for Mr. Bush. Or perhaps of walking again. Supposing she were to be wakened and told that her dear Miss Hurst, who she trusted completely, was a murderess!

For Jonathon would not mince words if he carried out his threat. It might be that she would be forced to tell Flora the whole story herself—and watch the child shrinking away from her, shocked and disillusioned, taking refuge in her invalidism, her chance of recovery postponed perhaps forever.

How could she have become so emotionally involved with this child, who in the sunlit square in Venice had been so unlikable? She had never dreamed this would happen, nor that her emotions could involve her in such a dangerous situation. What was she to do? Go on fending off that drunken man's advances, and praying for a miracle? But what was the miracle to be? She must, in the meantime, simply do as Daniel had asked and keep Flora happy. Then Christmas would be over, Simon and Edward would be at school, and Daniel would be free to wander Europe with his heiress daughter.

Christmas was never meant to be a menace nor life so cruel.

Disappointingly, in spite of daily massage and constant encouragement, Flora's legs remained stubbornly lifeless. Finally one day she had one of her outbursts of temper, and struck Lavinia's arm as she was rubbing the limp ankles.

"Oh, leave me alone, Miss Hurst! It's no use. I'm always going to be a cripple."

"I expect you are, if you want to be."

"Want to be!" Flora screeched. "How could anyone want to be ugly and horrid like this?"

"Perhaps they might think they get petted and pampered this way."

"But I don't! You scold me, and Papa goes out all day and takes Simon, and Mamma only wants Edward! I hate you! I hate everybody. I wish I were dead. I'd like to be buried with Great-aunt Tameson," she went on, beginning to enjoy her morbidity. "She was the only one who loved me. I could eat some poisonous berries like Willie Jones. Only I would have to make my will first, wouldn't I?"

"Flora, stop being so precocious! You're a silly little girl just showing off. Making your will, indeed!"

"I shan't put you in it if you're going to be so horrid. I shan't tell you who I'll put in it. I'll keep it a secret."

There was a commotion at the door as Edward banged on it unceremoniously and then burst in.

"I heard you saying you'd got a secret, Flora. I've got one, too."

"You have not. You're making that up," Flora said bad-temperedly.

"I am not. Mamma told me one."

"She did not."

"She did so. She told me an important one." His lively little face began to grow uncertain. "But I don't really want to go and live in London just with Mamma."

Flora pounced without mercy.

"Is that the secret? You see, you haven't kept it after all. What an untrustworthy little boy you are. Mamma ought to be more careful what she tells you." Her face tightened as she said suspiciously, "Why is Mamma taking just you away? Why are you to live in London?"

"I don't know. She said I could see the Household Cavalry ride past every day, and we'd go to pantomimes and things. But I thought I was to go to school with Simon."

Flora's mind was occupied broodingly on this startling information.

"I wouldn't care in the least for a hundred troops of Household Cavalry. Anyway, Papa would never allow you to go. Mamma's just making up a story."

"She said there'd be no one else, not even Cousin Jonathon." Edward was plainly worried. It didn't seem that he had invented this fantasy. "I'd rather there was someone else, even old Bushie. Are you hoping to talk to old Bushie at the party, Flora? He's hoping you will. He picked some berries and things for you to draw on our botany lesson this morning." Edward added, in a clever imitation of Mr. Bush's soft, hurrying voice, "I think these may provide a charming study for your sister, Master Edward. She's very clever with her pencils. You'd do well to imitate her industry."

Flora's bad temper was melting into blushes and giggles.

"You don't know what 'imitate her industry' means."

"No, and I don't care. Grown-up talk is tiresome. Mamma makes me stay while she and Cousin Jonathon are talking. She says I'm not to leave because she doesn't like to be alone with him."

"What nonsense. She's often alone with him. She rides with him and walks with him, and laughs as if she likes it."

"No, she does not. He follows her, she says, and she has to pretend to be polite. Anyway, he's getting married soon and going to America, and I'm jolly glad."

"Getting married! Cousin Jonathon!" Flora lifted her eyes to the ceiling. "I pity his bride. Who is she to be?"

"How should I know? He just keeps saying he is going to America to settle down with his wife, and then we'll never see him again. But he says it's a pity that steamship passages are so expensive, especially for two."

"What else does he say?" Lavinia thought that her voice was admirably casual.

"Nothing else. I don't listen much. I don't want to know about his old wife. Mamma doesn't either. She says 'the sooner the better' and why doesn't he go at once, and he says doesn't she remember she begged him to stay to make Christmas jollier after the sad death in the house. And then he kisses her hand and she cries."

"Why does she cry?" Flora demanded.

"I don't know. Perhaps he bites her finger."

"Edward!" Flora giggled irrepressibly. "Mamma can't cry because she's jealous of this wife he is to marry. After all she has Papa. I wonder who this lady is."

Not content with wondering, Flora decided to ask Jonathon point-blank. This she chose to do that day at luncheon.

"I hear you are to be married, Cousin Jonathon," she said in her most grown-up voice. "I congratulate you."

Jonathon bowed toward her. His eyes glinted with amusement. "Thank you, Flora. That's very civil of you, I'm sure."

"But it isn't fair that we shouldn't know who your wife is to be. Is it, Papa? Mamma?"

"Is this the spirited young lady you talked about?" Charlotte inquired. "I believe you likened her to a blood horse."

"Someone from these parts, my boy?" asked Sir Timothy, who liked to know what was going on.

Jonathon put his finger to his lips. "Silence!" he said. "I have promised the lady."

"There's some reason for secrecy?" Daniel asked, with interest.

"I bow to a feminine whim. But this can scarcely interest you. She isn't a lady whose family or background you know. I met her at her home in London quite some time ago. Since then, I have kept in touch. Ladies," he addressed Flora specifically, "enjoy being wooed."

"Are you dying of love for her?" Flora asked. Her antagonism was temporarily forgotten in this new development.

"I hope to survive. Though the lady in question has a fatal effect on men."

"Is she so beautiful?" Flora was impressed.

"When you see her at her best. Fatally beautiful."

Charlotte made a sudden exclamation. "Jonathon! You're being ridiculous. Don't fill the child's head with nonsense."

"But I wasn't joking, dear Charlotte. Upon my word!"

The result of that little exchange was that Flora informed Edward that Cousin Jonathon's betrothed was a mysterious beautiful lady like a blood horse, and Edward began to neigh and stamp and begged Flora to fall in love with him. Both children were put out when Lavinia sharply told them to be sensible and not play such a silly game.

"But, Miss Hurst, we're so happy that Cousin Jonathon is getting married and going away. Even if he is to marry a horse!"

The giggles broke out afresh and were unstoppable. Lavinia had to give up and let them go on with their nonsense. She supposed she had to be thankful that Jonathon's enigmatic remarks were not as appallingly clear to Flora and everyone else as they were to her. She fancied Daniel had been suspiciously silent. But she was fancying things about everyone. The strain was becoming unbearable. She wished a hundred times that she had not made a promise to stay until after Christmas. She would so dearly like to quietly disappear into an obscurity where no one would find her again. Then, a moment later, she would look across a room and see Daniel's preoccupied face—he was scarcely outdoors at all now; only she knew that he was quietly and unobtrusively keeping everyone under observation—and doubt whether she could ever bring herself to leave Winterwood. The party spirit had never seemed so impossible to capture.

To everyone's surprise, Charlotte announced her intention of making a journey to London to do some shopping for Christmas. Daniel protested, asking her why, when she hadn't accompanied him and Flora and Miss Hurst.

"Because now I have changed my mind," she said. Her voice was quite gay and good-tempered, but it seemed to have an underlying strain. Her fingers, Lavinia noticed, were never still. They fiddled with her rings, her pearl necklace, occasionally the small rosy pearls in her ears. "Anyway, my shopping is a secret. If everyone in this house is to have secrets, why shouldn't I?"

She would take Bertha, she said. They would stay overnight and return by the afternoon train the next day.

"She's going to find a house for her and Edward!" Flora hissed. "That's what she means by it being a secret."

"Nonsense! She wouldn't do that without telling Papa." Since Flora seriously believed the absurdity, Lavinia added, "Where would she get the money to buy a house?"

"She would sell some of her jewels."

"What a little romancer you are," Lavinia said, but privately she, too, was almost certain that it was not something so innocent as Christmas shopping that took Charlotte on a journey she hated in midwinter.

She was absent two days, and returned looking peaked and tired. She declared she was exhausted after that awful train journey; the carriage was full of soot and it was freezing cold. But she had accomplished her shopping successfully and no one was to ask a single question until Christmas Day.

Someone, however, did ask a question, and that was Jonathon. His conversation with Charlotte was obviously not meant for other ears, for they were both abruptly silent when Lavinia, wheeling Flora into the long gallery where they proposed to decorate the Christmas tree, came unexpectedly on them.

It had been impossible to hear the end of their conversation. "Not enough," said Jonathon genially. "Sorry."

Charlotte saw Lavinia and Flora approaching, and cried gaily, "Cousin Jonathon says I should have bought more baubles for the Christmas tree. He has such extravagant ideas."

"It's nothing to do with him," Flora said in some surprise. "Simon and Miss Hurst and I are decorating the tree. Why are you here, Mamma? You have never wanted to help before."

"Perhaps I do want to this year." Charlotte was twisting her hands nervously. Lavinia hoped Flora did not identify the peculiar light in her eyes as fear. It seemed very plain to her.

"Our dear Flora knows what she wants, as usual," observed Jonathon. "What an extraordinary daughter for you to have, Charlotte. You who never know your own mind. But that's your fascination. Do as Flora suggests. Leave the tree to her and the admirable Miss Hurst. Come and tell me more about your expedition to London. I'm beginning to hanker for the big cities myself, delightful as Winterwood is. After Christmas . . ."

Their voices died away. It seemed as if Charlotte were mesmerized into accompanying Jonathon to some other more private place where their conversation could be continued without interruption.

"After Christmas can't come quickly enough," said Flora, "if it means saying goodbye to that horrible Mr. Peate. Even if Mamma takes Edward to London, I shall be happy here with you and Papa. You don't dislike me quite so much now, do you, Miss Hurst?"

"I find you tolerable," Lavinia said gruffly.

Flora really had an extraordinarily sweet smile. Perhaps Lavinia found it so because it was uncannily like her father's.

"Oh, thank you, Miss Hurst. I really believe you are speaking the truth at last."

When had she ever been speaking the truth? Lavinia wondered that, miserably, when, dressed in the yellow taffeta gown for the Christmas party, Flora pronounced that she was as beautiful as she had been at the opera in Venice when they had first noticed her.

Lavinia twitched at the skirt uneasily.

"It's quite absurd, Flora, that I should dress like this. It's unsuitable, to say the least."

"But I have ordered you to wear the dress I gave you," Flora said regally. She sighed with sheer delight. "You really do look exceptionally well, Miss Hurst. Have you studied yourself in the mirror?"

Lavinia had done that and turned away from her reflection. Of what use to look her best? The man she loved could not look at her, and the one she hated would look all too long.

"I believe you are fatally beautiful like that lady Mr. Peate talks about," Flora mused, and was startled when Lavinia begged her not to talk like that. "Why not, Miss Hurst? I would adore to have a fatal beauty."

"Well, perhaps you will when you have your own party dress on," Lavinia said brusquely. "You have stared enough at me. Now let us attend to you. Would you like your hair up?"

Flora's cheeks went pink with pleasure.

"May I? Oh, I should like that above all things. It will compensate for having to sit in a chair. But if I am to have my hair up, aren't I too old to wear a pink sash? And must I wear that baby necklace of coral beads? I'd much prefer Great-aunt Tameson's diamonds. When shall I be old enough to wear them?"

"What about living in the present?" Lavinia suggested. "Putting your hair up is a big enough step for one day."

But when Flora was dressed in the stiff white dress, and her swept-up hair gave her narrow, delicate face a premature maturity and showed her long neck, very white and slender and young, she promptly burst into tears.

"What is the *use*, when I can't walk? I thought I would be able to walk for Christmas and I can't. Who is to admire me when I am a cripple?"

"Hush, love, hush! Indeed no one will admire you if your face is red from crying. Stop it at once. I'll get a little of my rice powder for your nose if you'll stop this minute."

With a tremendous effort Flora controlled her tears, though her thin bosom still heaved. She let Lavinia dab her nose with powder and managed a wan smile.

"But it is a tragedy all the same, Miss Hurst."

"Well, do you know, I think Mr. Bush would be too shy to talk to you if you were walking about like everyone else. As it is, I am sure he will sit beside you while the rest of us dance."

A little less mournful, Flora began to pat the neat cluster of ringlets tied with ribbon on the top of her head.

"Do you think he will notice that my hair is up?"

"We must assume he has remarkably poor sight if he doesn't."

"Like Uncle Timothy," Flora began to giggle. Then she had another of her mercurial changes of mood. "Oh, I do wish Great-aunt Tameson were here. She could have worn her violet velvet gown and all her jewels. She told me she loved parties. She used to have very grand ones in her *palazzo* in Venice. She said if the jewels of all the guests there were put in a gondola they would have sunk it. And there were thousands of candles and the floor of the ballroom was pink marble. All the same, Winterwood can be just as grand. I wish she were here tonight to see it."

Chapter 19

The candles on the Christmas tree were alight and radiant. Logs crackled in the huge fireplace. The damask curtains were drawn across the many windows of the long gallery, and the portrait of Daniel's mother, the girl with the curling dark hair and eyes that matched the gentians in her favorite blue garden, gleamed faintly. Shadows hung about the far end of the gallery, but here, in the center, gathered around the Christmas tree and the fireplace, all was warmth and color.

Charlotte had added to the color by wearing a dramatic crimson velvet gown, as if she had some private gloom she wanted to banish. Her jet black hair was piled high on her head; her eyes were shining, like colorless glass. Tonight her beauty had that touch of eeriness that was slightly repelling. Some emotion was held tight beneath the perfection of her flesh and bone.

Whatever the emotion was, it changed when Lavinia appeared.

"You are very grand, Miss Hurst. This is only a small family party. Not a night at the opera."

"Mamma, I made Miss Hurst wear her new gown," Flora said. "It is my Christmas gift to her. Doesn't she look beautiful in it? And have you noticed that I have my hair up?"

"That is ridiculous for a girl of twelve. Miss Hurst's influence again, I imagine?"

Extremely disappointed by her mother's disapproval, Flora looked about to weep. Daniel, more observant than he had appeared to be, said calmly, "Our daughter is growing up, my love. Shall we have our gifts off the tree before they catch on fire? Those candles look remarkably perilous to me. And then I believe Mr. Bush is going to play the piano for a little dancing. No doubt he will want your help to turn the pages, Flora."

Mr. Bush's fair skin colored much too easily. He murmured something about being delighted, and Flora's tears were banished by her own patent pleasure.

The gifts were handed out one by one by Sir Timothy, whose

privilege it was, as the oldest person present. He kept dropping his spectacles and misreading labels, but at last everyone had beribboned packages to open. Flora had a riding crop from her father. She looked about to burst into tears once more at this suggestion that she would soon be riding again. Then she forgot herself in her eagerness to watch the reception of her own lavish gifts. Perhaps she should not have been allowed so soon to display her riches. Edward and Simon, to be sure, were highly delighted with their extravagant gifts, but Charlotte held the little silver box on her lap and viewed it with a strange expression, almost of hate.

"Press the little button, Mamma," Flora begged.

Charlotte obeyed and gave a gasp as the small blackbird sprang out and whistled merrily.

"Do you like it, Mamma? Does it please you? Papa and I found it in a shop in the Burlington Arcade."

"It looks much too expensive," said Charlotte.

"But that doesn't matter. I could give you a hundred presents now I'm rich."

"It's vulgar to talk like that. And your aunt never expected her money to be wasted. Now don't look glum. It's just not suitable for a little girl to spend a lot of money. But the box is very pretty."

Sir Timothy, unaware of the small contretemps, saved the situation by saying that he fancied he had just heard a blackbird. Surely that was not possible in midwinter. He would have to write to the *Times*.

Flora screamed with laughter.

"Uncle Timothy, you are droll! Mamma has the blackbird here. But do open your own parcel. Tell me if the scarf is the right color. It is to put over your shoulders on cold days. You always complain that there are too many drafts."

Sir Timothy was delighted with his gift, as was Simon with his cricket bat and Edward with a train set that represented the Great Western Railway.

"I say, Flora, I like your being rich. I hope you always will be."

Charlotte's eyes rested broodingly on Edward's rosy face. Then, as if she must retain the gaiety at all costs, she commanded Mr. Bush to begin playing so that they could dance.

Lavinia's pleasure in the lovely room and the apparently happy family faded as she watched Daniel dancing with Charlotte. They looked so handsome, and even though they didn't talk, Charlotte's cheeks caught some of the color from her gown as they spun in a lively polka. Then Jonathon bowed over her, asking if he could have the pleasure. He was almost good-looking in his evening clothes, almost a gentleman.

But that impression quickly faded as he began to talk.

"I must admire your cleverness, Miss Hurst."

"My cleverness?" She frowned.

"I warrant that dress cost a pretty penny. There must have been other cheaper ones that our dear Flora would have thought quite as good. But you were wise to choose the best. Butter your bread while you can. And I must say you look ravishing. No wonder Cousin Charlotte is put out. I've told you before she can't hold a candle to you. Oh, she's pretty enough, but touch her and she'll break into a thousand pieces. I can't endure hysterical women. You have fire and calm. A very exciting combination. You deserve to be well-gowned and you must admit that your youthful mistress can well afford the cost of keeping her adored Miss Hurst. You can wrap her around your little finger, can't you, my sweet Lavinia? I've watched you for weeks. Your technique is superb."

As Lavinia stiffened in his arms, unable to escape this loathsome conversation without creating a scene, he went on, "It's almost a pity to kill the golden goose. You might have been able to equip yourself with a great many more things before you left Winterwood. But I regret to say I'm much too impatient. I can't wait that long— What the devil are you doing?"

Lavinia had broken away from him, careless of any scene.

"I am sorry, Mr. Peate. I would like to dance with Simon."

Simon, overhearing, came forward shyly, pleased.

"I think you will be much too expert for me, Miss Hurst. I am only learning."

"Then all the better to have a little practice."

She spun away with him, laughing to mask the reason for her heightened color. After he had settled down into the step, he said, "What was Cousin Jonathon talking to you about, Miss Hurst? You looked angry."

"Did I? Well, perhaps I find his compliments a little fulsome."

"To tell the truth I don't like him either. Why does Mamma want him here? He's been hanging round for an awfully long time. I thought he would go when Great-aunt Tameson died."

"Your mamma has been a little sad and gloomy since your aunt died and likes company. I think she is very much affected by events like that."

"Yes, she either laughs or cries. She always has. There ought to be an in-between state, oughtn't there?" Simon asked seriously.

"Yes, I suppose there ought."

"You have it, Miss Hurst." The boy blushed at his temerity. "I think you look very nice tonight. Not at all like a companion, really."

"Yes, that's what Mr. Peate was telling me," Lavinia said dryly. "He was quite right. I ought not to have worn this dress. I only did so to give Flora pleasure."

At that moment the music stopped. When it began again Charlotte, exclaiming that she had not known Simon had grown into such an expert dancer, whirled him away, and Daniel stood beside Lavinia. He didn't ask her to dance. Neither did he comment on the way she looked. Indeed, he seemed scarcely to have glanced at her. She might have been wearing her old woolen day dress for all he noticed.

"It was good of you to dance with Simon."

"I enjoyed it. I think he did, too."

"Naturally. You have a way with children."

"He's scarcely a child."

"No. Fortunately. I shall have no qualms about leaving him and Edward in the new year."

"While you travel with Flora?"

He nodded.

Wasn't he at all interested in what might become of her? Could he cast all thought of her out of his mind so easily?

"Then you still intend to do this? What about your wife?"

"I will arrange a companion for her. She has no desire to travel."

So he did suspect Charlotte of something devious. At least he was keeping to his intention to separate her from Flora.

"It will be difficult traveling with Flora still so helpless."

"We won't go far in the initial stages. Perhaps Switzerland for the winter. I shall find a good reliable nurse for her. Don't think I am dissatisfied with you. Far from it. If you were twenty years older and a married woman you would be ideal. As it is—"

"I would go with you no matter what anyone said," Lavinia said in a low, intense voice. "Please let me."

"Impossible."

"Oh, I believe it was you and not your grandfather who built that Temple of Virtue!" It was almost as if Mr. Bush, at the piano, read her thoughts, for he raised the tempo of his playing and under cover of the noise she was able to say, "You said you loved me. Have you forgotten?"

It was crazy of her to lose control of herself like this with everyone about them. How could she have done it? She had certainly earned his cool rebuke.

"I think you have had troubles enough in your life, Miss Hurst, without my adding to them. I should never have spoken. I think we both escaped from reality for a moment, but that won't happen again. I ask you to forgive me."

She was staring at him wide-eyed—what did he know about her troubles?—when Edward came up to demand that Papa come and look at his new train. Anyway, the music had stopped, and Flora was saying in her clear high voice that it was so sad Great-aunt Tameson had died, she would have enjoyed this party.

Her words seemed to break a spell, or cast a spell, for it was that moment which Mary uncannily chose to rush headlong into the long gallery, her cap ribbons flying, and to burst out breathlessly that the bell in Lady Tameson's room had been ringing.

"Twice!" she declared. "Sharp, like my lady used to ring it. Phoebe was too scared to answer it, and so was I, begging your pardon," Mary finished incoherently, and burst into tears. "It were a ghost," she whispered.

Chapter 20

THERE was no time to observe who was in the room, or who might have slipped in unobtrusively after Mary's sensational announcement. First, everyone's attention was taken by Charlotte, who gave a cry and looked about to have one of her collapses. Daniel's hand had been on Lavinia's arm, and now it tightened hard. She saw Jonathon standing near the doorway, his bland, amused look unchanged, and heard Sir Timothy exclaim, "Good God!" and saw him fumble for his spectacles as if the ghost of Lady Tameson might be present and visible. But a moment later the mysterious ringing of the bell was superseded in importance by another happening.

Flora was standing on her feet!

She stood, a thin wavering figure, her chair pushed away, her face illumined with triumph and fright. Then she was overcome by the enormity of her achievement and collapsed in a little heap. Mr. Bush acted in sheer surprise, lifting her into his arms and saying in panic that he thought she had fainted.

Daniel was there immediately to take her in his arms. He laid her on the couch by the fire and hung over her, saying with deep emotion, "It's happened! At last! A miracle."

Almost at once Flora recovered consciousness. Excitement leaped into her face, and she wanted to stand on her feet again at once. Daniel restrained her.

"Not yet, my pet. Rest first."

"But I can move my legs, Papa. Look!" She flung off the rug and, modesty forgotten, her skirts were pulled up to display her thin legs emerging from her starched white pantaloons. "Look!" she whispered again in sheer disbelief.

To Lavinia almost the best thing was the way tenderness had returned to Daniel's face. His eyes were very bright. They might have held tears.

"It's a miracle," he said again.

"No, it isn't, Papa. It's only Great-aunt Tameson telling me to

walk," Flora declared with certainty. "That's why she rang her bell.
She knew it would give me a fright and make me get out of my chair.
She always said I could if I tried."

"But her bell didn't ring!" Charlotte denied vehemently. "That
must have been pure imagination on the part of the servants."

"But I heard it, ma'am!" Everyone had forgotten Mary, who had
been responsible for the alarm. Shaken as she still was, she was not
going to have her story dismissed. Indignantly she repeated it. She
had heard the bell quite distinctly, and so had Phoebe.

"Bless my soul!" said Sir Timothy. "Then why didn't you answer
it? Aren't you trained to answer bells?"

"We was too scared, sir. I couldn't have laid hands on that door-
knob for all the tea in China. I came flying down here as fast as I
could."

"And Phoebe?" asked Daniel.

"I don't know where she went, sir. I didn't wait to see. For Mrs.
O'Shaughnessy, most likely."

"So that whoever was in the room could come out unnoticed."

"You mean—someone playing a prank!" said Charlotte, her relief
so obvious that it seemed she, too, for a moment must have believed
in Lady Tameson's ghost.

"Master Edward!" said Mr. Bush suddenly, his light eyebrows lifted
in accusation. He must have been driven to exasperation too often
to speak up so plainly in front of his employers. He was probably
remembering the tadpole episode.

But Edward heatedly denied his guilt.

"I was here all the time," he declared aggrievedly. "Wasn't I,
Papa? I was here playing with my train. Why should I go and ring
that old bell?"

"Then perhaps it was a burglar who stumbled in the dark," Simon
suggested. "Papa, shouldn't the house be searched?"

Daniel's eyes went over the company reflectively. They lingered
on Jonathon, who was the kind of person who enjoyed practical
jokes. Had he been out of the room and returned unnoticed?

"Can anyone here throw any light on this matter? If they can, it
would save a lot of trouble."

There was silence. Jonathon ground out a cigar in the ashtray
beside him. He lifted his eyes slowly and looked toward Charlotte.
She was sitting beside Flora holding her hand, seemingly intent
now on the miracle that had happened to her daughter.

"Then I agree with Simon," said Daniel. "The house had better be
searched. Look after Flora. Keep her on that couch. Come with me,

Simon. And ring for Joseph. What about your jewels, my love?" He looked at Charlotte's surprisingly unadorned neck. "You're not wearing your ruby pendant. Have you left it in your room?"

"It's in the bank, Daniel. Surely you know."

"I thought you kept it here."

"I don't, after that scare we had with Aunt Tameson's brooch. The one Eliza took. I only have a few not very valuable things in my room."

"Mamma, please! You're hurting!"

At Flora's protest Charlotte released her hand, with an extravagant apology.

"I'm sorry, darling. Did I squeeze too hard? It's only that I'm so delighted about you. If there is a burglar upstairs, he ought to be thanked. What do a few jewels matter compared to my darling child getting out of that horrid chair!"

"But I'm sure it wasn't a burglar who rang the bell," Flora said intensely. "It was Great-aunt Tameson's hand from the grave!"

Jonathon Peate laughed suddenly, loudly, and strangely enough it seemed to be that sound rather than the ghostly tinkling of the little silver bell beside Lady Tameson's bed that made Charlotte lose her self-control.

"How *dare* you laugh!" she cried.

"But, my dear sweet Charlotte"—Jonathon flung out his hands innocently—"such an absurdity as that remark of Flora's could only be treated as a joke. You couldn't take it seriously?"

The question hung in the air. It seemed that Charlotte had no answer to it. She gazed at him speechlessly, and he seemed to find her hypnotized look even more amusing, for he laughed again, and suggested that perhaps he should go and help Daniel and Simon and the servants search for the ghostly intruder.

The spell was broken by one of the servants coming in to announce that the Christmas carollers had arrived and were in the hall downstairs. Charlotte gladly welcomed the interruption.

"Come, Teddy, Simon, Flora—no, perhaps not you, darling." She bent swiftly over Flora to kiss her brow. "You're overexcited and must rest. Poor sweet, your little miracle has been overshadowed by all that silly talk of burglars. But Papa and I are so happy we could cry." Indeed, Charlotte's eyes were swimming with tears. "Can you still move your legs?"

"Yes, Mamma. I could walk right across the room if I tried."

"Well, don't try. Just lie still. Papa will send for Doctor Munro first thing in the morning. Stay with her, Miss Hurst. You can hear the carollers from here."

The sweet voices floated up into the long room. The candlelight shining on Flora's face made it look radiant but ethereal, all its sharp precocity melted into the awareness of her private miracle.

Once in royal David's city . . . sang the carollers, and Lavinia, looking down at Flora, said instinctively, "You look a Christmas angel."

Flora abruptly dispelled that sentimental illusion by sitting up and beginning to complain that no one was taking any notice of her.

"They say they care, but they don't. Papa goes off chasing burglars, and Mamma says everyone must listen to those silly carollers. And you, Miss Hurst, you look as if someone had died."

Lavinia made herself laugh. "Do I? I suppose I'm thinking that you won't be needing me any longer. You'll have a proper governess, not a nurse."

"Miss *Hurst!* I will not! If you say that I'll refuse to walk."

"I don't think so. You'll find it's too fascinating, being able to ride again, play games, dance, travel, perhaps. Your papa may take you back to Venice."

"Miss Hurst, *why* are you saying all that?"

"I'm just surmising." Lavinia suddenly knelt down and flung her arms around the slight figure. "Oh, darling! Little love! I'm so happy for you. That's why I'm crying. As if someone had died, indeed!"

Flora stirred in her arms. Her voice was unsure, afraid. "But Miss Hurst—who did ring Great-aunt Tameson's bell?"

It looked as if that puzzle were not to be solved. Daniel came back saying that the servants had been aroused and instructed to search the house completely. But what with the invasion of the carollers and all the subsequent noise it would have been easy for an intruder to escape. It was certainly true that the bell had rung, for it was found lying on the floor as if someone had knocked it down in the dark. It was a pity the maids had lost their heads and not waited to see who emerged from the room. It was very likely that someone had been playing a practical joke.

"Let's bless them for what they did," Daniel said, looking down at Flora. "If we catch a burglar I'll willingly let him go scot-free. Indeed, I'll put a sovereign in his pocket. Now let's get this child to bed."

"Oh, Papa! I'm far too happy to go to bed. I'll never sleep."

Lavinia doubted if anyone was going to sleep very much for the remainder of the night. But Flora's exhaustion proved greater than her excitement and soon she was settled and breathing quietly. Lavinia herself stood at the window and looked at the starlight shining over the quiet garden. Flora's blue garden, with the few gentians flowering in the wintry earth, the forlorn stone face of the infant lifted to the sky, the terrace with the sphinxes, the long shrubbery walk to the Temple of Virtue, concealed among the overgrown rhododendrons and the weeping willow, the lake water shining darkly at the bottom of the slope. The stable clock striking the hour, the white pigeons stirring and giving muffled croons, the roses in the rose garden pruned to a thorny austerity, the great yew shaped like a Chinese pagoda, inky black, the espaliered peach and apricot trees stretching in spider-webbed precision along the rosy brick wall, the far winter-brown fields, and the narrow silver line of sea on the horizon. The strange sadness of it all. For now she was never to see the peach tree burst into blossom, the blue haze of aubrietia and bluebells and forget-me-not come over Flora's garden, the blaze of rhododendrons in the shrubbery, and the sun shining on the lake.

The Christmas star shone, and the end had come for her.

She lit the candle again, and sat by the dying fire to write in her journal.

"Everyone has gone to bed, but I still sit here in this lovely extravagant gown Flora insisted I wear, looking not at all like a Cinderella with my feet in the ashes, but feeling more like one than I can describe. It is all over. If I have contributed toward Flora's recovery, then it has been worthwhile, even at the cost of my future happiness. Perhaps this is the way I was to make amends, just as poor Robin is making amends in prison. I don't doubt that Daniel will recover from whatever damage I have done to his feelings. Men do, I believe. But I? Shall I grow hard-faced from never laughing? Shall I torment the succession of innocent children or old ladies who will be my care for years to come?

"The Christmas star is shining. It means love, and I have to tear love out of my heart.

"Tomorrow Flora will walk again. Doctor Munro, that silly half-blind old man who couldn't diagnose what was the matter with Willie Jones, will pronounce his verdict. If it is favorable, Flora's father will prepare to take her on that long holiday abroad. The boys will go to school. Charlotte? What of Charlotte? Is she to be abandoned? Something *has* happened between her and Daniel. Did he, after all, not believe her story of taking the laudanum herself?

Is that why he is prepared to take no risks with Flora, who is such a rich little girl? Could he possibly believe . . . If he did, it is my fault. I sowed the suspicion. I encouraged him to believe that Charlotte, or her sinister cousin perhaps, was avaricious enough to— No, the thought is too terrible to put on paper. But Charlotte is unbalanced. Tonight there was that wildness in her eyes again. She looked so afraid, as if she really believed in ghosts. But ghosts who may have had reason to do her harm. Reason? What am I imagining now? Poor Lady Tameson may have had little affection for her, but why should she want to come back to do her harm?

"Someone, *not* a ghost, must have rung that bell tonight. It couldn't have been Eliza come back. Eliza, who had so missed Lady Tameson's bell-ringing. It is strange she didn't answer my letter. Perhaps it is too soon yet to expect an answer. I was hoping to see her at her sister's in Norfolk, and ask her advice about a new position. We are both casualties of Winterwood, if one could describe us so.

"I have so loved Winterwood . . ."

The fire gave a dying flicker and Lavinia laid down her pen to get her handkerchief. She was crying. Such a useless thing to do. This was not the moment to remember the touch of Daniel's lips against hers. She had to be practical, as Daniel had said she must, and face bleak reality.

She was about to get undressed at last when there was the sound of scratching at the door. At first she thought it was Sylvie wanting to get in, until she saw the little dog curled up in her basket as usual, though the sound had wakened her, and she was whimpering softly, her delicate nose quivering.

Daniel! The wild hope leaped in Lavinia, only to sink when she opened the door a cautious crack and saw Jonathon, still in evening dress, and carrying a candle in a silver candlestick. Behind its wavering flame his face looked curiously shadowed and a little grotesque. He was smiling, as always, and when Lavinia whispered, "What do you want?" he suggested that she come out and close the door lest Flora wake.

"I don't think you would like her to overhear our conversation."

Lavinia, about to shut the door in his face, realized that he was more than capable of creating a stir and waking not only Flora but everyone else.

She knew all too well why he had come. Christmas was over. He wanted his answer.

She knew that she would have to bargain. She had come to that decision some time ago.

She closed the door softly, and stood in the passage, shivering.

"Couldn't you have waited until the morning?"

"It is the morning." He laughed softly, and added, "I can see that you have been sitting up reflecting, just as I have. When the clock struck three, I realized that I couldn't wait a moment longer for your answer. What is it to be?"

"I am leaving here," she said rapidly. "Tomorrow I intend giving my notice to Mr. Meryon. If you will remain silent, I promise to meet you in London at a specified time and place."

"Oh, no, my dear, I will have nothing to do with a bargain like that. How do I know you will be at this specified place when I come?"

"I happen to keep a promise," Lavinia said frostily.

"Then how do I know what you will say? That you will have none of me, most likely."

She looked at him in disbelief.

"Can you really want a wife who marries you under threats?"

"When it is you, and it is the only way I can get you," he said coarsely. "No, the original arrangement remains. We leave Winterwood betrothed, or the whole sad story comes out."

"You are a monster!"

"Am I?" He seemed to enjoy her loathing. "I admit I would like you less if you meekly submitted. But you will submit, my dear. You won't leave Daniel and that spoiled brat in there with unpleasant memories of their dear Miss Hurst. You see, I know you very well. You are an idealist. A foolish and quite impractical thing to be."

"And how do you think you are going to look, telling this story about me?"

"Oh, a man in my position has nothing to lose. That's the advantage of it. Others have—a very great deal."

"Others? Such as Mrs. Meryon?"

He laughed less softly. His expelled breath nearly blew out the candle. She shrank against the door, fearful lest he should touch her. If he did, her control would break—as once before it had . . .

"Knowing secrets can be profitable," he said. "It's an invisible asset that I recommend. But you're shivering. I mustn't keep you here in the cold. It's Christmas morning, so I'll be generous. I'll wait until midday for your answer. I promise conversation won't lag at the luncheon table, for once. But it depends on you what turn it takes. Be kind to me, Miss Hurstmonceaux."

"I would rather die!"

"Hush! Such melodrama so early in the morning. It's tempting to tease you. Your eyes sparkle like very frosty stars. But I'll leave you in peace now. Good night, my love. Sleep well. Look your best tomorrow. I want to be proud of you."

Chapter 21

It was Christmas morning. Before breakfast Daniel said prayers, and then one by one the servants came forward to receive their gifts. There was a general air of excitement about the miracle that had happened to Miss Flora. Joseph carried her down as usual, but when, on her command, he set her in the middle of the room and, quite unsupported, she walked on thin unsteady legs to her chair, there was a plentiful mopping of eyes and exclamations of wonder.

Even more moving was Daniel's grave voice giving thanks in his prayers for her recovery. For a little while it seemed as if the queer cloud over Winterwood had lifted and a peaceful happy atmosphere prevailed. Lavinia avoided meeting Jonathon's eyes. That way, she could almost convince herself that nothing mattered except Flora's recovery. Nothing, at least, was more important, though she wasn't selfless enough to regard her own uncertain future as unimportant. Her sleepless night showed on her face, and even Flora, in spite of her absorption in herself, had wanted to know why she was so pale.

"You are not ill, Miss Hurst? You can't be ill when I am so happy!"

"I thought of you too much to sleep. There. Does that please you?"

"Oh, you always hide other feelings beneath what you say." Flora was too perceptive. And also maddeningly complacent this morning. "I expect you are still worrying that I won't need you anymore. I thought I had given you my assurance about that last night." Then Flora lost her precocious manner, and became a child again. "I shall be able to ride again. Isn't that truly wonderful? I shall ask Papa to find us two good horses so that you can always ride with me. You do ride, don't you, Miss Hurst?"

"I have ridden, yes."

"You will need a riding habit. We must go to Dover—"

"Flora! Stop treating me like a puppet to be clothed and to behave for your amusement! Don't you realize how unbearably patronizing you are?"

The words had burst out uncontrollably, but when Lavinia saw Flora wince she was instantly contrite.

"I'm sorry, I shouldn't have said that."

"No, you should not have. You are not employed to speak to me like that."

"Neither am I employed to accept constant presents from you."

"Other people like presents. Why are you so different?"

"Other people—this is a stupid conversation. Anyway, I am not other people."

Flora sulked for five minutes. Then she said in a small voice, "I didn't know I was being patronizing."

"Then let us say no more about it—except that I will not be needing a riding habit."

"Perhaps you will change your mind." Seeing Lavinia's look Flora added hastily, "It is wicked to quarrel on Christmas Day. We should be full of love."

In spite of that bad beginning it was Flora's day, and everyone did appear to be full of love for her. Charlotte kissed her tenderly; Sir Timothy said, "By Jove, Flora, tell me the secret and I might get back my eyesight," and Flora answered seriously that perhaps he had better say a prayer to Great-aunt Tameson.

"Yes, by Jove, perhaps she's not dead, after all. Ringing bells in the middle of the night. Deuced queer."

Jonathon Peate laughed loudly, as was to be expected. But a little later his ready laughter deserted him.

It happened when Daniel distributed the mail at the breakfast table. It had come up from the village last evening, and had been overlooked in the general excitement.

He delved into the bag and produced a handful of letters.

"Here's one for you with a foreign postmark, my love." He looked closer at the envelope. "Italian. Venezia. Who is writing to you from Venice?"

Charlotte opened the letter, looked at it, then let it flutter from her hands. She was ashen white. She could make no attempt to hide her shock.

"What is it?" Daniel asked.

"What is it, Mamma?" demanded Flora.

"From—from Aunt Tameson," Charlotte managed to say. "It must be a mistake."

Daniel stared.

"It certainly must. Dead women don't write letters. Let me see it. I suppose it has been lost in the post all these months."

"Foreign post offices," Sir Timothy said, as if no more comment were needed.

"She says she's coming," Charlotte said shakily. "The date is—only last week. Look, Daniel."

"December the twelfth," Daniel read. "Dear Charlotte, As I wrote to you earlier in the summer, I have a great wish to die in England and be laid to rest with my little Tom. I have now made my plans for traveling and hope to be seeing you within a very short time. But I beg you not to inconvenience yourself on my account. I shall arrive quietly and without any fuss. Forgive me for not writing more. I am not very strong; the weakness is particularly in my hands. It is the way my poor husband went, too. I am shutting up the palazzo. The pink jade cupid you admired I am bringing for you; other things are too large to travel with. I apologize for difficult writing. It is my bad hands. Your loving aunt, Tameson Barrata."

Flora suddenly began to whimper.

"You told me Great-aunt Tameson was dead!"

"So she is!" Charlotte cried violently. "This letter is a hoax. A horrible wicked hoax."

"Played by whom?" asked Daniel in a genuine mystification.

"How should I know?" Charlotte was twisting her hands agonizedly. "The only thing I do know is that it isn't from Aunt Tameson. How *could* it be? Did she get up off her deathbed? You saw her. Doctor Munro—Jonathon—you all saw her."

"What about the handwriting?"

"I don't know."

"Look at it."

Daniel thrust the sheet of paper before Charlotte and her curiously unwilling eyes stared at the awkward sprawling writing. Jonathon peered over her shoulder. He was no longer laughing. His coarsely handsome face had grown ugly. Only its jovial expression had ever saved it from ugliness, Lavinia realized. But now she saw it as it could be, just as the strain in Charlotte's face had edged its beauty into that uncomfortable eeriness. The two of them, the niece and nephew of the old lady in Venice, were highly disturbed.

"I suppose the writing is like—I'm not good at remembering. I destroyed the other letters I had from Aunt Tameson."

"What about the signature on her will? You watched that being made, Miss Hurst. What do you think?"

It was Lavinia's turn to look closely at the black scrawl. She lifted her eyes in deep perplexity.

"It's awfully similar. Without comparing them I would say they are the same. Could the Contessa have made a mistake in the dates, and written this letter before you were in Venice? Perhaps she forgot to post it. Perhaps someone found it and posted it only a week or so ago."

"That's what's happened," exclaimed Jonathon in patent relief. "Trust Miss Hurst's clever brain."

"Why, yes, it must be." Charlotte began to laugh shakily. "Well, what a fright we've all had."

"Then it isn't true that Great-aunt Tameson is alive?" Flora asked. "It wasn't her ringing her bell last night?"

"We must assume that was an accident," said Daniel. "Otherwise we have a practical joker both here and in Venice. A little unlikely, don't you think? Incidentally, Charlotte, was someone left living in the *palazzo*? I understood the Italian maid was to leave immediately after we did."

"Fernanda? So she was. But the place was to be put up for sale after Aunt Tameson's death. Mr. Mallinson knows all about that. I expect it has been opened up to show prospective buyers, and the letter was found."

"Perhaps. Perhaps." Daniel was still not satisfied. "We'll find out what Mallinson has done. But I can't understand the date on the letter. The twelfth of December. Thirteen days ago. Why on earth should your aunt, whose brain had remained quite unaffected by her illness, date a letter written in midsummer six months ahead?"

"The old lady was weak on figures," said Jonathon. "That I do know. She could scarcely add two and two. Edward could have done better."

"Adding figures is nothing to do with writing the name of the month," said Daniel coldly. He stared at Jonathon, seeming to expect to read something in his face.

"All that vagueness of the brain is connected. Surely you must know that medical fact."

"Perhaps. But whatever you say, this needs looking into. We need facts, not suppositions."

Charlotte sprang up.

"What are you going to do?"

"Write to Mallinson. See if he can throw any light on the matter. There's no doubt that the letter was posted in Venice. But by whom?"

It seemed that Flora, in wishing that Lady Tameson were there to share their party, had set some strange forces in motion. The old lady had returned to haunt Christmas.

Doctor Munro had been sent for to observe and pronounce on Flora's great improvement. The faithful old man was touched and delighted.

"So there you are, lassie. You've done for yourself what none of us slow old doctors could do. How did it happen, would you mind telling me?"

"Yes, Great-aunt Tameson rang her bell and I got such a fright I jumped up immediately."

"Aye. The shock would have done it. Released the paralysis, so to speak. But what is this you're saying? Did the old lady have her ghost conveniently to hand to pick up that bell?"

"It was an accident, doctor," Charlotte said quickly. "One of the servants knocked the bell over, and is afraid to admit to it since no one had any business in that room."

Doctor Munro nodded.

"Then I think you should seek out the culprit, Mrs. Meryon, and give her a medal. Poor Lady Tameson, eh? And she peaceful in her grave this three months."

But was she? The strange mystery, far from clearing, became intensified after a visit from the vicar, Mr. Clayton. He was extremely puzzled. He produced a letter written in the same shaky black writing as the one received by Charlotte and said that someone signing herself the Contessa Tameson Barrata was making inquiries about the grave of her son.

"She says she would like to be buried with her son, and intends to return to England to spend her last days. She inquires about the state of the grave. Is it tended properly?"

Charlotte had said frequently that Daniel had granted the living to a much too youthful vicar after the death of old Mr. Mansell, who would, incidentally, have remembered Lady Tameson when she was plain Tameson Peate. Certainly young Mr. Clayton was very much disturbed by the mysterious letter.

"You must tell me whom I have buried, sir! The church records must be kept accurately."

Daniel stiffened.

"You have buried the body of my wife's aunt. Who else did you think it could possibly be?"

Charlotte gave a high hysterical laugh, abruptly cut off.

"This extraordinarily morbid conversation! You will agree that I ought to know my own aunt, Mr. Clayton."

"But this letter, Mrs. Meryon! It carries a date only a fortnight old."

It was as well the children were not present. Charlotte and Daniel
had received Mr. Clayton in the library, where Lavinia had been
asked to help write letters about the strange matter, and told to remain when Mr. Clayton came in. She would like to have escaped the
morbidity herself. The cloud over Winterwood had lifted only very
slightly that morning. Now it was pressing down blackly, suffocat-
ingly. Odd disjointed memories were coming back to her. The
strange woman who had called, purporting to be an old servant, and
who had been astonished not to be remembered. Lady Tameson
saying in her vigorous manner, "I'll win. I always win." Eliza's story
of how she had fumbled for her crucifix when she was dying, she
who had never admitted to being a Catholic. The too-tight rings on
the wasted fingers. And the sound of her high cackle as she said that
cheating was to be recommended so long as one wasn't caught at it.

She heard Daniel telling Mr. Clayton to leave the matter with
him, and not to mention it to anybody.

"It's a hoax, I'm afraid. Someone with a very macabre imagination
is playing a game with us. We also had a letter this morning."

"You, too!" The young man was agog.

"That's why I say it's a hoax. But I'll get to the bottom of it."

"Then the grave is to be undisturbed?"

"Oh, good heavens, yes!" Charlotte cried. Her voice had the high
timbre of extreme tension. "It mustn't be touched. Daniel! Tell
him."

"There's no question of its being touched. Anyway, that would
require permission from the Home Secretary. Ignore this communica-
tion, Mr. Clayton, I beg you. This deplorable matter will be cleared
up within a few days. Thank you for calling. A glass of Madeira before you leave?"

Lavinia remembered her exploration of the dust-sheeted rooms
of the old *palazzo* on the Grand Canal. Had someone been hiding
in them, and living ever since in the silent shut-up house? Waiting
patiently to perpetrate this morbid joke that was more than a joke?
One would have known it would distress Charlotte, with her highly
nervous temperament, but the unexpected thing was that it distressed the Contessa's nephew, too. Although Lavinia had imagined
Jonathon to have nerves of iron, there was no doubt he was shaken
by the mysterious letters. So shaken that luncheon went by without
a glance from him, or one word about his promised threat to expose
her. Neither had he sought her out to demand her answer to his
proposal. She had a reprieve. She had to be grateful to the unknown
hoaxer for that.

Daniel dispatched the letter to Mr. Mallinson asking him to make urgent inquiries as to who had access to the *palazzo* in Venice, and whether anything of an irregular or puzzling nature had happened. He contemplated making a personal visit to London, then decided to wait for Mallinson's answer.

"It may mean I go to Venice instead," he said.

Charlotte sank back in her chair.

"Then you are taking this seriously?"

"The more I think of it, the less I like it."

"Why?" Charlotte's voice was almost inaudible.

"Blackmail is an ugly word."

"Blackmail!" Jonathon exclaimed. "Explain yourself, Meryon."

Ignoring him, Daniel continued speaking to Charlotte.

"Had your aunt any relatives besides yourself and your cousin?"

"You mean—someone who would have designs on her fortune?" Charlotte said faintly.

"Exactly that. After all, you were scarcely close to her. I understand you were to be her heir simply because you undertook to bring her back to England and care for her until she died, and then bury her with her son. Might there be another claimant who resented this?"

"Such as me?" Jonathon said crudely. "Only I'm right here so I couldn't have posted the letters."

"Another claimant such as your cousin here," Daniel went on, still addressing himself to Charlotte. "After all, you only made Jonathon's acquaintance in Venice. I believe you didn't know of one another's existence previously. Couldn't there be some other person similarly placed? You ought to know more about this than my wife, Peate."

It could never have been said that Daniel and Jonathon were on congenial terms, but now a cold formality seemed to have sprung up between them. It was as if it were no longer necessary to pretend a friendship they did not feel. But why? Blackmail was a word that could easily have fitted Jonathon Peate, Lavinia admitted, but it scarcely fitted now, for he was as badly shaken as Charlotte. She had never thought to see fear in that bold face.

"The old lady had no other relations," he said quite definitely. "Willie Peate had only one brother, my father. Charlotte knows the other side."

"There was my mother, and another sister who died young," Charlotte said. "Aunt Tameson was the eldest. There can't be any other relative, Daniel. Really there can't."

"Then a close friend whom perhaps she had promised to remember in her will?" Daniel persisted.

"She didn't seem to have any around her when we went to Venice. She seemed completely alone. That was after her companion had died." Charlotte shivered suddenly and violently, and said that she was thinking of that bizarre funeral they had gone to. The black-draped gondolas on the gay blue water. So incongruous. And all that sunshine and the blazing white monuments in the cemetery. No wonder Aunt Tameson had wanted to die in England.

"Perhaps," said Daniel thoughtfully. "Well, we must wait for Mallinson's answer. Miss Hurst, where are the children?"

"Mr. Bush has them in the schoolroom."

"It's time Flora had her rest. She must be particularly careful not to overdo things. Stay with her, Miss Hurst."

With that curt order he left the room. Lavinia gathered up her writing materials and prepared to follow him. In her haste she dropped her pen, and turning to pick it up she caught a strange conspiratorial look between Charlotte and Jonathon. A look of apprehension and fear and *knowledge*.

She was not an eavesdropper, and abhorred such a tendency. But under the present circumstances it was justifiable.

She deliberately refrained from completely closing the door, and paused to listen.

Charlotte spoke in so low a voice that her words were disappointingly inaudible. What she said, however, had a shattering impact on Jonathon, for he forgot all caution as he exclaimed, "You mean to tell me you didn't see it! You utter fool!"

Joseph was crossing the hall; Lavinia could not linger. What was she to do with this new cryptic information? Tell Daniel? See what he made of it? Or say nothing and wait for Mr. Mallinson's letter.

Say nothing, she thought wearily. She had already run to him with too many alarms. He must know there was some understanding between Charlotte and Jonathon. He was not blind.

It was a misty damp afternoon, not suitable for being outdoors. Nevertheless Charlotte ordered the brougham and drove off, telling no one where she was going. When she returned she did not come indoors immediately, but walked up and down the terrace in her long gray cloak and befurred bonnet. Mary had looked out of a window and seen her and said that the mistress was in one of her moods where she couldn't be still.

"Sometimes she walks up and down half the night, Bertha says. It's her nerves all ajar. They won't let her rest. That traveling abroad didn't agree with her. She's been in her queer moods off and on ever since."

As if something invisible were pursuing her, Lavinia thought, looking down at the tense, lonely figure. Then, suddenly, Charlotte looked up sharply as if she knew she were being watched. Lavinia drew back from the intense stare of the white face. But a moment later she knew that it was not this window but the next one at which Charlotte gazed. Poor Lady Tameson's window. As if she expected to see a ghost.

When she came in to tea she was shivering. She said she had been to put some flowers on her aunt's grave.

"It's a mistake to go to churchyards in the winter. They're so cold." She shivered and held out her visibly trembling hands to the fire. "So cold."

She asked Lavinia to pour the tea so she could drink some and compose herself before the men came in.

"Do you really believe those letters are a hoax, Miss Hurst?"

"I think they're a mistake. They must be."

"Whoever wrote them knew I had admired the jade cupid. How could anyone know that, except my aunt herself?"

"You mean—they've been written *after* you were in Venice?"

"Yes, didn't you realize that? I'd never seen the cupid until I was there. I don't think even my husband has seen the significance of that."

"So it must be someone playing a trick," Lavinia said in complete bewilderment. "Unless—"

"Unless what, Miss Hurst?"

"Unless it wasn't your aunt you brought to Winterwood."

There was a crash and the delicate Meissen cup and saucer lay in fragments on the hearth. There was spilled tea everywhere.

Charlotte sprang up, wringing her hands.

"Ring the bell. Get someone to clean this up. So clumsy of me. My hands were stiff with cold. Where's Daniel? Where's Jonathon? Where's *Jonathon?*"

It almost seemed as if she had expected Jonathon to mysteriously disappear. But he was very much with them still. He came in presently, and appeared to have recovered his familiar aplomb.

"I'm late," he said. "I apologize." He took the proffered cup of tea from Lavinia. "I'm neglecting you, Miss Hurst." His eyes gave her their specific message. "But that, I assure you, is only temporarily." A faint odor of whiskey hung about him. There had been no tributes on graves for him. He had been down to the village inn to bolster up his courage in another way. It was necessary for him, too, to blot out the thought of the mysterious woman in Venice—if there were a woman who wrote letters in the handwriting of someone already deceased.

Daniel didn't come in until tea was over. He was in riding clothes, and he, too, apologized for being late. He said he had ridden to Dover to put the letter to Mr. Mallinson on the train himself. He had contemplated going to London personally, but was afraid that, being Christmas, the old man might be away. In any case—his eyes went around the room—he preferred not to be away from home himself at this time of the year.

"Where's Flora, Miss Hurst?"

"She's resting, Mr. Meryon. She's tempted to be on her feet too much. She doesn't believe the miracle unless she constantly proves it. Mary's giving her her tea in her room."

"Daniel, why do you go on worrying about Flora?" Charlotte said irritably. "The time for that is over."

"I hope so," he said cryptically, giving her a long look.

If she had had a cup in her hand, Lavinia believed she would have dropped it again. Something had passed between her and Daniel. Was it acknowledged suspicion? Had Daniel, all the time, believed that fiction of the laudanum in Flora's chocolate?

"Charlotte's right," said Jonathon suddenly. "I can think of people more deserving of anxiety than your very pampered daughter." Then he dropped his bombshell. "Since this little matter in Venice seems to be on Charlotte's mind—and on mine, too, I grant you— I've decided to go and do a little personal investigation."

Charlotte was on her feet.

"Go to Venice! Then you do think it—more than a hoax?" Her voice trailed away.

"Let's just say I don't like being hoaxed."

Chapter 22

He really did mean to go. He had a servant pack his bags that night in readiness for his departure in the morning. The evening was passed in desultory conversation about the discomforts of traveling across Europe in midwinter. Sir Timothy had a lot to say about that, but no one paid much attention. Charlotte looked tired enough to drop. But when Daniel, who scarcely took his eyes off her, suggested that she retire, she denied vehemently that she was tired. She sat on over the dying fire, afraid to go upstairs.

Finally Jonathon said that if he were to travel the next day he thought he would get some sleep. The barest perceptible nod from Daniel indicated to Lavinia that she must go to her post beside Flora. Mary, who had been sitting up with her, would be nodding or perhaps sound asleep by the fire.

Jonathon must have guessed that she would follow him, for he was lingering in the passage. He had pulled back the curtain from one of the long windows and was looking out on the dark night.

"It's beginning to rain," he said. "If this wind gets up I'll have a damned unpleasant crossing."

"Are you a bad sailor? Is that all that worries you?"

"Was that a taunt, my pretty Lavinia? No, it's not all. Another thing that worries me is losing you. But we'll have to postpone that little affair until I return. In not less than ten days. Can you wait that long? I think you can. I think you will." The threat was plain enough in his voice, but it was overlaid by this other anxiety. It seemed that the mysterious trouble in Venice could be more important than she. Why wouldn't he say what it was? Why wouldn't Charlotte speak? Or did they truly not know?

It was not only Charlotte who dreaded the night.

Flora was sitting upright in bed, wide-awake, her eyes much too bright and apprehensive.

"Miss Hurst, at last you've remembered my existence. Why do you leave me alone with that good-for-nothing who just falls asleep?" For Mary, looking the child she was, her cap tilted sideways, her little work-roughened hands clasped on her apron, was sound asleep by the fire.

"Why aren't you asleep, too?" Lavinia asked Flora.

"Because my legs ache."

"You used them too much today. Didn't Doctor Munro warn you not to? The muscles are still too weak. You must be patient."

"Miss Hurst, don't scold! I dislike you very much when you behave like a governess."

"Then I shall behave like a nurse. Would you like some hot milk?"

"No."

"Then shall I rub your legs to ease them?" Lavinia began to shake Mary awake. But before the sleepy girl had stirred, Flora was saying, "Miss Hurst, what did they say downstairs tonight? Is it true Great-aunt Tameson is coming back?"

"Flora, of course not! She's dead."

"Edward thinks she is coming. You wouldn't believe how quiet he's become. He thinks she wants to punish him for playing tricks on her. Phoebe had to promise to sleep in his room. Would you believe it, a big boy like that!"

Flora was silent a moment, trying to retain her scorn. But it left her, and her voice was small. "I was not allowed to see her lying dead. Is it because—she wasn't?"

"I saw her," Lavinia said quietly. "She looked very peaceful and contented. Does that please you?"

"It would please me more if she were still here. I don't really want her money or her jewels. I'd gladly give them back. I don't need them now that I can walk."

"No, you don't," Lavinia agreed. "They're a—"

"They're what?" Flora asked, as she paused.

She had been going to say they were a curse. And that was true. For everything had happened since the old lady had changed her will. Everything sprang from that, even this strange haunting.

"There are many things more important than wealth," she said primly. "Now will you please lie down and go to sleep."

"If I can have Sylvie on my bed. Then I will feel safe. She barks if anyone strange comes in."

"Now whoever do you imagine is going to come in?"

Flora's overstrained eyes looked up from the pillow.

"Sylvie would regard Great-aunt Tameson as a stranger, I expect."

"Flora darling!"

To conceal her own agitation Lavinia briskly awoke Mary and sent her stumbling off to bed, then allowed the little dog, trembling with pleasure, to curl up beside Flora. Charlotte, she thought, would have appreciated Sylvie's company that night. But Charlotte had given her treasured pet to her daughter to prove how much she loved her—even though previously it had been quite obvious to everyone that she had a passionate unbalanced affection for Edward, and no one else, especially not her crippled, plain and difficult daughter. One could not change one's affections overnight simply because the daughter one had despised was suddenly immensely wealthy. But it might be politic for the world to think one could.

Lavinia didn't know why her quite unproven suspicions about Charlotte came back so vividly.

But yes, she did. For today it was as if a mask had slipped from Charlotte's face, and the haunted woman beneath it showed all too clearly.

There had always been a plot between her and Jonathon Peate. If she had received Lady Tameson's money, he had been going to share it for some private reason. But the plan had gone badly awry and had somehow to be retrieved.

So Charlotte lavished affection on Flora, and talked to Edward of going to live in London with only him, her best-loved child, and pretended to seek the company of the man who frightened her out of her wits. All contradictory behavior.

And now, most contradictory of all, the plotters themselves were frightened. Badly frightened.

The tap on the door an hour later scared her badly. Flora had at last fallen asleep, and she herself, from sheer exhaustion, was drowsing.

But in a moment she was sitting up, and Sylvie was growling softly.

Was it Jonathon again? This was more than she could stand.

It was Daniel.

He apologized for disturbing her. He only wanted to know if everything was well.

"With Flora? She's asleep."

"Good. Lavinia, I want you to take her away tomorrow. I will arrange lodgings for you. Somewhere quiet. Bournemouth, perhaps. Will you do that?"

"Has something happened?"

He gave a bleak smile. He looked very tired.

"Hasn't enough happened? No, nothing more. My wife will say nothing. Nothing at all. She merely assures me that I know as much as she does. When I point out that I am not collapsing from some secret fear, as she appears to be, she says that is merely her nervous condition. She has always been highly nervous, and a letter from the grave does nothing to improve her health."

"There is some reason for Mr. Peate to be going to Venice. Some urgent reason. Your wife must know what that is."

"Perhaps. Personally, any reason, no matter what it is, to get him out of my house pleases me. I should have made him leave long ago, and not listened to Charlotte's wishes."

"You think everything will be all right when he has gone? But you don't, or you would not want me to take Flora away."

"It will be good for Flora's health."

Lavinia put out her hand impulsively.

"Will you join us in Bournemouth?"

"Later. When we have finally ascertained who is buried in young Tom Peate's grave."

He had called her Lavinia again. That was the only glimmer of comfort she could get from the curiously shocking conversation.

She slept, to dream of Lady Tameson wearing all her jewels standing over her bed and demanding, in her hoarse autocratic voice, to be taken out of the cold English mud and returned to her grandeur in Venice. Then Jonathon Peate stood behind her giving his loud laugh and saying that he would take her if the weather were not too stormy, and the poor old lady screamed, awaking Lavinia to a chilly dark morning, and Flora shouting in her ear.

"Miss Hurst! You slept so soundly. I had to scream. Look, I got out of bed without help."

The little figure in her long white nightgown was so appealing after that nightmare that Lavinia threw her arms around her.

"Bless you, little love. I'm so happy for you."

"I'm happy, too, because Mr. Peate is leaving us. Did you know? His boxes have been carried down, Mary says. You have slept late, Miss Hurst. Hurry or you'll be late for breakfast. You may even be too late to say goodbye to Mr. Peate!"

"And that will not break my heart, as you well know."

Flora giggled. She seemed in high spirits.

"And I've also looked in Great-aunt Tameson's room and she hasn't come back. That was all imagination, wasn't it?"

"Certainly it was. Tell Mary to brush your hair while I dress. Then we may even be in time for prayers."

"Let us say a prayer that the Channel crossing is very rough."

Lavinia looked out of the window to see the storm-torn clouds.

"I think that will be unnecessary. But we could hope that Mr. Peate won't be a coward and refuse to go."

She was to remember that remark later.

Before breakfast was over, Joseph stood at the door saying in a flustered way that there was a young person arrived from London with a large package directed to the Contessa Barrata.

Charlotte was on her feet, her hand pressed to her heart.

"What is in this—mysterious package, Joseph?"

"The boy says it's a new gown, madam, made to my lady's order. It comes from Madame Hortense, who has always made for my lady."

"But why has it come *here*?"

Joseph looked bewildered and nervous.

"The boy said that was the directions. He's waiting in the servants' hall if you want to question him, madam."

Daniel threw down his napkin.

"I'll question him. Stay there, Charlotte."

Only Sir Timothy spoke while Daniel was gone.

"Curious," he said conversationally. "Poor Tameson overestimated her span of life. Waste, if it's an expensive gown. I suppose the dressmaker won't take it back." He chuckled appreciatively. "By Jove, the old lady kept her vanity until the end, didn't she? I wonder where she thought she would be wearing this new gown."

The gown was made in Lady Tameson's favorite violet-colored velvet. It was very grand indeed. There were yards of black braiding around the voluminous skirt, and some very handsome lace on the bodice. A letter enclosed with the garment apologized to the Contessa for not sending it in time for Christmas, but the order had only arrived from Venice on the twenty-third of December, so that it had been quite impossible to fulfill it so rapidly. In any case, perhaps the Contessa herself had not yet arrived. She had said she was about to leave, but dreaded traveling in midwinter, and would break her journey two or three times on the way. She expected to arrive in England on Christmas Day or possibly a day or two later. The bill, Madame Hortense was to send to her niece, Mrs. Daniel Meryon of Winterwood, and she was sure that Mrs. Meryon would also take care of the messenger's expenses.

Daniel put down the letter.

"What's it all about? You must know." He didn't call her Charlotte, or my love, or dearest, as was his usual custom. He simply addressed her in that cool hard way as if she were a stranger.

"I—know?" she faltered. "But I don't. I haven't the faintest idea—"

"Then you, Mr. Peate?" Daniel swung round on Jonathon, who was sitting rigid, dressed in his traveling clothes, his face calm enough but curiously mottled. "You are about to leave for Venice. Don't tell me this journey is a wild-goose chase. You are expecting to find some person—the person who has been writing these letters and ordering this gown. *Who is she?*"

"Dammit, how do I know? Someone with a peculiar sense of humor, to begin with. Certainly I was expecting to find someone. I don't imagine those letters were written by a ghost. But whoever it is, it's obviously too late to flush them out in Venice. They—he or she—appear to be on their way to England. Just about here, if that"—he pointed at the letter—"is to be believed."

Charlotte sprang up, then stood immobile as if unable to think what to do next.

Sir Timothy had put on his spectacles and was examining the dress, which Daniel had thrown over a chair.

"You must admit, Charlotte, this was Tameson's favorite color. She always smelled of violet scent, too, I noticed. It would be interesting to know what events in her life had given her this obsession about violets. Well, who's going to stand the bill for this creation?"

Abruptly Flora began to cry. This was the signal for Charlotte to spin around and cry in a rage, "Miss Hurst, haven't you the sense to take Flora out of here? This is not for children, this terrible joke. Daniel, that garment has got to go back to London at once. Madame whoever-she-is must be told it's a mistake."

She reached for the bell rope, but Daniel stopped her.

"What are you doing?"

"I'm ringing for this to be taken away and packed. The messenger mustn't be allowed to leave without it."

"Don't do that," said Daniel quietly. "Let us wait until its owner arrives."

"No one is coming! Who could be coming?"

Daniel turned his stony face to Jonathon.

"Have you ever noticed," he said conversationally, "that wherever there is a great deal of money the wolves gather? Or I believe the Contessa called them vultures. So let me persuade you to postpone your departure. I am sure our mysterious guest, who may be arriving at any moment"—he turned to glance out of the window—"will expect to find you here."

But Jonathon's face had gone an unpleasant yellow. The color of cowardice, Lavinia thought. She had a feeling of exultant revenge as she saw that it was his turn to be the one threatened. His eyes were hypnotized like a frightened animal's. He stared at the door as if expecting it at any moment to burst open and some terrible ghost appear. He was nothing but a craven, after all. He had visibly shrunk. The violet dress spread over the chair was the strange symbol of his downfall.

What could it mean to him? Was it proof of something he had feared?

At last he spoke, but not in answer to Daniel's question. He looked at his watch and said, "I must be off or I'll miss the ferry. May I call upon your generosity once more, Daniel, and borrow some conveyance to take me to the railway station?"

Charlotte sprang up. If Jonathon had gone pale with private fear, she was a wraith, wild-eyed, ashen.

"Jonathon, you can't go! You can't leave me now."

He gave her one glance and started for the door.

"Jonathon—"

"Don't bother about the conveyance after all," he said in haste. "I can't wait for it to be brought round. My own legs will take me faster."

The door slammed behind him.

Charlotte sank into a chair. "You coward!" she whispered. "You coward!"

Daniel, not gently, pulled her trembling hands from her face.

"The time has come for an end to these mysteries," he said harshly. "Don't let us waste time weeping for that rogue. Let him run away with the furies at his heels. Don't you agree, Miss Hurst?"

Lavinia could scarcely express her thankfulness. Although the gale still raged, the morning seemed lighter, brighter, gayer.

"I do, indeed."

"He has escaped too lightly, I think, but at least he has gone without what he came here for. Isn't that so, Charlotte?" He crossed over to the door and locked it. "I believe you know the whole story, and you will not leave this room until you have told it. Uncle Timothy, Miss Hurst, sit down. Now we are alone. The truth, Charlotte. At once."

Even then, in spite of the unaccustomed cold anger in her husband's voice, it was some time before Charlotte could speak. She was literally bereft of words. Several times her trembling lips opened, only to close soundlessly. She, too, was hypnotized by the dress lying across the chair. By the dilated look of her eyes, she seemed to be seeing a ghostly Lady Tameson in it.

When at last she began to talk, it was in a disjointed monotone, like someone muttering in her sleep. Something about a funeral. At first Lavinia thought she meant Lady Tameson's at the church in the village, but then she spoke about the cypress trees being so dark, the sun so hot.

"She wanted the nice cool earth," she kept muttering. "And I pretended—"

"Pretended what?" Daniel was close, trying to understand the restless, whispering voice.

"It was too late," said Charlotte, suddenly opening her eyes wide. She saw Lavinia and seemed surprised, as if she had been completely lost in her nightmare.

"Miss Hurst! Why aren't you with Flora? Are you sure it's safe to leave her? I thought you were afraid. She's much too rich for a child. A child who can't walk. A cripple. And she gets the fortune while Teddy—my darling Teddy—"

The wandering voice died away. But the terrible question had been answered at last. There had been an attempt on Flora's life. By Jonathon Peate? By her own mother?

Pain creased Charlotte's forehead.

"Jonathon made me do that—with the laudanum. It was horrible. But he threatened. He wanted so much. He talked of nothing but money."

"How could he demand money from you?" Daniel asked. "What right had he to? Was it because of something that happened in Venice? Because that's where it began, isn't it? Tell us, Charlotte."

For a little while it seemed again as if Charlotte was not going to be able to speak. But presently she overcame her agitation and began to tell the strange story in a low but unexpectedly composed voice.

There had been a dead body when she had arrived at her aunt's *palazzo* in Venice. The old woman there told Charlotte she had arrived too late. Her aunt was dead. It was a great pity, because there had been no time to remake her will, as she had promised to do, in Charlotte's favor. As it stood, all her fortune went to various charities.

The old woman had been Lady Tameson's companion, an Englishwoman whose name was Sprott. She had one son, Jonathon. He, too, had been at the *palazzo* when Charlotte had arrived. It was he who had made the clever plan that was going to enrich both Charlotte and himself.

His mother had heart trouble and was unlikely to live very long.

So why should she not impersonate the dead Contessa, who lay upstairs awaiting her funeral? Indeed, the impersonation had already begun, for the doctor who had attended the Contessa and signed her death certificate had been informed that his patient had been Mrs. Amelia Sprott. Jonathon had instigated the deception. He had anticipated Charlotte's agreeing with him that it would be a disastrous shame if all that fortune went to charity. It belonged rightfully to Charlotte, and of course to him, Jonathon, for his help in such a daring plot. Though he promised not to be greedy. He would demand only a small share, perhaps twenty thousand pounds. When he received it, he would disappear out of Charlotte's life forever. She could rely on him.

So the funeral of the supposed Mrs. Sprott had taken place. The new Aunt Tameson waited in her *palazzo* to be transported to England. There was only one important thing for her to do. Imitate the Contessa's handwriting. She had to practice a great deal. Everything else was easy. She relished wearing the jewelry and the good clothes and preparing to die a countess. It was true that she had been afraid, at first. She seemed to be intimidated by her son, but the histrionic had an appeal to her, and she had obtained a macabre pleasure from her role.

But there was one thing no one had anticipated—that she would begin to find Charlotte's and Jonathon's scheming too distasteful, that she would despise Edward as a spoiled rude child, and that she would grow to love Flora.

She had quarreled with her son when he came to see her at Winterwood because of his greedy demands. This had made her suddenly decide to play her own game. Flora, the sensitive crippled child, should get the fortune that was not hers to give.

This scheme successfully accomplished and the will accepted as legitimate, Jonathon, in a fury, still demanded his due. Charlotte must provide it somehow; otherwise he would expose her, and she would not only face criminal charges but all that great fortune would disappear from the Meryon family forever. However, if Flora were to accidentally die, Jonathon pointed out diabolically, and what was she but a poor useless cripple, the money would remain in the family, and accessible.

When the clumsy plot on Flora's life failed, Charlotte was sickened, and tried to placate Jonathon by going to London, taking her jewelry from the bank and giving it to him to sell in New York. There were wealthy men in New York, the new railroad and oil tycoons, who would pay large sums for genuine ancestral diamonds to hang around their wives' necks. At last Jonathon, perhaps a little cowardly himself about such a dangerous scheme as child murder, agreed to accept this payment and leave. But he refused to leave before Christmas because he had other business to complete, more romantic business. He had made a proposal of marriage.

So they would be gay until Christmas. Charlotte would wear her beautiful gowns to drive away gloom, and Jonathon would enjoy the hospitality of Winterwood to the full for these last days.

But again their plans had gone awry. The letters had begun to come from Venice.

Who had been buried in Venice? Was the Contessa not dead at all?

Charlotte had thought the letters another trick of Jonathon's to frighten her into obtaining more money. There was no doubt it was he who had slipped upstairs and rung the little silver bell in Lady Tameson's room and, counting on the servants' alarm, had been able to leave the room unnoticed. But these letters were another thing. They had come direct from Venice. Had his mother tricked him, and the woman who had died not been the Contessa at all? Was she due to arrive at Winterwood, as the letters said?

Even Charlotte, sitting there like a ghost, talking now as if she could not stop about the coffin, the jewels, the gondolas making a black shadow on the blue water, the laudanum to make one sleep, the carelessly shrilling cicadas, Jonathon's voice constantly in her ear demanding more and more, could not answer the final question. There was nothing to do but wait and see who might arrive.

The morning was endless. Lavinia didn't suppose five minutes went by without someone jumping up to look out of the window. But the drive, curving away beneath the leafless trees, remained empty. It continued to rain, water dripping off the sphinxes' heads, and lying in glassy pools on the paving stones and the rose garden. The day was gray and brown and dull amber. Fires crackled cheerfully in all the rooms, but the wind howled in the chimneys and the heavy depression was indoors as well as out.

Lavinia kept Flora in the yellow parlor, and at her request Mr. Bush brought Edward there, too. The young man was ingenious at inventing informative games to be played with pencil and paper, but for once Flora failed to respond pleasurably to this activity. She was as much on tenterhooks as everyone else.

The day wore on and there was no sound of carriage wheels, no vehicle laden with traveling boxes and a mysterious occupant coming up the drive. They were waiting for a ghost.

Just before dusk Charlotte's control broke. She disappeared upstairs and came down in her riding habit. She said she was suffocating, she must get out, she must ride.

"Don't be mad! It's blowing a gale," Daniel protested.

"But I am mad," she shouted back at him, laughing, her eyes shining in her white face. "You've always known that. Haven't you, my love?"

"Charlotte, I forbid you to go out alone."

"Oh, I'm not alone. Peters is here with my horse."

"Then keep him with you."

"Of course. Why are you fussing so? You know I can ride, gale or no gale."

She could, too. She looked superb as she galloped away, a slim upright figure completely at one with the horse. Lavinia saw Flora watching her, her face tight and still, and knew suddenly why the child had once ridden so recklessly and fallen. She had been competing with her beautiful mother.

Daniel put his arm around her shoulders.

"We'll have you mounted again in a few weeks, my pet."

"A few weeks! Why not this week, Papa?"

"You may be walked around on Nicky, certainly."

"Nicky! My old pony! Papa, are you crazy?"

"No. And neither do I intend you to be. You will have patience."

But although his voice was kind, it was abstracted. His mind had followed Charlotte on her wild gallop. Did he think he should have prevented her going, or at least gone with her to protect her? But could anyone protect her from the furies that must now pursue her?

Another slow hour went by. Sir Timothy came in to report that he and Simon had finished their game of chess, and Simon had won. The boy was getting too good.

"By Jove, Daniel, this house is like a morgue today. Everyone sitting about as if they expect the crack of doom. No sign of our anticipated traveler yet?"

"No," said Daniel shortly.

"Then we can give her up for today."

"Why do you imagine the sex of this person is feminine, Sir Timothy?" Lavinia asked.

"There's no question about it, Miss Hurst. Only a woman would behave in such a devious way. Anonymous letters, violet velvet gowns! That only comes from a most romantic mind. This is a damn bad business all round. I don't know what's to come of it."

Daniel turned from the window and came to kiss Flora on the forehead.

"Upstairs with you."

"Oh, Papa, no!" Flora's eyes were wide with alarm. "Why am I to be sent away? Am I not allowed to see the lady who arrives?"

"It is highly doubtful any lady will be arriving. Do as I say."

Flora knew her father well enough to realize that this was one occasion when blandishments would not sway him. In any case, she had to admit that she was extremely tired, and would be glad if Joseph would carry her up the stairs.

"For quite the last time," she assured him. "Tomorrow I will be much stronger."

Lavinia, gathering up Flora's belongings to follow, lingered long enough to hear Daniel calling for a hurricane lamp. He was worried about Charlotte.

But a moment later Charlotte came in. She was dripping and exhausted. She allowed her wet riding habit and her boots to be taken off, and then sank back on the couch.

"I only went to the village." There was a curious furtive look in her eyes. She said petulantly, "Why do you all stare at me? Has something happened while I was out?"

"No, nothing."

"Then no one is coming. The hoaxer—"

Her words were cut off as there came a sound of horses trotting and wheels crunching on gravel. The horses slowed to a walk, stopped. Someone was tugging the doorbell. The clamor sounded through the hall.

Charlotte was on her feet, her hand to her throat. She gave a stifled exclamation and suddenly, like Jonathon Peate, fled. But there was no ferry steamer and a passage to the Continent for her. She could only go upstairs and cower in her bedroom, probably behind a locked door.

No one followed her, for they were all waiting breathlessly to see who was to be admitted.

Daniel himself had swung the door open. And in stumbled a small figure, black-bonneted and caped. At first she looked around nervously, not lifting her veil. Then she saw Lavinia, and for some reason this gave her confidence, for she flung back her veil and hurried forward.

"Oh, Miss Hurst, I'm so glad you're still here. I had to come back to see if everything was all right. I had your letter saying you was so worried about Miss Flora. It was that which made me go to

Venice. I was so shocked with what you said about the laudanum and all. I'd never have thought I had the courage to make such a journey, but that gave it to me."

Then she realized she was standing immediately in front of Daniel, and hastily bobbed him a curtsey.

The visitor was no mysterious countess, no threatening villain. She was only Eliza.

"I'd have been back sooner, but that dreadful storm delayed the steamer. As it was, the crossing was something fearful. I was prostrate. But I'm recovered now. Miss Hurst, tell me quickly, is Miss Flora all right?"

Lavinia flung her arms round the little figure. Her face was radiant with relief.

"Mr. Meryon, I see it all now. It's Eliza who has been to Venice, and sending those letters. Isn't that so, Eliza?"

Eliza nodded. "And such a journey it was, all alone. I only did it because my lady had asked me to. Not long before she died, sir. She wrote those letters and said if I thought things was not all they should be at Winterwood I was to travel to Venice and post them. They was to give certain people a fright. She said she could have her joke, too. She'd be laughing in her grave, she said. But I do hope, sir, the letters didn't do harm. No more than a little fright they were meant to be. I think that was to be mostly for her nephew, Mr. Peate. She had taken a dislike to him in her last days. Is that all they did, sir? Give Mr. Peate a fright?"

"They did that, Eliza," Daniel said gravely. "We must hear more about this. But later. I'm sure you're tired from your journey. Go and get a meal, and then I expect you'd like your old room back."

"You mean I'm to stay, sir? But the mistress—"

"I mean you to stay, Eliza. I can appreciate loyalty as well as Lady Tameson could. By the way, you must be recompensed for your traveling expenses."

"Oh, no sir. The diamond brooch was for that. That was my lady's instructions. I was to sell it. I did, and got a hundred pounds for it, though I fancy I should have got more. But there wasn't time to fiddle-faddle about that. So there's no expenses, sir. I only hope my lady did some good. She meant to, poor soul."

"More good than she knew," said Daniel dryly. "She has benefited various charities to the extent of a fortune. And my daughter is no longer burdened with wealth. So the old lady can rest peacefully. Both of them can."

"Both of them, sir?"

"I see you don't know the whole story, Eliza. Perhaps Miss Hurst will take you upstairs and tell it to you."

Lavinia put her arm around the little weary figure.

"Yes, indeed, Eliza. And Flora will be overjoyed to see you."

Eliza had one more question to ask.

"The mistress, sir? Is she all right?"

Daniel's mouth tightened.

"Yes, she's well, Eliza. She's been riding in the rain, as she likes to do. She's gone up to rest."

He moved toward the fire, obviously not intending to put Charlotte out of her suspense at once. Perhaps he thought she deserved a great deal more suspense than the next hour or two spent trembling behind a locked door. She had admitted attempting to murder her own daughter. How could he ever forgive her, or live with her again?

Flora was indeed overjoyed to see Eliza. She flung her arms about her, exclaiming, "Do you mean you have been writing those mysterious letters? Oh, Eliza, how wicked!"

"I only posted them, Miss Flora."

"What an odd thing for Great-aunt Tameson to ask you to do. But I am sure, if she told you to, you were right to obey." Then Flora, no longer interested in a problem that was solved, had to burst out with her own news. "Eliza, did you know that I can walk again?"

"Well, I never did!"

"I'll show you. And that horrid Mr. Peate has left us. So now we can all be happy. Isn't that wonderful?"

Eliza exchanged a glance with Lavinia. Happy, it said, you poor little thing, when your own mother wanted to do away with you.

She was longing to hear the whole story, but the long journey had taken its toll. She was nodding in her chair. Lavinia ordered her to go to bed at once, and the same thing applied to Flora.

"Oh, Miss Hurst! You're behaving just like a mother," was the last thing Flora murmured sleepily.

So it happened that Lavinia was the only one awake when Daniel's urgent voice at the door whispered, "Miss Hurst! Can you come? We can't rouse Charlotte."

He was in the passage, his face wild with shock. He held an empty bottle in his hands. It bore the familiar red label indicating poison.

"I should have guessed. She said she had ridden to the village. She went to get more laudanum. When she heard the cab arriving with Eliza and rushed upstairs, she must have taken it. We had to get into her bedroom through the dressing room, breaking the lock of the door."

The locked door between herself and her husband. That, too, he was admitting in his distress.

"Is she—dead?"

"I fear so."

Lavinia put her hand in his.

"She may only have meant to sleep. To escape for a little while. As she has at other times."

"Perhaps. Joseph has gone for the doctor."

"Can I go up to her?"

"No, no. Bertha is with her. I won't have you distressed. You have suffered far too much for us already."

He had not let her hand go and now she drew him to the stairs.

"Then let us go down and wait for the doctor. I think you have suffered enough, too."

"So long as you stay by me. You will do that, Lavinia?"

"Always," she said steadily.

Chapter 23

It seemed as if the children would never let her out of their sight, even the quiet, uncommunicative Simon. Edward had grown subdued and quite tractable. He obeyed Mr. Bush at last, and hadn't teased Flora for days. He was too young to fully understand what had happened and seemed only relieved that now he would not have to live in London alone with Mamma.

Charlotte's undisciplined love had imposed a too heavy burden on the little boy, Lavinia realized. That must have been the reason for the wild rages and tantrums. Now he was cautiously beginning to enjoy the peaceful routine so necessary to a happy childhood.

Flora, too, after her first shocked grief, had grown quieter, older, and touchingly dignified.

"We must look after Papa, Miss Hurst," she had said at the very beginning.

"Yes, but—"

"You can't think of leaving, Miss Hurst. You can never leave us now."

She had promised on that fatal night to stay by Daniel. But she had only meant that to be over the worst days of the funeral and the inquest. The verdict had been death by misadventure. It seemed that most of the servants knew of Charlotte's weakness for the soothing effects of small doses of laudanum, and it was assumed that on this occasion, owing to her agitation, she had accidentally taken too much.

The truth would never be known. And that, Lavinia thought, seemed unimportant. Charlotte had threatened the life of her own daughter, and now, by some ironic justice, was dead herself. The fact was all that mattered.

But their own lives had to go on, hers, the children's, Daniel's. Only a little healing time could go by until decisions were made.

Daniel, however, did not intend to wait for anything like the usual period of mourning. Only a week after the funeral he sent for Lavinia.

She stood in the familiar study, seeing the firelight wash over the ceiling and the paneled walls, and thought only that a man should not have aged so much in so short a time. Robin had done so in prison, but Daniel had not been in prison. Except the one of his own making. For suddenly he began to tell Lavinia about his marriage to Charlotte.

"I loved her once. We were both very young, she only seventeen. She was like quicksilver, thistledown. She wasn't really made for touching. She hated having babies, hated marriage. When one finds out these things too late—it is a tragedy. Then this mental instability began. I was never easy about her. She was always unpredictable, doing and saying wild things, making scenes constantly, upsetting the children or the servants. I haven't been in love with her for a very long time. Is that a terrible thing to say about one's wife?"

"Not when it's true. And not to me."

"No, not to you." He gave a half smile, grateful, tender. "What would I have done without you?"

"I promised to stay with you." But now her words were automatic, for she knew what was coming. He was about to ask her to be his wife, and what would he say when he knew the truth about her, the fatal stain on her character? Would she be a fitter mistress of Winterwood than poor Charlotte with her wild and criminal behavior?

He crossed over to her, looking down at her quizzically.

"Are you regretting that promise? You suddenly look unhappy."

"No, I'm not regretting it."

"Then will you regret it if I ask you to be my wife?"

"Oh, Daniel!" Her voice choked. At last he had said the words she had thought could never be said. But they could not be answered until her carefully guarded secret had been told. She knew now that there must be absolute truth between them.

"Then answer me, Lavinia. I didn't expect you to hesitate. Is it too soon after Charlotte's death? Have I offended your sense of decorum?"

She gave a short laugh at that. "You will scarcely think I care about decorum when I have told you my story. I should have told it to you long ago. I should never have deceived you."

He took her hands, his eyes still quizzical, even faintly amused. "What is this terrible story?"

She began to relate it quickly, the whole sordid scandal, her brother in Pentonville prison awaiting transfer to Dartmoor, where he would finish his seven years' sentence for manslaughter, herself the chief witness in the trial, her character in shreds as she had stood day after day being ruthlessly cross-examined.

After the trial she had resigned herself to her life being ruined, she admitted.

"But poor Robin has much the worst part," she said. "Seven years in prison."

"He deserves it."

"Oh, but he was only reckless and hot-headed. He loves me dearly."

"It would not be the way I would love a sister."

Lavinia looked at his angry face and her heart sank.

"I only ask that Flora not be told this story. I would like her to go on thinking well of me after I have gone."

"After you have gone! But what of your promise to stay?"

Lavinia made herself look at him steadily.

"When I gave it you didn't know this lamentable story of mine. I absolve you completely from your offer since you made it in ignorance."

"Ignorance!" His eyes were positively twinkling. "My dearest innocent Lavinia, I have always known your past."

She stared at him in amazement.

"I have wanted to protect you ever since. Don't look so unbelieving, my love. Did you think your Cousin Marion could refrain from telling it to me at the first opportunity in Venice? Such a wonderful malicious story about the beautiful young woman she was so jealous of. Come, darling, you really must acquaint yourself more completely with human nature if you are to bring up my children. And later, God willing, our own."

"You knew it—all the time!" she whispered.

He smiled again before taking her in his arms.

"Our children we must wait for, but for this"—his lips were on hers—"I wait no longer."